COLD AIM

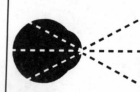

This Large Print Book carries the
Seal of Approval of N.A.V.H.

THE LINE OF DUTY SERIES, BOOK 3

COLD AIM

JANICE CANTORE

THORNDIKE PRESS
A part of Gale, a Cengage Company

Farmington Hills, Mich • San Francisco • New York • Waterville, Maine
Meriden, Conn • Mason, Ohio • Chicago

Copyright © 2019 by Janice Cantore.

The Line of Duty #3.

Unless otherwise indicated, all Scripture quotations are taken from The Holy Bible, English Standard Version® (ESV®), copyright © 2001 by Crossway, a publishing ministry of Good News Publishers. Used by permission. All rights reserved.

Scripture quotations marked AMP are taken from the Amplified® Bible, copyright © 2015 by The Lockman Foundation. Used by permission. www.Lockman.org.

Scripture quotations marked NLT are taken from the Holy Bible, New Living Translation, copyright © 1996, 2004, 2015 by Tyndale House Foundation. Used by permission of Tyndale House Publishers, Inc., Carol Stream, Illinois 60188. All rights reserved.

Thorndike Press, a part of Gale, a Cengage Company.

Thorndike Press® Large Print Christian Mystery.

The text of this Large Print edition is unabridged.

Other aspects of the book may vary from the original edition.

Set in 16 pt. Plantin.

LIBRARY OF CONGRESS CIP DATA ON FILE.
CATALOGUING IN PUBLICATION FOR THIS BOOK
IS AVAILABLE FROM THE LIBRARY OF CONGRESS

ISBN-13: 978-1-4328-6869-7 (hardcover alk. paper)

Published in 2019 by arrangement with Tyndale Publishers, Inc.

Printed in the United States of America
1 2 3 4 5 6 7 23 22 21 20 19

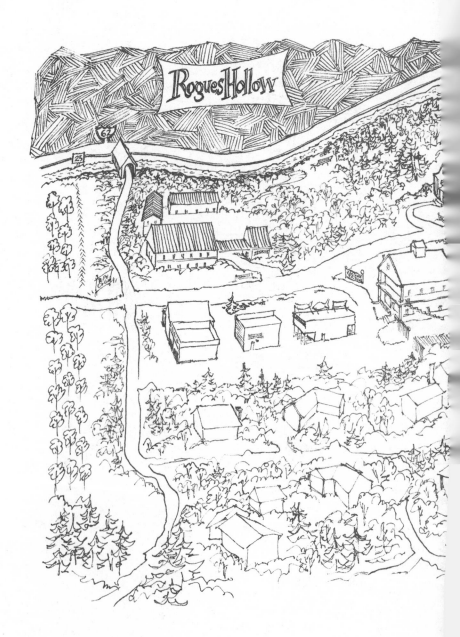

DEDICATED TO THE VICTIMS OF
HUMAN TRAFFICKING, WITH
PRAYERS FOR THEIR SWIFT
RESCUE AND RECOVERY.

ACKNOWLEDGMENTS

I'd like to acknowledge Idele Collins, Darrell and Gail Wiltrout, and all the members of the prayer team who have shown me the power of prayer.

"FOR NOTHING IS HIDDEN, EXCEPT TO BE REVEALED; NOR HAS ANYTHING BEEN KEPT SECRET, BUT THAT IT WOULD COME TO LIGHT [THAT IS, THINGS ARE HIDDEN ONLY TEMPORARILY, UNTIL THE APPROPRIATE TIME COMES FOR THEM TO BE KNOWN]."

MARK 4:22, AMP

"BUT THE EYES OF THE WICKED WILL FAIL, AND THEY WILL NOT ESCAPE [THE JUSTICE OF GOD]; AND THEIR HOPE IS TO BREATHE THEIR LAST [AND DIE]."

JOB 11:20, AMP

"THERE IS NO FEAR IN LOVE, BUT PERFECT LOVE CASTS OUT FEAR."

1 JOHN 4:18A

PROLOGUE

Twenty-Five Years Ago
Royal's knuckles were white with his grip on the door handle, nervousness and irritation jacking him up as if he'd just mainlined some speed. Devo, the skinny coke freak driving the car, kept rapping the same song lyrics over and over:

"Now that the party is jumping,
With the bass kicked in, the fingers are
    pumping. . . .
Ice, ice, baby, too cold.
Ice, ice, baby, too cold, too cold. . . ."

Royal hadn't cared for the song when it came out a couple years ago, and the fact that Devo was not a singer, had no rhythm, and kept repeating the same thing over and over while tapping on the steering wheel with his large brass ring was aggravating to say the least. But Royal bit his tongue. This

15

gig was the biggest thing to drop in his lap ever, and he vowed not to fail. Devo had the experience and was leading the gig, so Royal would listen, follow instructions, and do the job he was hired to do, for more money than he'd ever seen.

"You have poise for a kid, so I'm trusting you here." The words of the man paying for the job echoed in his mind. They called him Boss Cross. *"I see big things for you, Royal, so prove yourself with this task. You do that, and the sky is the limit."*

At eighteen the praise and confidence the man put in him had Royal's chest puffed with pride. He'd do anything to make the man proud, anything. *"The sky is the limit."*

"It's ice time, baby." Devo came to a stop, and Royal refocused on him. They'd cruised through a quiet neighborhood in San Pedro, pulled into an alley, and parked next to a cinder-block wall. It was close to 2:30 a.m. on a pitch-black, moonless night, with cloud cover. Rain had just started to fall. Big drops splattered on the windshield. Royal heard in them the same rap rhythm Devo had been tapping.

"You ready, kid?" Devo asked.

Royal looked across the car and nodded. "I'm ready," he said, ignoring the silliness of the question because as soon as Boss

16

Cross had found out from his friend the girl's secret shelter, they'd planned and practiced this job so many times that Royal was fairly certain he could perform his part with his eyes closed.

"Need a little boost?" Devo pulled a baggie out of his pocket and held it out.

Royal held a hand up. "No thanks, man. Want a clear head."

"Suit yourself." Devo dug into the bag, and Royal looked away as the guy snorted the coke. He wasn't even tempted to indulge. Royal felt as if he were stepping into a new life, and he was going to experience it all without being messed up.

Devo finished and sniffled, licked his fingers, then said, "Okay, check your watch. The two-minute rule applies. I kill the alarm, and once the door is open, we are in and out in two minutes — got it?"

Royal nodded and held his fist out. Devo bumped it and opened his car door. Royal followed, pulling his hoodie up as the rain pelted down. Devo made a stop at the back of the car to open the trunk. The plan was to grab the girl, toss her in the trunk, and get out of Dodge as fast as possible.

Devo then stepped up to a padlock securing a wrought iron gate in the center of the cinder-block wall. He cut the lock easily

17

with the small bolt cutters he had with him, opening the gate to a modest, neatly kept backyard. They'd studied the target address extensively. Royal knew the layout by heart. Devo was inside the yard quickly with Royal on his heels. They reached the back door of the small, Spanish-style stucco dwelling, and Devo stopped. He held an index finger to his lips.

Royal nodded and drew a small five-shot .38 revolver from his waistband. Devo trotted off to disable the alarm — that was Devo's specialty, anything electronic, any kind of lock — and Royal moved to the left of the back door, taking shelter under the eaves.

Heather sat on the bed, arms wrapped around her bent legs, head resting on her knees. She was in a room decorated for a little girl because according to her benefactor, small female cousins usually stayed in the room. The decor was all pink and frilly, dolls and stuffed animals neatly arranged, and while at eighteen she wasn't that far from being a little girl, she felt old, ancient, and devoid of any hope or joy reflected in the decor. Next to her on the bed was a calendar, days until the grand jury was seated marked off in black ink, only two remaining yet to be crossed off.

The closer the day came, the more her despair deepened. She was set to testify in front of a grand jury against the man who stole her innocence, the man who sweet-talked and conned her into the sex trade. At one time she believed and trusted him, maybe even loved him, until he crudely shoved her aside and sold her to the highest bidders, keeping her a prisoner for three long years, using and abusing her and letting others do the same. Ironically it was being arrested for prostitution that saved her. That and Sergeant Isaac Pink, the one cop who believed her, the one cop who pushed back on the charges against her and turned the focus of his investigation onto her captor, exploiter, and the real criminal, Porter Cross.

Heather knew Sergeant Pink had fought hard for her, and he still believed in the institutions she'd long since lost faith in.

"You testify, tell the truth, look into the jury's eyes, and this evil man will go down. I promise you."

Heather reluctantly agreed, and Pink even gave her shelter, housing her in his downstairs guest room to keep her safe until the grand jury.

But was she safe?

Tonight, fear kept her from sleep, kept her tense. Porter Cross was a rich, powerful movie producer, a famous and ruthless man. He had no shortage of wealthy, connected friends who were equally wicked. If she did reach the grand jury, would those law-abiding, normal people truly believe her, a woman arrested for prostitution, over Cross?

Out of respect for Pink and all he had done for her, Heather dutifully crossed off the days until the jury convened, but now, two days out, her courage failed her. She'd packed a bag and was ready to flee, take her chances out in the world and try as best she could to forget Porter Cross. Would Pink understand?

In the end, it didn't matter if he understood. He thought that Heather's being here was a big secret. The trouble was, Heather knew big secrets never stayed buried.

Time ticked away as Heather waited for the sounds to subside upstairs, something that would indicate that Pink and his family had dropped off to sleep. She knew the alarm code, though he'd been careful not to show her, and she could quietly let herself out. One thing the past few weeks in Pink's house had taught Heather was that she had a gift for computers and electronics. Porter

Cross had had a computer and he worked on it constantly, but he wouldn't let Heather touch it. Isaac Pink had one also, and Heather had spent hours learning from him how it worked and why. She wished she could take it with her.

It was important not to have to explain to Sergeant Pink why she had to leave because she knew she'd lose her nerve as soon as she saw his face. But she also knew that even if the grand jury believed her — and that was a big *if* — any trial for Cross would be a joke and the man would walk. Where would she be in Pink's eyes then? She certainly couldn't live with him and his family forever.

There were other reasons she had to leave. She'd heard Pink on the phone when she wasn't supposed to be listening. He feared that Cross was actively searching for her, trying to locate her hiding place, and if he found her, Cross would kill her. Pink didn't have to convince Heather of that; she was certain Cross would kill her when he found her, and there was nothing that would stop him from killing Pink as well. Heather was putting him and his family in danger the longer she stayed.

Sometime after two in the morning, Heather got up from bed. She peered out into the dark night and saw that rain was falling. Pulling on a thin windbreaker over her sweater, she zipped it up and grabbed her backpack. Something fell onto the floor, sounding like a tremendous explosion to her oversensitive ears, and she held her breath before slowly picking it up. It was the small Bible Mrs. Pink had given her.

"Read it, dear. It will give you peace."

Heather had tried to read it. She'd even asked Mrs. Pink to explain a paragraph or two to her, and a couple of passages she'd read had warmed her heart. After all, God was supposed to defend the fatherless. But the book hadn't stopped her fear. Still, she opened her backpack and shoved it inside, then zipped it back up. Slinging the pack onto one shoulder, she opened her bedroom door and stepped into the kitchen, wincing when the floorboard creaked. After a minute, hearing no other sound, she continued forward.

She'd already written an apology note for Pink for what she was planning. Stepping into the pantry, she pulled down the jar Mrs. Pink kept emergency cash in. There was a little over five hundred dollars inside, and Heather took it all, replacing it with the note and putting it carefully back on the shelf. She'd stuffed the cash into her jeans and turned to leave the pantry when she heard the stairs creak.

Someone was coming.

Sucking in a breath, Heather quietly pulled the pantry door closed and stepped as far back inside as she could, hoping that whoever was awake, it wasn't because they were hungry, and they wouldn't look inside the pantry.

"Gravy, I've got a bad feeling about this." Heather heard Pink's voice, a whisper. He was talking to his partner, Graves, a man he always called Gravy. He'd probably come downstairs so as not to wake Mrs. Pink.

Footsteps told her that Pink was in the small kitchen, pacing from one end to the other.

"No, no, I get that. I'm being an old woman, but I can't help it. I —"

The whisper stopped and so did the pacing.

"Hey, something's up. The alarm panel just went dead. I saw the light wink out. No, it's not the power — fridge is still on. I gotta go, man. Send me help."

The rain fell harder, and Royal pulled on gloves. His pulse increased, and he worked to calm the shudder in his hands. He was ready for this, he told himself. Failure was

23

not an option.

Suddenly Devo was next to him, looking and smelling like a wet dog. "Child's play," he whispered. "Ice, baby, ice."

He went to work on the back door and had it open in a matter of seconds. Once Royal stepped inside, he knew the next few minutes would change his life forever.

Devo moved in first, two steps ahead of Royal. And that was when it all went wrong.

"Boom! Boom!" The report of a gun sounded like a cannon, and Devo went down. Somehow, someway, the man had been waiting for them.

All instinct and reflex, Royal crouched and stepped to his right, firing back in the direction of the sound. He emptied his gun and heard a muffled "Oomph," then a thud.

Breath coming fast and ears ringing from the gunfire, Royal stepped forward, *Get the girl* singing in his mind. A big man was down on the floor, moaning. Royal knew it was the police officer who lived here, the man hiding the girl.

Shoving his own small, empty .38 into his waistband, Royal ripped the man's shiny revolver from his grasp and shot him again. The moaning stopped. He then pivoted toward the room off the kitchen, where they'd been told the girl would be.

Operating on pure adrenaline, internal clock telling him time was ticking away, Royal pushed open the door and clicked on the light. The room was empty. Eyes sweeping the area, he stepped forward and threw open the closet door. Nothing but clothes.

He heard the floor creak. Did someone call out? The girl must be upstairs. Swirling back out of the room, Royal jogged for the stairs. Ears ringing from the gunfire, he thought he heard someone, but he didn't hesitate. When he saw a woman, the cop's wife, Royal fired without hesitation, feeling in a groove now. The woman went down, and he leaped over her. Upstairs, he found the couple's daughter hiding under the bed and he shot her.

But the girl he'd come for, the one he wanted, was nowhere.

Heather heard Sergeant Pink move again, but he didn't go back upstairs. She hunkered down, more fearful now. What was happening?

She struggled to stay still, to not fidget, and then she heard the back door open.

A floorboard protested.

Boom! Boom! Two shots blasted her eardrums, and Heather jumped, nearly wetting her pants and smacking into a shelf, knocking a container of cereal onto the floor. Even as she stiffened, gripping her backpack in front of her with both hands, Heather thought of poor Mrs. Pink having to clean up the mess.

Bang, bang, bang, bang, bang. More shots, and Heather heard a thud, then groaning. Was it Sergeant Pink?

She held her breath as footsteps sounded in the kitchen. Another gunshot, and the groaning stopped.

The footsteps crossed in front of the pantry, toward Heather's room. The door was thrown open.

They were here for her.

It took all her strength to stay still. Very faintly, she heard Mrs. Pink call out, "Isaac?"

She wanted to scream a warning, something, anything, to save the woman who'd been only kind to her.

The footsteps passed in front of the pantry again, moving to the stairs. More gunshots.

Paralyzed by fear, Heather stood frozen, but the fear evaporated as a sense of self-preservation and fight or flight kicked in. She knew she had to move or be slaughtered. She opened the pantry door and darted out, stumbling when she saw the still form of Isaac Pink on his kitchen floor. Horror brought tears in a rush, and she bit her tongue to keep from screaming. But street-smart pragmatism told her there was nothing she could do for him or his wife.

She cursed Porter Cross and hurried toward the back door. There was another body there. *Devo.* He belonged to Cross. At least Sergeant Pink got one.

Trembling, she stepped over him and out the back door into the driving rain, taking her one brief chance to flee and save her life by never looking back.

Cursing, certain his two minutes were up, Royal did what life on the streets had taught him to do well: he thought on his feet. He bounded back down the stairs two at a time and returned to the kitchen, where he checked Devo, who was twitching. Putting his newly acquired handgun in the waistband at the small of his back, Royal grabbed Devo and swung the thin man up over his shoulder. Devo made no sound, not then and not when Royal dumped him into the trunk, where the girl should have gone, and slammed it shut.

He slid behind the wheel and forced himself to drive slowly out of the alley. The rain was pounding, a Southern California gutter buster of a storm, and even with the pummeling of the water, he thought he heard sirens. Winding out of the San Pedro neighborhood, Royal found his way to the Gerald Desmond Bridge and back into Long Beach. He drove to Sixth Street, where he could park under an overpass, out of sight of traffic, got out of the car, and threw up.

When his stomach was completely empty, he stepped out from under the overpass and let the rain pound him until he was soaked through. Only then was his head clear enough to consider what he must do next. They'd failed where the girl was concerned, and Royal was not about to add to it by getting arrested. He checked on Devo again. The cokehead was dead, already cold to the touch.

Considering the car, which was stolen, and poor dead Devo, Royal had an idea. He knew how to get up on the bike path that ran along the flood control channel. With this rain, the channel would be rushing, engorged with runoff, if not now, soon.

Hopping back in the car, Royal drove up onto the bike path. He cautiously turned the car wheels down the steep concrete bank, toward the rushing water, which was halfway up the bank, left the car in drive, and leaped out, hitting the wet pavement so hard his teeth jarred. The vehicle rolled forward and down into the dark, debris-clogged water. In the darkness, the car disappeared quickly.

Royal didn't know where it would end up, but he knew the water and the elements would erase any evidence tying him to the car. As an afterthought, he tossed his little .38 into the water after the car. He examined the gun he'd taken from the cop. Shiny, it was a larger revolver with hard rubber grips, and it felt like it was made for his hand. *I'll keep this,* he thought. *Scratch off the serial number . . . it will be a good piece.*

He then hurried away, back down to the access road and into downtown Long Beach. Royal was so wet he didn't even feel the rain anymore, which was showing no signs of letting up. He found a phone and called Boss Cross, the man he'd failed.

The boss listened as Royal told him everything that had happened, without embellishment or excuse.

"Sit tight. I'll send a car."

The car, a limo, came a while later, with a bag of dry clothes waiting for him in the back. The rain had finally lessened, and the sun was trying to brighten the sky. Tired and cold now, and wondering about his fate, Royal changed as the driver took him to a gated residence in Rancho Palos Verdes.

Hair still wet on his collar, Royal was led into the TV room, where Cross, his right-hand man Digger, and his business associate Cyrus, sat watching an early morning news broadcast. Royal didn't know Cyrus very well, but he admired what he did know. Cyrus was younger than Cross, and he had style. He was a big spender and liked a lot of the same stuff Cross did. Digger was a tough guy, a Vietnam vet and a martial arts expert, one of the scariest guys he'd ever met. Digger had taught Royal a few moves and promised to work with him more if Royal proved himself.

"You did good, kid." Cross held out a beer, Royal's favorite, and Cyrus beamed, nodding in agreement. Digger's expression, as usual, was unreadable.

Floored and a little speechless, Royal took the beer. "But we didn't get the girl and Devo is dead."

"Devo sacrificed himself for the rest of us," Cross said. "But I'm impressed by the way you handled yourself, how you impro-vised. You didn't panic. Well done."

Royal swallowed, in awe now. "Th-th-thanks."

He was offered a seat on the couch and he took it, chugging the beer. As he watched the news reports on TV, he understood. The cops had no idea where the girl was. She'd been a witness in hiding, and now the cop and his family hiding her were dead and she was nowhere to be found. The cops were clearly ready to blame the girl.

Cross laughed, and he and Cyrus clinked glasses. "We'll find her eventually. But there'll be no trial, that's for sure. You certainly have proved that you have a cool head in stressful situations. You've earned yourself a nickname — given any thought to one?"

Royal considered the question for a brief moment. "Yeah, I have. You can call me Ice."

1

Present Day

Today should have been the day of her baptism. But instead of being dunked in the cool water of the church's baptismal, Police Chief Tess O'Rourke coughed, eyes squinted and burning because of the hot smoke swirling everywhere. She wore a nose and mouth mask, but it barely helped. A lightning strike fire was raging. Half of Rogue's Hollow was under a mandatory evacuation order.

She hopped back in her patrol vehicle as the Coopers, the second-to-last holdout family on this rural road she was evacuating, grabbed their kids and a dog, climbed into their truck, and reluctantly left their property. The husband, Garrett Cooper, wanted to stay and defend the home, and he'd slowed Tess down considerably, eating into her margin of safety.

"The house is a hundred years old — we can't just leave it!"

"Garrett, the house can be replaced, possessions can be replaced — your life can't be." Tess tried to reason with him and got nowhere. It was Janie refusing to leave without him that finally worked to change his mind. Tess witnessed a tense fight between the pair that ended when Cooper recognized that his wife wasn't going anywhere without him. And fighting to save a hundred-year-old structure on two wooded and brush-choked acres, with the wind driving the flames this way, was foolhardy to say the least. Finally common sense won out. The only way he'd save his brand-new pickup was to drive it out with his family in it.

Even now, in spite of helicopter and plane water drops, Tess could see the flames swirling and consuming on a seemingly unstoppable march. They were off to her left now, roughly behind Arthur Goding's place, and the wind was driving them along the ridge of hills that bracketed the boundaries of Rogue's Hollow. Arthur had left his home without argument, taking his dog and loading his livestock into a large trailer.

"Have to trust this all to the Lord," he'd said.

The property next to Arthur's, a onetime pot farm, was vacant, so no worries there.

Nearly everyone else, including Bart Dover, who owned the property at the end of the road, had already evacuated as well. Dover's farm was at the western boundary of Rogue's Hollow. He hadn't wanted to wait or to take a chance, so he left with his family at the first sign of trouble. Tess wished everyone had been so easy. There was one last resident Tess had not been able to contact — at the end of Juniper, a gravel road that cut south, between here and the Dover place. Fighting with Garrett Cooper had put Tess on the razor's edge of danger; the safe time cushion the fire captain had given her was expiring.

"Edward-1." The radio crackled with her call sign.

Tess yanked off the mask to answer. "Edward-1, copy."

"Fire is advising that you hurry. The wind has shifted, and they can't guarantee you won't be cut off."

"I've got one more home. Five, ten minutes, max."

"10-4, will advise."

Tess wiped sweat from her brow as she pressed the accelerator, able to breathe again inside her air-conditioned SUV. She followed the Coopers' truck down the long, bumpy driveway. They turned right to head to town and safety, while she turned left.

The last property on Juniper was the largest at 105 acres, and it backed up to a hillside that could erupt into flames any minute. Tess was barely acquainted with the person who lived there. A bona fide recluse, Livie Harp was sometimes the lead topic on all channels of the Rogue telegraph, the thread of gossip that wound itself everywhere through the Upper Rogue valley.

That gossipy thread told Tess that Harp had bought the property in cash, several years ago, before Tess came to Oregon. Everyone labeled Harp a "prepper" because she'd spent months having the property renovated and "fortified," as Tess's friend Casey Reno liked to say. The Harp property was as off the grid as possible with solar panels, well water, a septic system, a greenhouse for vegetables, and no listed phone. Tess had heard that Harp even butchered her own meat.

Tess learned from Pastor Oliver Macpherson that Harp seemed to be trying to come out of her shell.

"Twice now she's come to church. She comes late, sits in the back, and leaves early, but at least she's putting her toe in the water."

Tess had worked in the Hollow for over a year and had seen the woman only a couple of times, in her car, an old-style Land Rover that almost looked armor-plated, driving back to her place.

In southern Oregon, a lot of large properties tended to look like they were built — and stuck — in the nineteenth century. But Harp's place was all twenty-first century. One of the improvements she added to her property was strong metal fencing and an equally heavy security gate. Tess had heard that she had an intercom system and cameras everywhere, and that when she transacted business online and deliveries came, they didn't get past the gate. She'd provided a chute for packages to be pushed through, so they were safe on the other side of the gate. Livie herself would come and get the package only after the delivery person had left.

Tess wasn't certain how much the gossip she heard could be trusted, but as she pulled up to the gate now, it was obvious that the security here was formidable. Mindful of the cameras on either side of the fence, she punched the intercom.

The minute or so before there was a response seemed like an hour. Tess was about to punch it again.

"Can I help you?"

"This is Chief O'Rourke. Ms. Harp, there

is an out-of-control forest fire heading your way. I'm ordering a mandatory evacuation."

"I have no intention of leaving."

"Maybe you didn't hear me. There's a raging fire —"

"I heard you. I'm not deaf or stupid. I'm also not leaving my home, my property."

"Fire personnel will not be able to respond to your residence in the event you need help."

"I'll be fine. I'm not asking for help. I can take care of myself. I have defensible space."

The intercom clicked off. Tess had only a second of openmouthed shock before her phone rang. It was Oliver. He hadn't wanted her to go, telling her that she'd already completed her duty when it came to warning people and facilitating evacuation. A recent fast-moving fire in northern California had amped up his angst; people there lost their lives when the fires moved toward them so fast they had no chance to get away. Putting herself directly in harm's way was not in her job description.

"Tess, you need to get back here now!" The emotion in his voice touched her deep inside, making her wish she could hold his face in both hands and assure him that she was fine.

Tess heard debris smack her car, and she

felt it move as a strong wind gust slammed into it. She'd been in a car pelted with sand during a sandstorm in the Arizona desert years ago, and that was what this felt like.

"I'm heading back now," she said and then realized the phone was dead, the connection dropped. She plopped the phone on the seat next to her, frowning because she knew Oliver was justifiably worried. Briefly, she considered a radio call to the incident command center so someone could let him know that she was okay.

Tess looked in her rearview mirror and saw a tornado of flames. She was certain the house she'd just left was lost. The flames were angry, clawing at the sky, and the smoke dark and ominous. She jammed her car into reverse as a large explosion rent the air, deafening even to her with her windows rolled up. The Coopers' propane tank must have exploded. As if shot from a flame-thrower, fire squirted across the road. Tess was cut off.

She reached out and punched the intercom again. There was no choice but to hunker down with the recluse.

But would the woman open the gate?

Tess waited for a response even as her rearview mirror showed a wall of smoke and flames coming closer.

2

Oliver Macpherson stared at his phone as his connection to Tess dropped. Cell phone reception was spotty at times in Rogue's Hollow as it was, but with two fires raging, and one close to the nearest cell tower, fire personnel had told him that coverage might be affected.

Is Tess okay?

The fire incident commander had warned her not to go, since the fire was moving fast and was too unpredictable. Oliver asked her not to go. She was the police chief; surely she could let the fire department see to evacuations. But Tess was Tess, fearless and a little reckless at times. He couldn't deny that those same qualities that attracted him to her also frustrated and terrified him at times.

"At the rate this fire is moving, you have at best ten minutes," the fire commander had told her.

"Please don't push it," Oliver had pleaded. *"Pay attention to the clock."*

"I'm not stopping to socialize. I'll be fine."

In the end they'd set a safe time parameter, but Tess was way past that now.

He was across the street from his church — all services had been canceled today — and stood near the Hollow bridge, looking down River Drive. The wind whipped around him as he tried to get a better view of the road she should be coming down if she followed the last evacuee. The truck he knew as belonging to Janie and Garrett Cooper appeared, passed him, and turned in to the already-crowded church lot. Rogue's Hollow Community Church was a certified shelter for those complying with the evacuation orders. Though only half the town was threatened and the wind-whipped fire was swirling away from downtown Rogue's Hollow, it seemed as though the whole town was here at the church and mobilized to help.

That was what Oliver loved about this place and the people he called friends and parishioners — they were always ready and able to help. There were trailers used to help move threatened livestock, RVs loaned in case people were out of their homes for an extended period of time, and food and food preparers ready and able to start serving up meals.

Knowing that all he could do right now was commit Tess to prayer, Oliver crossed the street and walked back to his church and all the activity there. The fire department had set up a command post in the lot. Emergency personnel, volunteers, and displaced residents milled about. Arthur Goding, looking distraught, was talking to the incident commander. The last communiqué from a helicopter pilot dropping water in the area was that the old logging camp behind his house had gone up in flames. Arthur was more concerned about the camp than he was his own home.

"I can rebuild my house, but that camp is irreplaceable because of the history there."

In all the years Oliver had lived in Rogue's Hollow, he'd never seen such a hot and fast fire as he was seeing today. Started by an early fall thunderstorm on Bureau of Land Management property yesterday, the flames spread quickly over summer-dried brush as the same wind that moved the thunderstorms along spread the fire.

Oliver felt bad for Arthur. As he fought back his continuing worry for Tess, he shoved his phone in his pocket and went to speak to the Coopers.

"She headed to the mystery mansion," Garrett Cooper said. His wife was sniffling; it was obvious she'd been crying.

Their house was surely lost, Oliver thought, stifling the urge to turn and look down the road again. The growing and moving cloud of smoke would only heighten his anxiety about Tess.

The "mystery mansion" was what locals called the home of Livie Harp. She was the area's most elusive resident. No one really knew much about her except what was gossip. Oliver remembered when she moved to the Upper Rogue. She'd spent a lot of money remodeling the old farmhouse she purchased, practically rebuilding it, hiring out-of-the-area contractors and making them sign nondisclosure agreements. At the time, it created quite a sensation in town, and the gossip threads had fascinated him.

Oliver had spoken to her at length once, when she came to him late one night about a month after she'd moved in and asked that the meeting be confidential. She took him by surprise, sort of like a sneaker wave at the beach, and even after he began to speak with her, he wasn't certain that his legs were under him. He let her ask the questions, trying to gauge what was really going on with the woman.

"I've listened to a couple of your messages on the Internet. You talk a good game," she said, refusing his offer of a chair.

"I share a Good News message —"

"Good news? That's what people call the Bible, right?"

"Right."

"You believe the Bible? All of it?"

"I do."

She stopped pacing and stared at him. Then the questions came rapid-fire.

"How can you be so certain the book is true and not fairy tales? How can you be so sure? Do you really believe there is a God?"

"Let me take those one at a time." Oliver swallowed. *"I do believe the Bible is true. I've studied the book for most of my life. It's consistent, historical, and it brings a clear Good News message of salvation for mankind. There's historical evidence as well, but my guess is that isn't what you are looking for — dry history."*

"I want some proof." She banged her closed fist into an open palm.

"I can't pull a rabbit out of my hat, if that's what you want, but if you're truly looking for God, he's not hard to find. The proof is all around us. Seek him honestly; he's there, in those pages."

"He may be there in those pages, but he's

44

certainly not present in this world. How can he be? There is so much evil, so much pain. How do you explain that?"

"I won't argue that the world isn't broken. But it's not the absence of God; it's the presence of sin that's responsible for the pain and suffering here. God's presence gives us hope. The Good News of the gospel is the story of God —"

"That doesn't answer my question. Why doesn't he just stop it all, stop all the suffering? If he's all-powerful, he could."

Oliver could see that underneath all the nervous energy was a lot of pain. What had hurt this woman so deeply? he wondered. He struggled to find the right words, to know exactly what would impact her.

"And he will. I don't claim to understand all the ways of God. But I trust that he knows what's best. Besides the Bible, another way to learn about God's character, his purpose, is to be around people committed to him. Why don't you join us for service on Sunday?"

She struck him as a true seeker, but she flatly rejected his invitation. *"I don't do well in crowds."*

He tried again. *"I'll pray with you. I'll help you understand the passages in the Bible you struggle with, and I'll point you to comforting passages, but trying to work this out on your own won't give you the whole picture. It's been my experience that it helps to be around and involved with God's people."*

"It's been my experience that it's best to not trust people at all. I'll keep to myself, thank you."

She'd left, and he'd never spoken to her again. He wasn't certain he'd helped her, and he wondered what had happened in her life to make her so closed off. But recently he had hope that some of what he'd said had sunk in and borne fruit. Harp was venturing out more and more — he'd heard as much from others in his congregation. She'd even been seen flitting through the market in town. When she did come and go, she did so quietly, and a lot of the chatter about her had died down. Since their first meeting perhaps four years ago, Oliver had Livie Harp on his prayer list. He prayed that she'd keep searching and find what she was looking for.

Would she stay in her home with the fire advancing that way?

Boom! The sound of an explosion in the distance made Oliver duck reflexively. He turned, but all he could see from here was wildfire smoke. As he recalled, several people out that way had propane. A propane tank explosion would only exacerbate an already-dicey situation.

Oliver hurried back to the incident command post, which was a flurry of activity. There he heard the words that just about made his heart stop.

"The fires have crossed the road. Chief O'Rourke and any other resident beyond the junction of Juniper and River Drive are cut off."

3

Tess turned away from the flames, heart pounding. She gripped the steering wheel and looked up as the gate slowly swung open. As soon as the opening was large enough, she pressed the accelerator and shot up the gravel driveway, smoke swirling in the air like a murky, flowing curtain. Powerful sprinklers engaged on either side of her, sputtering at first and then shooting out strong jets of water. Livie Harp was prepared.

Noting cameras every several feet, Tess drove, elevation increasing, for about three-quarters of a mile before Harp's house came into view. Fear of the fire fled as an overwhelming curiosity about this mysterious woman took over.

She knew that preppers were not uncommon around the area, even extreme preppers like Harp. Though all the other properties she knew as belonging to preppers were occupied by groups, families, not single recluses. Large properties with good wells seemed to attract people who feared some disastrous worldwide catastrophe on the horizon. She'd been told that many people in the area drove old cars, vehicles that operated with carburetors, not computers, in the event of an electromagnetic pulse attack that would destroy the electrical grid and render computers and the cars they controlled useless.

Was that Harp's story?

At the end of the drive stood an impressive two-story log home, shrouded in smoke and surrounded by another security fence, with a large wraparound porch and the mountain behind. The word *defensible* popped into Tess's head. Solar panels, a water tank behind some trees, and what Tess believed was a greenhouse were visible. There was also a huge barn and corral, set up with a circular walker for horses, with Harp's Land Rover and a horse trailer parked in front. More gossip came to mind, about Harp patrolling the perimeter of her property on horseback, shotgun at the ready. Everything but the old Rover looked state-of-the-art, and Tess couldn't help but wonder how on earth Harp supported herself.

A second gate swung open and she drove through. A woman Tess pegged as Harp stood on the porch, holding a shotgun.

Tess's radio crackled. It wasn't dispatch; she recognized Oliver's voice and she heard the panic there.

"Tess! The fire has crossed Juniper. Where are you?"

She picked up the mike and took a moment to calm her own voice. "I'm fine," she said, hoping to defuse his panic. "I'm at the Harp property. Looks like we'll both ride this out here. I think the Coopers' propane tank just exploded."

"We heard it all the way down at the church. The wind finally seems to be letting up, and a C-130 is on the way. They hope to knock a lot of the fire down. Stay safe."

"I will." Tess disconnected, glad that he sounded calmer. She parked her car and undid the seat belt.

Harp hadn't moved. She stood on the porch, watching Tess.

Tess opened the door and climbed out. "Thank you for letting me in here," Tess said as she approached the stairs.

"I'm sorry you felt the need to come here. I can take care of myself no matter what."

"It's my job to make sure people are safe.

The evacuation order was made yesterday
—"

"I will not evacuate." She stepped back as Tess reached the top of the porch.

"Now there's no choice," Tess countered.

Tess regarded the mysterious prepper for a moment. Harp was taller than Tess, but not by much. And she was older, Tess guessed by at least ten years. She also looked lithe and fit, reminding Tess a little of Linda Hamilton from the Terminator movies, wearing dark jeans and a dark tank top. Her gray-streaked hair was pulled back into a ponytail. And there was an energy about her like she was a coiled spring, ready to explode. Tess had seen energy like that in good cops and in bad criminals. It had to do with a sure sense of purpose. Harp was confident and assured, ready for anything. That made Tess more curious, not less, and she wondered what the next hours would bring.

She made a mental note to do as much digging into the woman's background as possible — if they survived the fire.

"We'll be fine," Harp said as if reading Tess's mind. She looked away and gestured with the shotgun barrel. "My livestock are out of harm's way, and I've got all the space cleared of brush around my home, a good well, and cisterns full of water. I'm prepared for any contingency."

Tess coughed as a blast of smoke rolled over them. Briefly she wondered if the wind had weakened as Oliver said. If it had, that would certainly help the fighting effort. The flames were visible through the eerie smoke haze, off to the left, on the hillside, running this way. She heard a chopper and then saw it drop a load of water on the leading edge of the flames.

Harp set the shotgun down. "We may need to man some fire lines. Are you up for that?"

Tess nodded as a dry pine tree caught fire to their right, crackling and popping as the flames took hold. She followed Harp as the woman jumped off the porch and jogged to a heavy-duty diesel-powered ATV. On the back was a spool of thick fire hose.

"Hop on," she said to Tess. As Tess climbed onto the vehicle, Harp turned on a valve. She then hopped into the driver's seat, and they headed for the fire.

The hose wound off the spool and Harp stopped a short distance away from the tree. Tess got out of the vehicle and followed Harp's lead, helping to draw out hose on this end. Tess felt the heat of flames and struggled to breathe amid the swirling smoke. She pulled the mask that was around her neck up over her mouth and nose.

"Open that water valve," Harp ordered, coughing and nodding toward a lever.

Tess did as instructed, switching on the water, and the hose plumped, charged with water.

Harp pointed at the closest flames as Tess helped her pull the water line along.

Her eyes burned, and her lungs felt as if they'd burst. She wondered if the two of them could survive before the C-130 made its appearance and dropped its load. She did something she was very rusty at but was working on, trying to remember what her father had taught her years ago and what Oliver was trying to reteach her . . . She prayed.

4

San Jose, California
Ice looked around him at the mess ac-
cumulated after the party last night.
Granted, the house was no palace to begin
with — it was a boarded-up foreclosure the
man he was looking for had broken into a
week ago — but now it looked as if a bomb
had exploded. Along with the beer cans,
half-finished drinks, and half-eaten pieces
of pizza, partygoers who hadn't made it
home slept here and there. There were two
on the couch, several on the floor, and a
couple in the corner. From the smell,
someone had vomited somewhere, but he
wasn't looking for that.

He was here to clean up a mess, though
not the vomit, stale pizza, and discarded
cups and plates. This wasn't Ice's normal
gig. His was the con, the smile, the look,
the story that strung the merchandise along.
But something had happened that pulled

him away from his normal job, and now he needed to solve a problem, a worthless employee, someone who had double-crossed him. Ice's partner had called, explaining that this man had poached the merchandise Ice had provided.

Ice drew in several deep, calming breaths to tamp down his anger, knowing he shouldn't act on emotion. There was no room for mistakes, and acting emotionally led to mistakes. This was business. He'd procured a young girl for his partner and passed her to a middleman. The middleman was to move her right along, and he hadn't done that. He'd violated the terms of his contract, and Ice would mete out justice.

Ice had been watching the man, waiting for the right time to approach. When the party started, he thought perhaps the cops would enter the picture. So he waited for them to bust the party and take care of the problem for him. But that hadn't happened. It was seven in the morning now, and Ice had come back to survey the damage and take care of the guy himself.

His eyes roamed the room, and then he found him. The guy was in the corner, arms wrapped around Ice's "loner," a San Quentin quail, the one girl he had procured on this trip for the partner. The sight obliterated his calm and made him so angry, if he'd had a bat in his hands, he'd have been hitting home runs on people's heads.

Ice trafficked in girls but, like a drug dealer, didn't want employees sampling the product. The girl was meant for the man who paid all the bills, and this jerk should never have gotten involved with the merchandise.

He walked to the corner and stood looking down at the pair for a minute, hands on hips, trying to decide how best to handle the situation.

He'd met the girl four days ago. It had been easy to gain her trust and voluntary compliance. Though in his early forties and far from being a teen, Ice was youthful-looking, and he knew it. With sharp blue eyes, sandy-blond hair he liked to wear long, and sculpted features, he'd been told by more than one female that he looked like a young Brad Pitt, only better.

And he used it.

He'd seen this girl at the mall by herself, looking lonely and more than a little angry. Those were the easiest to score. He'd started with a nonthreatening smile. Before long he was buying her a soda and listening compassionately to her pour out her teen-age angst and fury at her mother, who still treated her like a baby. Dad had left and was married to a wicked stepmother. She hated them all. Ice had heard so many similar stories over the years. Listening was important — listening and gaining trust. With this cute little brunette, a charming dimple in her chin, all it took was that afternoon chat, and she was in his van with him, ready to leave it all behind.

He'd delivered her to the middleman, who should have been long gone to Arizona with his cargo. Ice knew telephone poles and storefronts all over were being plastered with pictures of the girl, "Have you see her?" posters. He didn't want to leave without her; that would be leaving money. To Ice, the girls were simply a commodity, a product he provided to clamoring clients. This young one was particularly suited for Ice's partner. She was so anxious to get away, she'd complied, no force needed.

It didn't matter to Ice one way or another. Compliance was nice, but if there was no compliance, he'd apply force quickly and ruthlessly.

He heard voices and stepped to the window. Cops. From what Ice could make out, someone had called them because a party attendee had left his car blocking a driveway. They were at the curb.

He cursed. Being rushed was never a good thing. He pulled his handgun from behind his back. He'd already constructed a home-made suppressor from a soda bottle and, with his gloved hands, attached it to the barrel of his gun. He always used a revolver so as not to leave any brass lying around. The cop would hear something — a suppressor never completely muffled all sound — but the shot would be dampened. Ice knew their procedures. They'd step back a minute or two to try to determine what they'd heard, giving him time to flee.

He put the gun to the betrayer's head and fired. The girl stirred, but she was probably too drugged to have any clue about what was happening.

He discarded the bottle, grabbed his bag, and headed for the back door. At this point the girl would only slow him down. He'd cleaned up the mess; that would soften the blow of losing her. It was too hot for him here now. Time to leave the state for Nevada, maybe Oregon.

5

Dusty, smoky, sweaty, and tired, Tess climbed out of her SUV sometime after 10 p.m. She'd fought the fire beside Harp and then fought Harp about letting the firefighters onto her property to ensure all the hot spots were out.

"You can't stay awake forever," Tess had argued, *"and you have a big piece of property. Suppose the wind kicks up again and ignites an ember somewhere. You'd have no chance."*

Harp relented but insisted Tess stay as long as the firefighters were on her land and escort them off. They'd covered all the ground the fire incident commander thought was at risk, and thankfully, it looked like, with the weather cooperating, Harp would be just fine.

Tess was as surprised as anyone when Harp thanked her. *"Chief, I've heard good things about you, and I'm glad they all proved true. While I wish the circumstances were dif-*

ferent, I appreciate your help, and I'm glad I got this chance to work with you."

Shocked, all Tess could think to say was "You're welcome. There are a lot of good people in town. I hope you'll see fit to be a little less closed off."

With the fire around Harp's place beaten back, the immediate threat to Rogue's Hollow was also ended. When the road reopened and Tess drove back to town, she felt as if she could finally relax.

A large tent had been set up in the parking lot of the church as part of the command post for the fire. She'd come to debrief with the fire incident commander and find out how the battle was progressing overall. To her surprise and delight, Oliver was still there waiting for her. He stepped forward and grabbed her in a hug, lifting her off her feet.

A tidal wave of emotions swirled through her exhausted soul. She and Oliver had been an unofficial item for a couple of months. And she was happy with the way things were going. But this was the first public display of affection on either of their parts. Tess closed her eyes and relished the hug and Oliver's comforting strength. Would this take their relationship to another level?

After a minute, he set her down and she

opened her eyes, recognizing they were creating a spectacle in front of volunteers and the other emergency personnel hydrating and debriefing after a tough couple of days.

Stepping back, she smiled. "Hey, I'm a mess, and I just got you all dirty."

"Doesn't bother me at all. I'm just glad you're okay." He leaned back and looked her over, his eyes warm and full of sparkle, and for a minute Tess thought he'd kiss her. A combination of fear, embarrassment, and excitement twisted up inside her like a tornado. Then he said, "Things got a little close out there, didn't they?"

"Yes and no." She pushed back some hair that had fallen over what she was certain was a sooty forehead, disappointed and relieved at the same time that the moment had passed. "Livie Harp is stubborn and completely prepared for any and all contingencies."

"I bet. And I want to hear all about it. But first, there's sandwiches and drinks over here."

"Great. I'm famished." Tess followed him to a large table set up with food and drinks for all the first responders. She washed her hands and then grabbed a sandwich, some chips, and a drink. Firefighters, cops, and volunteers ringed the tables, and Oliver found them a place to sit.

Tess munched her food and between bites told him about her interaction with Livie Harp, in the back of her mind wondering about the forward movement of their relationship. It was a good thing, right?

Two days later, the smell of smoke still hung in the air. There were still a couple of hot spots here and there, but the fire danger to residents was finally over. Oliver looked forward to the day all the smoke would be gone, and he'd see his beautiful Oregon blue sky again. Because of the fire emergency, he'd missed a couple of regular appointments. Now that the worst had passed and the fire was on its way to being completely extinguished, he was able to reschedule one of the important ones. This meeting brought him to the Jackson County Jail, where he was led to an attorney-client room to meet with a convicted felon awaiting trial on new charges.

Oliver had met Don Cherry a couple of months ago, when the man had ostensibly been in the employ of a local pot farm. In reality, he worked for a drug lord, a man who was out to kill Tess O'Rourke. Thinking about that order still gave Oliver the shivers. The drug lord was eventually captured after a shoot-out at a local residence, and now he was in custody in a federal prison in California. But long before the shoot-out, Cherry had been paying Oliver visits for questions and conversations. At the time, Oliver believed Cherry was struggling with fully trusting in God; he wanted to have faith, but a hard life, including time in prison and an affiliation with a violent street gang, had clouded and stunted his ability to believe.

In spite of Cherry's gang tattoos and scary demeanor — an FBI agent once made the comment, "One glare from that guy could scare the white off rice" — Oliver saw good in the man who'd been hardened over time. His insight proved golden when Cherry actually saved his life. The drug lord had ordered Cherry to kill Oliver and two other people, but instead, Cherry hid them and saved them all.

After the shoot-out, when Cherry was taken into custody along with the drug lord, Oliver didn't end his relationship with the man; rather, he made a point to try to visit him at least once a week. Since that time he'd had many interesting conversations with Don, including one where Cherry confessed faith in Christ and a desire to lead a Spirit-filled life.

Cherry was cooperating with federal and state authorities and had been placed in protective custody until his day in court because there was a bounty on his head, courtesy of the Mexican mafia. Plus, the drug lord he once worked for had issued many threats to kill Cherry. The threats seemed to not faze Don at all. He was calm, full of questions about the Bible, and clearly at peace with all the life decisions he was currently making. He would eventually be transferred to federal custody, but until that happened, Oliver was committed to doing all that he could to help the man.

"Good morning, Don," Oliver said as deputies brought the large man into the room. Cherry, broad and strongly muscled, towered over Oliver. He nodded to Oliver and sat still while the deputies shackled the belly belt he wore to the floor. They unshackled his hands, a concession to Oliver because Cherry brought with him his Bible and a notebook.

How could they do a Bible study if his hands remained shackled? Oliver had argued. The sheriff had eventually relented, and for the past month, they'd had many productive study sessions.

Once he was settled, the deputies left the

room and Oliver opened in prayer.

"Father, we ask for your presence in this room as we study your Word. Open our eyes and hearts to your truth."

"Amen," Cherry said. "I missed our visit. Glad you could reschedule."

"It's been a rough few days." Oliver gave him a sketch of the brief but destructive fire in the Hollow.

"Everyone okay?"

"No lives lost, but a lot of destruction. Tess handled the crisis well."

At the mention of Tess, Cherry showed the hint of a smile, all the emotion he ever revealed, Oliver had learned.

"That chief, your lady, she's a tough cookie. Is she too tough for you?"

"I don't know that I'd use the word *tough,* but she is dedicated."

"I wouldn't have said that a cop and a padre would mix." Then he grinned. "One is all about putting people in jail, and the other is all about setting people free. Justice and mercy — ain't that opposite ends of the spectrum?"

Oliver couldn't suppress his own grin. Don had a point. "Not really opposite. All fair justice is dispensed with some mercy, I think. And, uh, we mix fine. We both help people, just in different ways."

The big man considered this. "I guess you could say that. I never thought of arresting people as helping them. But in my case, you two were a great tag team. Her arresting me and you explaining God to me . . . well, you needed a captive audience, and you got it."

Oliver laughed. "God will use whatever it takes, Don." He switched the subject away from his personal life to the portion of Scripture they were set to study. But it was hard to concentrate on 1 Samuel. Cherry hit a nerve, as he often did. Was Tess, the dedicated and courageous chief of police, too tough for him to handle? *"Opposite ends of the spectrum"?*

6

Tess's throat was still sore from all the smoke she'd inhaled two days ago, and her muscles protested vehemently after the work she'd put them through in the smoky heat of the fire. Her mind had worked as hard as her muscles that day. Livie Harp was as big an enigma as anyone Tess had ever met. She was still trying to wrap her brain around the woman. She didn't remember ever meeting anyone so stubborn or evasive. Of course, her first thought was that Harp was a fugitive from justice — why else would she be so fiercely protective of her privacy? But as she observed Harp over the few hours she worked with her, Tess's instincts didn't ping *criminal*. She couldn't put her finger on it, but it seemed as if there was more hurt in Harp, not criminality or meanness. And there was nothing on her property to indicate criminal activity, only a perfectly self-contained setup, and here in this part of Oregon, that was not uncommon or illegal.

In any event, Harp's defensible space helped the firefighting effort. Tess saw the clear line of demarcation at the edge of her property, and that enabled them to do battle, jumping from dry tree to dry tree just outside the property boundary. Then, when she feared she was at the end of her strength, help came in the form of a C-130 dropping fire retardant. It was almost as scary as the fire, watching the huge plane deliver a load of fire retardant a scant few feet away, but it saved the Harp property, and Rogue's Hollow, from further devastation and protected the recluse's house from flames. As it dropped a cloud of reddish retardant, Tess could only gape in awe. The landscape looked otherworldly, engulfed in a reddish, smoky haze. Two more drops and they were winning. The fact that the wind had died also aided the fight.

In the end, Livie Harp lost a couple of pine trees and some perimeter brush. Tess had tried to engage the woman in conversation, but it was obvious that she played everything close to the vest.

"How do you support yourself out here, all alone?"

"I do Internet security. I test secure banking

*websites for flaws, find them, then tell compa-
nies how to make their sites more secure. I
work from home. No need to travel anywhere."*

"Aren't you lonely out here by yourself?"
Tess had asked.

Harp offered the vaguest of smiles. *"Life is
easiest and safest when I'm around people I
trust. I trust Livie Harp."*

That was the extent of what Tess learned,
along with Harp's website. It was something
Tess wanted to look into as soon as possible.

Now, two days later, with the fires largely
out, damage was being assessed. Since the
fire had impacted the most rural segment of
Rogue's Hollow, it looked as if only four
homes were lost — no people or livestock
had died, thank goodness — along with the
old logging camp behind Arthur's home.
But his home was spared, as was the vacant
property next door. Not all evacuation
orders had been lifted, as firefighters were
still working hard to put out random hot
spots on BLM property, but the capricious
weather was turning cool. Rain was in the
forecast, and Tess expected that sometime
today everyone would be let back into their
neighborhoods and homes.

She bought a cup of coffee from the Hollow Grind, nodding and talking to people

here and there. After a year she'd come to know a lot of the coffee shop regulars and felt welcome and at home. Everyone seemed to be in good spirits despite the ordeal of the last few days. The emergency served to bring people together, she noticed. She even saw some neighbors who'd been torn apart by the contentious issue of recreational pot sitting and enjoying coffee together.

Oliver would be happy to see that, she thought. Oliver and his church were working overtime to help everyone they could.

Thinking of Oliver made her smile. His unrestrained bear hug when she returned to the command post after the odd encounter with Livie Harp still made Tess flush warm. True, they'd been seeing each other for a couple of months, ever since the gunfight at Arthur's home, when Tess had faced off against a wanted drug dealer, but they hadn't been at all demonstrative in public. It was an adjustment to be together, for him because he'd been widowed only the year before and for Tess because the idea of trusting God and stepping back into a lifestyle she'd abandoned years ago was still very new. But he'd whisked her up into his arms before she could say a word, and she hadn't protested. It felt good to be in his arms and wonderful to know how much he cared.

In her heart of hearts, Tess knew her feelings for him were just as strong.

Memories of the shoot-out at Arthur Goding's house with a corrupt DEA agent and a wanted drug lord surfaced. She knew Oliver had a morning meeting at the jail with one of the main players in the incident from a couple months ago. She didn't see Don Cherry the same way Oliver did. Oliver saw him as a soul to save, and while Tess didn't think that would hurt, she'd never get as comfortable with the man as Oliver had. Even after Oliver jumped Cherry and punched him out to save Tess, the two men called each other friends.

The memory brought on a happy hum as she continued down the street and stepped into the station. But the sound died in her throat when she saw what was awaiting her in the lobby.

Sheila nodded her way. "This gentleman has been waiting to speak with you."

The man stood. He was tall and fit, with a bearing that said cop or military. Wearing cargo pants and a dark T-shirt under a light jacket, he was either undercover or off duty.

"Chief O'Rourke?"

"That's me."

He held up his ID. "Agent Alonzo Bass, FBI, out of Phoenix, Arizona."

Tess studied the ID for a moment. "Hello, Agent Bass, you're a long way from home. How can I help you?"

"It's Lon, and I have a situation to bring to your attention. Is there a place we can talk?"

"Sure." Tess nodded and pointed the way to her office. Once they were inside, she closed the door. "Does this have anything to do with the incident here in July?"

"Yes and no. It has to do with a case wrapping up in Mesa, Arizona. It's not big news yet, but it will hit tomorrow." He opened the briefcase he had with him and pulled out a standard FBI press release. "As to what happened here three months ago, I know Marcus Ledge. I've talked at length about the incident you two were involved in and done my own study of the area here. He says you're to be trusted, that you're good at what you do. That goes a long way with me."

"Hmm." Tess studied him for a moment, remembering DEA Agent Ledge and his corrupt partner. Then she directed her attention to the press release, which concerned a sting operation and the shutting down of a child trafficking ring based out of a mansion in Mesa. Four minor girls and one adult female were liberated, and eight adults arrested.

"Wow. But what does this have to do with me?"

"One of the rescued girls, the eighteen-year-old, is going to be our star witness. She was closest to our target, and she acquired an iPad with information implicating a high-powered person involved in this ring. There's a lot of money tangled up in the case and possibly a lot of politics. My partner and I have been tasked with keeping the girl safe."

"You? Wouldn't that normally fall to the US Marshals?"

"Ordinarily, yes. But when this hits the media and you see who our main target is, you'll understand why we're going outside channels." He stood, hands in pockets, jiggling keys and change. "Chief, my research of Jackson County in general and Rogue's Hollow in particular turned up a few things besides sterling endorsements of you and the way you work. There's a battered women's shelter here in town, correct?"

Tess bit back a response. The shelter was supposed to be a secret, but she'd quickly learned that in a small valley, it was impossible to keep any secrets, especially a big

73

one. While it was irritating that this outsider had easily discovered the place, she knew there wasn't a lot she could do, short of moving the shelter, and that wouldn't happen.

"Yes, we do."

"With your permission, I'd like to contact the couple who run the place and ask if they're willing to provide shelter for the girl, our witness, while we provide security."

"Why do you need my permission?"

He took a photo and slid it across her desk. Tess picked it up. She recognized the man but said nothing.

"This is the man we believe headed up the trafficking ring. The man I want to bring down."

Tess brought a hand to her mouth, hoping she controlled the shock that she felt. To say that Cyrus Beck was a well-known public figure was an understatement. He was middle-aged, sixty at most, but his face was smooth and unlined. In the picture, he was wearing casual clothes and still appeared trim and fit. At least six feet tall, with his sandy-brown hair perfectly trimmed, Beck might be considered a handsome man by some, Tess supposed. But to her, his eyes were insolent, and there was a cruel smirk to the turn of his lips. Maybe she read what she knew about him into her perusal, but she'd never be attracted in any way to a man like Cyrus Beck.

In shock she asked, "He's not unknown to me, but human trafficking?"

"I intend to prove that his legal activities and outspoken activism provide cover for his baser hobbies," Bass said.

Tess took a deep breath. This was big. Among other things, Beck was a vocal environmentalist and one of the richest men in the country, maybe the world. In law enforcement circles he was what was considered a high-profile agitator. He would hire protesters to vocalize his beliefs, and he didn't care if his hires got violent — which they did, more often than not. She'd worked a couple of those incidents years ago, with Long Beach PD, and faced rioters behind riot shields.

One particular day stood out, a protest she'd worked down in the Long Beach harbor. Beck wasn't there, but it was well known he'd financed the activity. The group was protesting a Chinese company Beck accused of using manufacturing processes that contributed to global warming. Among other incendiary activities, they attempted to board container ships from China.

That day in the harbor a man died when

the brakes on the truck he was driving failed and the vehicle slammed into a wall. The brake lines had been cut. Such sabotage was something Beck's protesters routinely engaged in. Unfortunately, no arrests were ever made. And now this man she considered an irritant and provocateur was being charged with human trafficking.

As far as Tess knew, Beck's money was mostly inherited, but she'd read somewhere that he was a savvy investor and he also published a couple of magazines devoted to conservation. Tess believed in conservation, but she was not on the drive-only-electric-cars-or-only-ride-a-bike bandwagon. Cyrus Beck claimed to be passionate about ending all dependence on fossil fuels. Yet he was a jet-setter, from what she knew, flying all over the world on a private plane — talk about a carbon footprint. He threw his money behind any politician who shared his views, and he himself had stated in interviews that he believed in fomenting change, "by any means necessary."

This was where Tess had a major problem with the man. He endorsed violent revolt in the name of his cause. As a law enforcement professional, Tess hated it when the line between legal protests and violent riots became blurred.

It was the elephant in the room. Everyone knew that Beck, or one of the many non-profits he financed, paid the agitators, and they did damage, hurt people, destroyed businesses, not only in Long Beach, but all over the country. Yet he was never indicted for his role, never made to pay for the havoc he created. And scant few of the protesters were ever held accountable either, which always rubbed Tess raw.

Tess never understood it but knew it was political. All a cop could do when politics was involved was follow orders and policies and procedures to the letter.

She looked from the press release back to Bass, his expression unreadable. "You're sure?"

Bass nodded. "It will be all over the news tomorrow or the next day. I believe I have probable cause to ask a judge for an arrest warrant for Beck. Our girl has testimony and evidence that could put Beck away for a long time. I need to keep her safe, locked away. An Oregon battered women's shelter is the last place anyone would look."

"Doesn't the FBI have safe houses? Closer, maybe somewhere in Arizona or Nevada?" Tess's knee-jerk response was, *After the episode with the DEA rolling in for a high-profile search and arrest, did she really*

77

want to put her little hamlet through something similar again?

"Let's just say I'm afraid that the kind of money Beck has can buy information. He might own someone in Arizona law enforcement — I don't know for sure. I want my wit as off the radar as possible."

Something about the request bothered Tess. She glanced to the list of her life rules, framed and hanging in her office, a gift from Oliver. Rule #1: "Listen. Think. Speak. LTS." She sipped her coffee. Lately, she'd been working a lot with one federal agency or another.

"How long would you expect to keep her hidden?"

"I can't say. It depends on the court process. You know as well as I do things can drag out once his lawyers are in play." He hiked a shoulder.

Yes, Tess did know how things could drag out. "Do you need an answer right this minute?"

He sighed, clearly impatient. "Right now, my partner is with the girl in a hotel in White City. We have, at most, forty-eight hours to secure the witness. Time is a luxury."

"I understand, Agent Bass, but we just survived a big fire, we've yet to lift all the evacuation orders, and after what happened here this summer, I'm reluctant to put the people in my community at any further risk if I can avoid it. Let me speak to the people at the shelter. And I'll have to notify the sheriff. It's a county facility."

He held his hands up. "Speak to the couple, but I'm asking that you not notify the county. I realize that's putting you in a tough position, but seriously, the fewer people who know about this, the better. I'm sure I don't have to tell you how far and quick even the most unintended slip can spread. If Beck gets even a hint . . ."

Tess regarded Bass. He was right, she knew it, but now he was asking her to lay her butt on the line. She had a good working relationship with the Jackson County Sheriff's Office — did she really want to jeopardize it?

She wanted to talk to Oliver, Rogue's Hollow PD's official chaplain. She wanted to think about this for a good long time.

"I'll drive out there now. They weren't ordered to evacuate. I'll be as quick as I can, but I'm not going to make a decision this minute. And I need to read the department chaplain in on this. He's made aware of every woman who goes to Faith's Place in case they request spiritual help. I won't deny this victim that."

Bass frowned. "Will he keep his mouth shut?"

"I trust him."

After a long moment, he nodded. "Fair enough." He dropped a card on her desk. "That's me if you need to call and check up on me. Won't tell you who to talk to, but you can call the Phoenix office. Just don't mention the domestic violence shelter or my wit — and especially not in the same sentence — okay?"

"Gotcha."

"Do you mind if I go get a cup of coffee and come back in a bit?"

"I'll find you."

7

After Bass left, Tess sat at her desk for a minute. She'd planned on researching Livie Harp this morning, but instead she looked into Alonzo Bass. She couldn't help it; after coming face-to-face with a dirty DEA agent, one who nearly killed her, she wasn't going to take anything at face value. She called the Phoenix office and confirmed what Bass had told her. He was who he said he was, and he was part of a human trafficking task force. Tess skimmed the preliminary press release Bass had given her, still amazed that they were going to arrest Cyrus Beck.

She almost called Faith's Place, the domestic violence shelter, to speak to the couple who ran the place, Bronwyn and Nye Scales, give them a heads-up. But she put the phone down, deciding to drop in unannounced. Everything in Rogue's Hollow was a few minutes away. Tess finished her coffee as her phone beeped with a text. It was Oliver's good morning text. He was on his way back to the Hollow after the visit with Cherry.

Tess smiled and returned the message, at the last minute adding a question. When you get back, will you have a few minutes to take a drive with me?

Love to.

I'll be at the church and wait for you there.

Fifteen minutes later, with Oliver in the car, Tess started toward Faith's Place and told him about Agent Bass. He couldn't get past Cyrus Beck.

"Beck? Are you kidding me?"

"No, not at all." She cast a glance across the car. Oliver was certainly animated. "You sound as if you know him."

"In a way, I do. For a while, he was public enemy number one here in Oregon."

"What? Here? Why?"

"He was born and raised in Eugene. From what I've heard, his father owned a large logging operation. Beck Senior had his hands in a lot of different businesses. He was also an avid hunter, fisherman, out-doorsman."

"You're kidding me. Cyrus Beck is definitely not a chip off the old block."

"True. From what I've heard, he hated hunting and logging long before his father died. In fact, Beck Senior was killed in a freak accident while on a hunting trip. The story goes that as soon as Cyrus got control of the estate, he sold all interests in the logging operation and then set out to put all logging out of business. He organized protests in the forests, had people living in trees to save them, and started a save the spotted owl campaign and all that. A lot of old-timers blame him for the practice of spiking trees. When I first came here, his face was on a lot of shooting targets."

"Spiking trees?" Tess frowned. She'd heard the term but didn't remember where.

"A vicious tactic. Protesters would nail large spikes into trees. His stated reason for spiking trees was to make them worthless if cut. And when loggers did cut the trees, running a saw through a spiked tree became deadly. The saw blade would explode, and anyone nearby could be seriously hurt. A logger in California was almost killed. Beck was unrepentant. You can probably find videos on the Internet of him instructing people on how to spike trees."

"Charming. He's obviously graduated to more heinous crimes if he's involved in human trafficking."

"Jethro used to talk about the guy a lot. He knew the elder Beck and Cyrus, when he was a kid. Cyrus was spoiled, given anything and everything he ever wanted. He's never been held accountable for anything. . . . This is absolutely amazing if he's really going to finally be charged with a crime."

"A big-league crime at that," Tess added.

She had to pull over for a fire truck to pass on the narrow road they traveled. She nodded to the driver.

"When I first started at the church, in the children's ministry, Jethro often warned parents about indulging kids. In his mind that was what ruined Cyrus."

"Really? Sounds as if Jethro was really close to the Beck family."

"He was. He and the elder Beck served in the Army together. He always said Cyrus was Senior's blind spot. If you get him going, he'll tell you story after story about what a great man Senior was."

"I'd like to hear those stories."

"It's been at least ten years since Beck or his protesters have been in Oregon. I imagine Jethro will have a lot to say about Cyrus being arrested. He'll probably say it's poetic justice that we might keep a witness safe who could possibly serve up justice to him."

Tess shrugged. Though she firmly believed in the justice system, she couldn't deny that sometimes, people were able to buy justice. But human trafficking was a lot more serious and heinous than political agitating. Could this really be Beck's undoing?

She pulled up to the gate barring access to the shelter's driveway. Though Faith's Place was secure, it was not as secure as Livie Harp's compound. There was only a small camera at the intercom for IDs. And even though its location was a poorly kept secret, Tess had only heard of one incident here, several years ago, when a husband tried to get his wife out. Ken Blakely had broken his wife's jaw and disappeared before officers could arrest him. When his wife was released from the hospital, she was one of the first women to be housed at the shelter. Blakely ran his car through the gate, which at that time was wood, and tried to get into the house, but Rogue's Hollow officers arrived quickly and took him into custody. He ended up serving five years in prison for the incident and for injuries caused in a road rage encounter on the way to Faith's Place.

Tess had the code, and she punched it in and the gate swung open.

The battered women's shelter was in a part of the Hollow where no lot was less than an acre and the largest was five. The shelter itself had three acres. Tess knew that at one time the place had been part of a working farm, but the owners lost the business after some bad financial decisions, and the property was split up and stayed vacant for years. Bronwyn and Nye Scales had cleaned it up and set it up to rescue horses at first. When their daughter, Faith, was beaten to death by an abusive boyfriend, they set up a foundation in her name and remodeled the bedrooms to take in battered women. They kept up the horse rescue because Bronwyn couldn't say no to any hurting horse and they'd found this odd synergy in their quest to restore broken creatures: battered horses helped battered women recover and vice versa.

Tess felt a kinship with Bronwyn and Nye. She knew from experience how deadly domestic violence was. She'd lost her father when he responded to a domestic violence call. When the abusive husband raised his weapon to shoot his wife, Tess's dad stepped in the way and took the bullet, saving the woman's life and losing his own. Abused women needed a safe place to regroup and recognize that the abuse had to stop.

She pulled into the circular driveway and parked. The structure was a long, rambling house, the decoration and landscaping done in a Texas ranch style, right down to the long horns mounted over the front door and the large tree stump carving of a rearing horse on the right side of the driveway. Off to the left she saw Bronwyn working with a horse in the corral. The animal was thin and limping, Tess noted as she climbed out of the car. There was also an assortment of cows and goats in the front pasture area, animals rescued and kept safe from the fire, no doubt. Since Faith's Place had only been on standby for evacuation, the Nyes had taken in some livestock from places that had been required to vacate.

Tess and Oliver walked over to the corral.

"That a new acquisition?" Oliver asked.

"Yeah, she came in a couple of weeks ago. She's just calming down. The fires spooked everyone. I'm calling her Lollypop. Not sure what's up with her leg; have a vet coming out later this afternoon." Bronwyn led the animal to a trough, where Lollypop immediately stuck her nose in a pile of feed and began to munch.

After she tied the animal down and exited the corral, Bronwyn turned to Tess and Oliver. "What brings you two out here? Fire's out, and right now, I don't have any residents."

"We might have a resident for you."

Tess explained about the eighteen-year-old witness and the request for protection. And the secrecy involved. To Tess's surprise, Bronwyn knew about Beck. Not his past and not the environmental issues, but about the trafficking.

"I've heard whispers about that man. I attend a lot of domestic violence conferences all over the world. Lately, they intersect with this growing worldwide human trafficking problem. Gossip has been floating around about him for years."

"Really?" Tess was floored. She considered herself up to speed on law enforcement issues, but she'd not heard a whisper linking Beck to human trafficking.

Bronwyn nodded. "He's cagey. Scary too. There's a lot of fear about him. I met a woman from Malaysia, and she was convinced that Beck, or someone from his entourage, kidnapped girls from a small village there. Two villagers, mothers who wanted their daughters back, tried to complain to the government and were brutally murdered, and the story died. And it's not an isolated incident. I've heard similar ones from the Philippines, Pakistan, and India. He picks places where the authorities are easily bribed."

"So this could be a very dangerous proposition for you to house this girl," Oliver said.

Bronwyn hiked a shoulder.

"No pressure," Tess said. "I'll tell the agent no if you have any reservations."

Bronwyn's husband, Nye, walked up. "Reservations about what?"

Bronwyn filled him in. He smiled. "We're all about rescuing women. If this girl can put a bad man in jail, we'll help. We can't turn this one away, now can we?"

Bronwyn nodded. "I'll get a room ready straightaway."

8

"You don't think it's a good idea for them to house the girl?" Oliver asked as Tess drove back to town.

Tess tapped absentmindedly on the steering wheel. "Besides the fact that everything I now know about Beck is dangerous and disturbing, I don't really like leaving the sheriff in the dark. I don't know what to think. Beck has a lot of money. If he found out where the girl was and he wanted to cause problems here for Nye and Bronwyn, he certainly could."

"They don't seem to have a problem with the risk."

"No, they don't, but maybe they don't know what they're getting into."

"What has you so bothered?"

Tess blew out a breath. What did bother her? That something out of a suspense novel could happen? That Beck could send waves of hit men into Rogue's Hollow to locate and murder the witness, taking innocent people as well? That some horrible disaster was in the wings because of the power and reach that Beck had?

"I've just got a bad feeling about this. Maybe it's just coming too close on the heels of what we went through with DEA Agent Ledge and his crooked partner. I can't really verbalize a solid reason why I don't like the idea."

"Generally, I would agree with your hunches and feelings, but I think we should help this girl. We should help every girl or boy impacted by the evil and dehumanizing practice of human trafficking. It's a scourge on humanity that needs to be eradicated completely."

Tess looked across the car at Oliver and smiled as a warmth enveloped her. Oliver was the real deal when it came to helping others and to rescuing those in need. As a cop, Tess was used to helping people, but it was always surface aid because she had to move on, she couldn't get involved. With Oliver, his help went deeper. He truly cared about the souls of the people he assisted. Bottom line, he was genuine, and Tess loved that about him. He was her sounding board on a lot of things.

"I agree. Human trafficking is worse than

drug trafficking, a horrible plague on humanity. But after subjecting this town to a bloody shoot-out and two weeks of federal authorities looking into everything . . ." She patted the steering wheel with her palm. "Part of me wants everything to settle down. I've come to appreciate the quiet in small-town Rogue's Hollow."

"The shoot-out wasn't your fault. And look at the bright side — consider all the business those Feds brought to the town. Business is good even for a small town." He grinned.

"Good point. Casey even sold a record number of books during those two weeks."

"For two weeks Rogue's Hollow was on the map."

"I just want the Hollow on the map for positive reasons: the river, the Stairsteps, our wonderful lodging, not crime and chaos."

"Keeping this girl safe to testify and putting a predator in jail would be extremely positive. In the national arena." Oliver held his hand out and Tess put hers in it.

She couldn't argue with him there.

"The chaos, I trust you to handle," he said with a smile.

She returned the smile. "All right. I'll locate Agent Bass and tell him it's a go."

■ ■ ■ ■

Tess didn't have to look far for Bass. He was waiting for her at the station.

"I hope you have good news for me."

"I do. The Scaleses have agreed to house your witness. But before you jump for joy, I need to know all the particulars about the case and exactly what Beck is being charged with. And if anything goes right rudder, I'm letting the sheriff in."

"Fair enough. If you have the time, I'll show you everything."

"I'll make the time." Tess led the agent into her office and sat while he opened his briefcase and passed her a file.

"First, I'll admit that this ball got rolling because of a stroke of luck. For the past couple of years, we've been conducting training with the airlines on what to look for regarding human trafficking. Traffickers are brazen at times and will fly with girls across country, even out of the country. A flight attendant on a flight from New York to Phoenix noticed something odd about a threesome in first class. She thought the girls looked out of place with the man they were traveling with. She phoned ahead, and Homeland Security in Phoenix met the trio at the gate. Turns out, the girls were being trafficked. One was missing out of Tulsa, and the other from Florida. The man with them couldn't tell us much — he'd been given the girls by someone else — but he was taking them to the compound in Mesa. That gave us enough probable cause for the raid there.

"At the compound, we found three more girls. Two were Mexican nationals, the other from California. The disturbing thing is, all the girls went to the compound voluntarily."

Tess nodded. "They were runaways. I bet the person who brought them there promised them work or a better life or something."

"Exactly, and interestingly enough, they all described being recruited in a way, by a man who promised them high-paying jobs. Once in the compound, they were groomed for something else."

"This compound, it belonged to Beck?"

"Yeah, but it took a while to ferret that out. There were layers of shell companies, fake names —" he waved a hand — "but we figured it out. All the money trails lead to Beck. But it was talking to our adult victim that opened the floodgates. Chevy — that's what she likes to be called — was brought to Beck's brothel when she was fifteen. She became his favorite. That is, until she turned eighteen and was too old for him. She wasn't being altruistic or brave when she stole the iPad; she was jealous because she knew she was about to be replaced. Our raid coincided with her theft, and the tablet is now in our custody."

Tess frowned. "He left his tablet out where one of his victims could get to it?"

"No, she stole it."

"That sounds too convenient." Tess hated coincidences, especially when they were attached to such a large and complex operation. Right now rule #7 said, "Trust but verify." Should it be *"Trust but verify every coincidence"?*

"I'll take it, whatever you want to call it. We have the cause to ask a judge to issue a warrant for Beck. Evidence is stacking up. We're hopeful that once we retrieve the information on the tablet, there will be enough evidence to arrest him without bail as a flight risk. While there's a lot of circumstantial evidence, Chevy is the icing on the cake. She can tell a jury firsthand who Beck really is."

"I hope you're right."

"I am. And I'll tell you, Beck has been at this for a long time. Do you remember the name Porter Cross?"

Tess leaned back. The name was familiar, and then it clicked. He was a movie producer who, years ago, fell in a hard, public way. "Yes, I do remember that name. I think I was in the academy when he killed himself."

"Remember the name Isaac Pink?"

Tess nodded. "Every cop in Southern California knows that name. He and his family were murdered in their home. The killer or killers were never caught." She sat up. "Wait — Pink was sheltering a witness, a woman who supposedly had testimony to implicate Cross in a prostitution ring. Are you drawing a parallel here?"

"Not necessarily a parallel. More like a straight line. That case was the bureau's first stab at Cross and the first time Cyrus Beck came to our attention outside of environmental issues. The witness had been arrested for prostitution in San Pedro. Pink was a vice sergeant; he interviewed her. Heather Harrison was her name. He believed her when she told him she was being trafficked and forced into prostitution against her will. He contacted the FBI because she claimed she'd been moved from state to state, which made it a federal crime. She gave him the name Porter Cross and mentioned someone named Cyrus she didn't know as well."

"I don't recall Beck being attached to the Pink case at all."

"He wasn't. Other than the fact that he was a known associate of Cross — they were often photographed at the same Hollywood parties — there was no hard evidence tying him to anything illegal. At the time, the bureau already had an open file on Cross — a lot of smoke, but again, no actionable evidence. Heather didn't know his last name, but Cyrus was eventually determined to be Beck, and that was a new wrinkle."

He sighed and rubbed his forehead. "Back then, trafficking was not understood well, and it was often the women being exploited who suffered the full force of the law and not the traffickers. Sure, the occasional street pimp fell, but there were a lot of others who escaped the long arm of the law. It would have been standard operating procedure for Harrison to be charged and tried for prostitution because of the sweep, with no one considering that maybe it had never been her choice. In one way it was lucky for her that Isaac Pink was the vice cop who interviewed her."

"Lucky for her, not for him. Pink and his whole family were murdered with his service revolver, and she disappeared. She's the prime suspect in the murders. She had access."

Tess frowned as she remembered the manhunt for Pink's killer. Though she was not yet a cop herself at the time, her father was involved; he'd known Pink. And after the case was long cold, Pink's partner, Aaron Graves, gave a presentation on the investigation to her academy class. He was convinced that Heather Harrison was complicit in the murder but conceded that she hadn't worked alone. Tess had read that Graves died a couple of years ago, and his dying wish was that no one would forget Pink or stop looking for his killer.

"That was the line of thinking back then," Bass said. "When the girl disappeared, the grand jury was canceled. And the case against Cross disintegrated."

"Heather Harrison would have to have been a cold character. Along with Pink and his wife, his twelve-year-old daughter was executed that night," Tess mused out loud.

"If you truly believe she was the killer."

"You doubt that?"

He shrugged. "There are just a lot of blank spots in the case. Back then, Harrison was not the only potential witness against Cross who disappeared. Twice before, he was implicated in crimes, not pandering, but murder. Once in Florida, a woman who'd been seen with him ended up murdered. Unfortunately, so did the person who could put them together. No charges filed. Then in Mexico he was involved in the deaths of two women. Mexican authorities tried to extradite him, but the case fell apart when the witnesses recanted or disappeared."

"I hadn't heard about those cases."

"They are still open and cold. When Pink contacted the bureau about Harrison, agents tried to stay out of things, make the case look local, so Cross wouldn't be alerted too soon. But they worried enough about what could happen that they even set up a fake safe house, hoping if Cross did get wind of the investigation, it would draw him out, and maybe they'd catch him in the act coming for the witness."

"That was why Pink gave Harrison shelter in his own home."

Bass nodded.

"There was a leak," Tess said.

"Yeah, Cross never fell for the fake safe house. The whole thing was only supposed to be for a short time, while a grand jury was seated. Everyone thought the security was tight enough, that Cross was in the dark. But two days before Harrison was set to testify for the grand jury, Pink and his family were murdered, and she disappeared."

Hearing his words, Tess felt punched in the stomach, reliving, in a sense, that day the news broke about Pink's murder. Her father had been livid, inconsolable. Police work was a brotherhood. When a cop fell in the line of duty, it impacted everyone who wore the uniform. And Isaac Pink was slain in his own home with his family — that was particularly heinous. Daniel O'Rourke would have been upset even if he hadn't known Pink; as it was, they'd attended a couple of training classes together.

"He was one of the really good guys," he'd said just before he left to help with the eventually fruitless manhunt.

Pink died protecting a victim, and not too long after that, her father would be dead protecting a victim. Tess had to swallow and regroup her thoughts. Cops sometimes died protecting people — it was a fact of life.

"The evidence at the scene was confused and confusing," Bass continued. "There was no sign of Harrison, but she'd left a note in a jar where the Pink family kept extra cash. The cash was gone, and she apologized for taking it."

Tess frowned. "As I recall, that's one of

the reasons they named her as suspect number one."

Bass nodded. "It was an emotionally charged investigation. Everyone knew Pink. He was respected and well liked. The viciousness of the crime scene ramped everyone up. Pink's department conducted a full-on manhunt for the girl. Well, you know every agency in the state was on the hunt for the killer. The agents on the case sat back and let the locals run with it. When Harrison was named as the prime suspect, they hoped it would flush her out, if she were still alive. After all, she stole the money, and Pink's gun was never recovered."

"The case is cold now, still unsolved. But somehow I get the impression you don't think Harrison is the assassin."

"No, I don't. The man I took over for on the task force was convinced Cross was behind the murders, and I think the evidence backs up that theory. Forensics has come a long way in twenty-five years. Pink's gun was a .357 caliber revolver. One such slug was removed from his body, but other slugs were recovered as well, from him and the wall behind him, .38 caliber, indicating a second shooter."

"Harrison could have had a gun no one

knew about."

"I'll concede that. But later we discovered the .38 slugs matched ballistics in other murders in LA. There was also blood evidence by the back door, blood that didn't belong to any of the Pinks. And Isaac had been on the phone moments before being shot, talking to his partner. He told his partner the house alarm had been disconnected before hanging up, so . . ." Bass shrugged.

Tess considered this as a memory surfaced. "My dad never believed that Harrison could have killed Pink. The sergeant was too savvy to be shot to death by the girl he was sheltering. Pops believed they were looking for someone completely cold-blooded."

"Your pops was wise."

Tess shared another of her father's theories. "Do you think Harrison was killed as well and dumped somewhere else?"

Bass spread his hands. "She never resurfaced. My guess is, yes, she's dead. The bureau kept on the case after Cross. He left the country for a time, tried to live off the radar, but ten years later, his appetites eventually betrayed him. He came back to the States, and we caught him for kiddie porn. I was part of the child pornography task force that arrested him. When we caught him, he had more pornography on his computer and in his possession than any person I'd ever investigated."

"How did you catch him with the porn?"

"We got an anonymous tip, then set up a sting. I hate dealing with kiddie porn, but the guy was truly a sick puppy. He fell, hook, line and sinker."

"I remember his pretrial press conference. He cried and swore that he was innocent."

Bass rolled his eyes. "After his arrest we were flooded with complaints — women, girls, boys, all with stories about what a sick puppy he was and how they'd been exploited. He'd put fear into all of them. Some claimed to know of people he'd murdered to keep them from talking to the cops. Him being in custody made them brave."

"Were you ever able to substantiate any of the claims?"

"A lot of molestation, some rape, but we could never prove any murders. But now we get to the reason I bring Cross up at all. Like I said, Cyrus Beck was one of his closest friends — until, of course, the arrest."

Tess nodded, trying to remember more from that time period. It was big news when Cross was arrested.

Bass continued. "Twenty-five years ago,

like now, Beck had a lot of juice. Two years after Pink's death, an FBI agent working out of the LA office was arrested for being on the take. He was thought to have passed information about federal investigations to several people, one of whom was Cyrus Beck. And this agent was privy to the case involving Harrison."

"Beck was the one to compromise Sergeant Pink?"

"A possibility we could never prove. The agent refused to cooperate, but he was eventually convicted and sent to federal prison. He was killed in a fight after six months in custody."

"Wow" was all Tess could say.

"When I began to poke around into Beck's association with Cross and started to see some red flags and irregularities — he traveled a lot to Malaysia, Vietnam, countries with reputations for child trafficking — the task force was disbanded under the guise of budget cuts, and I was told to back off. I can't prove it, but I believe Beck got the door closed on that investigation."

Tess nodded. Unfortunately, she believed that was entirely possible. Money could and did circumvent justice.

"I kept after him anyway, on my own time. I built a file on Beck." Bass showed her some timelines, a chronological record of the investigation of Cyrus Beck.

"You're certain that Beck has been involved in criminal activity for at least twenty-five years." Tess's stomach turned at the thought of over two decades of depravity.

"I am. I haven't had the hard evidence to prove it in court. Beck and Cross were thick as thieves for a long time before Cross's death. He had the power to shut down my investigation for a time. But fast-forward to the present, because human trafficking is growing exponentially, it's in the news all the time now, and another task force was formed. We scooped up Chevy and discovered that she had the iPad."

Tess studied the timelines and the accompanying FBI notes. It wasn't long before she saw a pattern. With every protest Beck sponsored, girls went missing. All over the world, he used his supposed environmental awareness to victimize women. Mesa, where Chevy was apprehended, was also where Beck's main US home was located. She could see it wasn't far from the compound that was raided. The photos of the place were impressive. It was everything you'd expect a multimillionaire to have. She bet the estate, spread along a ridgeline, was at least six thousand square feet of living space. She counted three chimneys, a manicured yard, and two swimming pools.

"He ran a brothel out of his home?"

Bass shook his head. "The compound in Mesa has no direct links to him — at first glance. It took a lot of digging, but we discovered that one of Beck's shell companies was listed as owning the property. We believe that because he's gone untouched for so long, he's begun to think he's untouchable. There is also a money trail from Beck to the man detained at the airport."

"He'll flee."

"He may try, but we'll impound his plane when the warrant is issued, and then when we bring him in, we'll take his passport."

Tess glanced at the list of charges. "You have him for murder?"

"Two prior witnesses, women who contacted the FBI in Arizona about the compound and Beck, have disappeared. We've found blood evidence in the compound that leads us to believe they were murdered there. It's so Hollywood, but there's a trail of missing women I've been following." Bass shuffled some of the papers from his briefcase. "Something else interesting has come up, something I think exonerates Heather Harrison. For a while now the bureau has been consulting with agencies in Phoenix regarding some unsolved murders of women in the area."

"In the past, I've heard Phoenix called the unsolved murder capital of the country. A lot of the unsolved cases have female victims, but not many have been proven to be connected."

"We've linked seven unsolved murders to the same weapon, a .357 Magnum. Isaac Pink's stolen handgun."

Tess sucked in a breath.

"Right. Unless Harrison has evaded capture all these years and is killing women with Pink's gun, someone else is. I believe that someone is the person who killed Pink twenty-five years ago."

"That's a leap. Playing devil's advocate here — Harrison could have given the gun to someone, lost it, or tossed it, even. Or if she is still alive, it could have been taken from her."

"Maybe. But I still think it's a bigger stretch to believe she was involved in any way with Sergeant Pink's death. And interestingly, Beck has owned this compound in Mesa for as long as Phoenix has been dealing with these record numbers of unsolved murder cases involving women."

Another horrific coincidence.

"I believe all these murders are the work of a man who is employed by Beck now and probably was associated with Cross back then." Bass pulled out a composite sketch of a man. "We call this guy the Piper."

She picked the sketch up. "Like the Pied Piper?"

"Yeah. Based on what the girls we just rescued say, he's the recruiter. He picks up women — girls really — and delivers them to Beck. And when Beck is done with the girl, the Piper takes care of things."

Studying the picture, Tess saw a strong jaw, steady gaze, and chiseled features that indicated this guy was probably good-looking. But it was also a generic drawing, could be made to fit a lot of men.

Bass nodded, seemingly reading her mind. "I know, I know. It's not a perfect ID. But I've been on Beck's trail for practically my entire career. Chevy has helped fill in a lot of blank spots, and we're close, finally, to putting a true predator and his entourage in jail."

She pushed the drawing back across the desk. "That's a goal I can get behind."

9

All evacuation orders were lifted a little before 1 p.m., shortly after Tess dropped Oliver back at the church after the Faith's Place visit. Power had been restored to all of Rogue's Hollow, and while it saddened Oliver to see anyone lose a home, it was truly a miracle no more than four homes had been lost. And it was wonderful that no lives were lost. The families who still had a dwelling to go to packed up their belongings, grateful their houses were spared. Oliver helped several people gather their things and leave the church as soon as he'd heard.

One family that was not so lucky, Oliver was working hard to help in any way he could. Janie Cooper was inconsolable about the loss of a home that had been in her family for a hundred years. Once all the evac orders were lifted, Oliver and Garrett had driven out to the Coopers' property to take stock of the damage. If you didn't know a house had been on the lot, you certainly wouldn't have been able to tell.

Garrett cursed and kicked some charred wood around. "This was everything we had, Pastor. Everything."

Oliver chose his words carefully. He knew Garrett was a hothead, in and out of jobs, and that the only reason he hadn't lost the house to the bank was because the paid-off home had been willed to his wife when her mother died. The family scratched out a living mostly on Janie's small but steady paycheck from Walmart.

"We'll help all we can to get you back on your feet, Garrett. You can stay at a property the church owns until something more permanent is found."

"I never should have left. I should have stayed and fought that fire with my own hose and well water."

"The house can be replaced —"

"Stop saying that!" Garrett turned, fury etched on his face. "Everyone keeps saying that, and it's not true! You can never replace what I had in that house. I should have died trying to protect it." He stalked past Oliver, brushing his shoulder as he did. "Let's get out of here."

Praying silently, wondering at the fury and whether or not there was something else at the bottom of Garrett's rage, Oliver followed Garrett back to the car.

It was after 2:30 p.m. before Agent Bass and Tess got his witness, Roberta Impala, aka Chevy, comfortably, if reluctantly, ensconced in Faith's Place. The girl was small and slight, but there was a strength about her that surprised Tess. Nothing about her posture or attitude said victim. She had long, brown, smooth and sleek hair pulled back into a ponytail. It shone as if she spent a lot of time brushing it. She wore dark tights and a hoodie with *Denver* emblazoned across the front. She had with her a backpack of belongings and a new Kindle Bass had given her. She was discouraged from using the Internet at all, and Bass requested Bronwyn purchase any books that Chevy requested.

There was also a simmering petulance that Tess sensed in the girl. She was wound tight with anger and frustration. Her large brown eyes, her expression, and her entire visage looked more mature than eighteen years, and that saddened Tess. Chevy's youth had been stolen from her. In spite of how together she looked, how much unobservable damage was present and permanent? And surprisingly, Chevy was not happy with the situation she was now in.

"I'm going from one prison to the next," she groused.

"We've been through this," Bass said soothingly. "You're doing the right thing, and with luck, it will all be over soon, and you'll have your life back."

Chevy gave him a look filled with teenage cockiness and then announced that she was tired and wanted a nap.

Bronwyn showed her to her room. When she came back out, she shot a bemused glance Tess's way.

"You might have your hands full," Tess said.

"I can handle it," she said with a smile. "Nothing like a teenage girl to electrify a home."

Tess gave a wry smile before her attention was directed elsewhere.

"She's tucked away safe and sound. Why is there a need for me to stay here as well?"

The protest was coming from Alonzo's partner, Mia Takano, a small, compact woman. Tess could read the agent's tense body language.

"Mia, we've had this discussion before." Bass pulled her to the side. Tess tried not to eavesdrop, but she bet the issue was that the assignment was basically glorified babysitting, and Takano did not want to be stuck out in the wilderness like this. Takano thought Bass was overreacting, that there was no need to keep the witness away from the US Marshals.

Tess could sympathize. There were a lot of exciting, challenging duties in police work, but there was also plenty of grunt work: standing perimeters, waiting for coroners, babysitting prisoners. Most cops would rather get the challenging duty. And the trafficking case was big and challenging. If Tess were Mia, she'd prefer to be somewhere else, in the thick of the investigation, rather than sidelined with a teenager, even though all of the duty helped make the case. Takano would have to bend to authority and settle into the job.

Bass was the senior agent, and he won in the end. It was an unhappy Agent Takano who dragged her suitcase into the shelter as Tess and Bass left the area. Before Bass left, he gave Tess a thumb drive — "The sum total of my investigation into Cyrus Beck." Tess hoped to have time to look through it all carefully.

While the decision to house the girl had been Bronwyn and Nye's, and they were both more than capable, Tess felt a rising anxiety and a strong premonition that she should have tried harder to talk them out of it.

After all, Isaac Pink was a trained cop, and look what had happened to him and his family when he'd tried to shelter a witness. Tess prayed history would not repeat itself and vowed she would do all in her power to keep everyone safe.

10

Bass had been gone about an hour when a familiar face knocked on Tess's door.

"Got a minute, Chief?"

Tess looked up and smiled at Sergeant Steve Logan, a man she had dated when she first came to Rogue's Hollow, and someone she still considered a good friend at the sheriff's department. But Tess was wary. What if he'd heard about the witness? She was not about to lie straight to his face.

"Sure, Steve, what's up?"

He stepped into her office and she saw he wasn't alone. Behind him came a fish and game officer Tess knew but didn't like. Win Yarrow was taciturn and disagreeable. He was also old-school and chauvinistic. Tess hadn't had much contact with him but got the distinct impression that he did not care for her. Besides, she could never compete with him when it came to knowledge of the outdoors and the issues he dealt with on a

115

daily basis.

"It's because you aren't a native Oregonian," RHPD Officer Bender had told her. "Don't take it personal."

She tried not to, but at times the man was openly hostile.

"Win and I have had a busy morning," Steve said.

"I can smell that," she said, making a face. Both men were smudged with soot, and they brought with them the smoky odor of fire and burning wood. They'd been in the burn area for some reason.

Tess knew Steve had been tasked with assisting Yarrow. Over the summer there had been a spike in poaching on BLM property. Somebody very good with a hunting or sniper rifle had been killing and butchering wildlife. Yarrow had his hands full. He'd even gotten fish and game to offer a $25,000 reward for information leading to the arrest of the poacher.

While Tess didn't respond to any of the poaching because it was out of her jurisdiction, there had been two disturbing calls in the Hollow at small family farms, where in one incident two lambs were shot and in another, two lambs and a calf were killed. All the animals, domestic as well as wild, were killed by a high-powered rifle according to Yarrow, so his theory was that the poacher was killing the farm animals as well.

Yarrow's poacher was prolific, with kills all over the county, but most of them on BLM land bordering the Hollow and Butte Falls. Coincidentally, the man Yarrow suspected of being the poacher was Rogue's Hollow resident Ken Blakely, the one and only man who'd tried to break into Faith's Place to get to his wife. Right before the fire Yarrow had informed Tess that he planned to serve a warrant on the suspect's home. He'd asked that she stand by.

"Is this about the warrant? I'm so sorry, but with the fire —"

Yarrow held a hand up. "I understand why you missed our appointment. I know you've had your hands full the last few days. Sergeant Logan was there, and I had a couple of state cops with me." He grimaced. "We came up empty. Nada. Zip. Zero. I'm still certain Blakely is our guy, but he outplayed me this round."

"I second that," Steve said. "I wouldn't put it past him to have hidden the evidence somewhere else. He's sneaky and mean, especially since his release from prison, so he's not a novice."

"He's my only suspect. I have no choice but to keep after him," Yarrow said.

"He's savvy — that's for sure — knows how to play the system," Tess said. She and Blakely had crossed paths several times, usually because someone was complaining about him or something rude that he'd done. He lived in Rogue's Hollow's only apartment complex, a couple of streets behind the station. He was the neighbor nobody wanted to have. "Does not play well with others" applied to him in spades. His hatred of cops was not even thinly veiled. Poacher or no, since he was an ex-felon, he could not legally own a firearm and certainly not a high-powered rifle. She felt it was best to keep an eye on him, but not to crowd.

"He'll be here filing harassment complaints if you're not careful."

"I'll be careful, but I won't back off because we found some more kills." He handed Tess some photos. "Turns out the fire uncovered more poached carcasses."

Tess glanced at the photos, trying with all her might to fight the shock and nausea. Born and raised in Southern California, a region not all that hunter friendly, Tess was new to the hunting culture. At first, the animal lover in her had screamed for Bambi, but hunting friends like Victor Camus clued her in to the sport and to the fact that 99 percent of the hunters in her jurisdiction hunted not only for the sport, but for the meat. They ate venison and elk, and if they didn't, they found someone who did. Poachers were the one percent who wasted and killed for the wrong reasons. Yarrow had been trying to catch this particular offender all summer long.

Whether the pictures before her were the work of poachers, Tess couldn't say; she'd have to take Yarrow's word for it. From what she could see — and she wasn't certain because the animals were charred and burnt — there was a headless deer, a headless elk, and what looked like the body of a dog.

"He shot a dog?"

"It's a wolf, one of my marked wolves. He killed him and skinned him. These photos were taken up on the ridge around the boundary of Rogue's Hollow and BLM land. This guy kills whatever crosses his path."

Tess glanced from Yarrow to Logan, remembering the poor dead lambs. "So does this confirm that he's also responsible for the dead livestock?"

Steve nodded. "Some bullet fragments taken from poached bears were similar to fragments taken from one of the dead lambs."

Tess shook her head. "Any idea why he'd

target domestic animals as well?"

Yarrow shrugged. "I think the guy is just plain mean."

"Hard to tell his motive for the farm animals," Steve said. "But it could be spite. Blakely is the most disagreeable man I've ever known."

"Yes, that's Blakely," Tess conceded. "Is there a lot of money in poaching?"

"The wolf pelts maybe. But he's killed five black bears, gutted them, and removed their gallbladders. There's a heavy black-market demand for those."

Tess had read something about that. Bear gallbladders were supposed to be a cure for many diseases.

"He might leave an online trail for that. He's not selling bear gallbladders in the Hollow."

"He claims he doesn't own a computer or a cell phone. Says he doesn't know how to use them. In our search, we didn't recover a computer. And unfortunately, I don't have the resources or the tech skills to dig around online."

"What's good about finding these old kills —" Steve held up an evidence bag — "is we recovered more bullet fragments. They can be compared against everything else we've recovered. There will be a landslide of evidence when we catch him."

"All you need is the gun," Tess observed. "What exactly is the profile of a poacher?" she asked.

"Blakely." Steve and Yarrow spoke in unison.

"Ken's no dummy." Steve cast a glance at Yarrow. "He was born and raised here, probably knows the terrain better than anyone. I grew up with him. He killed his first deer when we were twelve."

"He worked at the butcher shop before he got arrested and sent to prison," Yarrow added, "so he knows how to cut up an animal. I'm convinced he has his weapon or weapons stashed somewhere. There's also a good chance that he's set up a hunting blind in the forest, and that's where he's hiding stuff. I'll find it if it's the last thing I do."

Steve hooked his thumbs in his belt. "I can't say I know everyone in Rogue's Hollow, but no one name jumps out at me like Ken's. He came out of prison a different man, more angry and difficult. Living on disability now, claims he can't work because of headaches. Poaching would supplement his income. Just to cover all the bases, we're going to talk to Victor Camus. He might have heard something different, or maybe he's noticed something off. He's in the forest a lot."

Tess agreed with that. As a local hunting guide, Victor knew the forest even better than Yarrow. "What should I be looking for?"

"Someone like Ken who doesn't work suddenly having money," Yarrow said. "That's an expensive truck he drives around. Someone good with a gun — the newer kills were spot-on; the guy's aim is dead-on."

"Ken was always a good shot."

Yarrow nodded in agreement. "I want to put up some trail cams."

He walked to the map of Jackson County hanging on Tess's office wall. He pointed to a couple of spots on the border of Rogue's Hollow and BLM property. It was rough country and had partially escaped the fire. "Because of the fire, he's lost some hunting ground. If he is based here in the Hollow, odds are good that he'll make his way along these trails eventually. They lead to bear territory."

"Fine, I don't have a problem with that."

"Thanks," Yarrow said.

"Is there anything else I can help you with?" Tess asked.

"I'll be sure and let you know if I think of something," he said and left.

Logan lingered. "How are you doing, Tess?

That fire was something."

"Oh yeah. It could have been much worse. We were lucky that the resources were close, and it was a freak late-season fire."

"I hear you met the hermit."

"Ah." Tess smiled. Just about everyone wanted to know about Livie Harp. "The Rogue telegraph spreads the news. I did. She's impressive, but quite the enigma."

"I remember when she moved up here. The telegraph was on fire. I would have bet that she was in witness protection, but —" he arched an eyebrow — "I'm not sure that makes sense. You have any thoughts?"

"To be honest, I've been trying to dig into her background, figure out what gives. I haven't had any luck. She certainly is off the grid and self-sustained. But she doesn't cause any problems for me, that's for sure."

"Well, if you get a chance to visit her again, think of your old friend Steve Logan, okay?" He spread his hands. "I'd like to get a read on her. She takes prepping to the next level."

"You got it."

Steve gave a thumbs-up and left her office.

Tess brooded. She'd wanted to tell him about the witness being sheltered and hoped he'd forgive her if he had to learn about it in a different manner.

11

Ice cooled his heels in Reno for a few days. While he waited for the incident in San Jose to calm down, he'd changed his appearance. He studied his face in the hotel mirror as if memorizing his new look. He'd buzzed his hair and then dyed what remained jet-black and left his beard to grow a bit. He didn't care for this look, but it was necessary. He'd changed his appearance many times over the years, ever since he'd shed the name Royal for Ice. He wasn't even averse to makeup or color-tinted contacts. He'd gotten good with makeup and fancied himself a master of disguise. It had to be done, so he'd live with this new change as long as he needed to.

From what he read on the San Jose news sites, the girl he'd left next to the dead cheater had given the police a good description of him, but not perfect. It helped that the cheater had drugged her enough to make her unsure of just about everything. He didn't like to waste time on regrets, so he didn't go down the road that said he should have killed her too. At any rate, that was miles behind him now. He was hunkered down at a cheap hotel in downtown Reno. The secret to staying free was to move fast and without hesitation. It always took the cops a while to catch up, so he was used to moving along. And he never used credit cards; his life operated on untraceable cash.

He checked his phone. There was a page of requests — clients looking for girls, and one urgent request from his best client, probably the only person in the world he would call a friend. Cyrus. That was the one he called back.

"What's up?"

His client cursed. "You heard about the bust?"

Ice shook his head, though he was on the phone. "I've been traveling."

"Ice, we have a problem. They took down a whole cell. Mesa is gone."

Ice sat. This was big. A lot of his girls went straight to Mesa; it was like an airport hub for his clients. This was going to hurt business, that was for sure.

"Wow, how'd that happen?"

"Feds got lucky. Look, that's not important. I've got a job for you."

"I'll be collecting girls as —"

"No, put that on hold. I want you to find a piece of merchandise the Feds took from the compound in Mesa. Chevy took something that belongs to me and I want it back."

Ice knew that name. Chevy, aka Roberta. He'd procured her for Cyrus . . . he had to think about how long ago. Two, maybe three years — it all ran together. She was trouble from the beginning, too smart for her own good, and Cyrus had let her get too close, the silly old fool. Chevy had almost been allowed into the inner circle. Ice had noticed that as Cyrus aged, he was taking more and more chances, getting more and more sloppy. Now his little pet had taken something from Cyrus and presumably given it to the Feds. Ice digested this information. The Feds took everything when they served a warrant and pounced on anything incriminating.

"How do you know she didn't already give it to the cops?" he asked.

"I'm talking to you, aren't I? Besides, it compromises you as well."

Ice felt anger surge as it often did when his safety was threatened by other people's stupidity. Even though this man was a friend, Ice really only trusted himself. That was why he liked to work alone. He counted to ten as he realized that he couldn't be compromised that much. His clients didn't really know him — they only thought they did. Even his friend only knew a fraction about him and what he did with his time.

"What is it?"

"My iPad with all my business information on it. Get it back. This is worth a couple of rocks to me. An extra one if you terminate the thief. I'm not even concerned about collateral damage. Do what you need to do. Scorched-earth time."

Three rocks. Briefly, Ice saw all those zeros and held his breath. *Three million dollars.* The figure even chased away the question of how Cyrus was stupid enough to leave his tablet where the girl could get it. Ice waited a beat, never wanting to appear overeager. But that was enough money to buy himself some leisure. The older he got, the more he thought about fading into the sunset on some tropical island somewhere. Now was his chance, if he could find the tablet and the girl.

"You have any information about where the girl was taken?"

"She's on the West Coast somewhere, I think. I'm priming the pump. I'll find out soon enough. I've got Digger out beating the bushes. I'll text you any information I get."

"All right, I'm in. I'll contact you on a different phone when it's done."

"Good. I'll send you a down payment. Terminate the brat. I want pictures."

A few minutes later Ice watched the balance in his bank account swell. Then he went to work, hacking, digging, determined to find out all the particulars of the Feds' case against Cyrus and the girl who'd just earned him so much money.

When he stopped to eat and finish the rest of a cold pizza, Ice turned on the news. There was still a trickle about him and the murder in an abandoned house. The cops in San Jose were asking for help and had set up a tip line, but he could tell interest was already fading. The first forty-eight were rapidly ticking away. They'd never find him.

He picked up his tablet again and searched every site he could for more information on the bust in Mesa. For the first time in a long while Ice felt fear. Not fear for himself — he could disappear and never be found; no one really knew him — but fear for his best client. Cyrus was really more than a client; he was a surrogate father as far as Ice was concerned. The Feds were hot on his trail, that was for sure, and if this news report was accurate, they'd built quite a strong case against him.

He almost picked up the phone to warn Cyrus, but stopped. Cyrus must know the danger he was in. That was why he wanted Chevy and everyone around her dealt with. He had contingency plans. He might have already flown out of the country. The girl was a small part of the whole case. Taking her out might not help the larger fight.

But it was personal now — Ice understood that. The girl had betrayed Cyrus in a big way. She deserved her fate. And there would be collateral damage, Ice could see that already. The Feds were obviously trying to hide her. She would be guarded. None of that mattered to Ice. He'd track her down and take care of the problem. He'd worked for too long with Cyrus. Failure was not an option.

Ice opened a beer. Cyrus had sounded more agitated than Ice had ever heard him. Sitting on the bed, he muted the sound on the television to think, watching the screen but not really seeing it. His thoughts took him back over the years to when he and Cyrus had met. It was through Boss Cross, the man who had literally pulled him up out of the gutter. Ice had grown up as Royal Redd. As the son of two drug addicts, he'd never really known his parents. They'd surrendered their parental rights when he was three years old. For six years he lived with his alcoholic maternal grandmother. But her death to cancer when he was nine was the end of any charade of stability.

It was also the end of his conscience. Tossed into a foster home with the first name *Royal* and the last name *Redd,* he was teased mercilessly. He learned to fight and steal to survive. A boy named Sue had nothing on a boy named Royal Redd.

He bounced from foster home to foster home until he turned seventeen. By then he'd learned to support himself by theft and con. Con especially energized Royal. He'd honed his ability to sell any illusion he tried and to make people believe him. The most important discovery he made was that his looks got him things from women. At eighteen he'd had three women strung out and turning tricks for him. That was where he'd met Cross.

Cross had pulled up in a stretch limo looking for girls. Girls, not women. Royal found him one, and a partnership was born. Royal learned to do whatever Cross asked: procure girls, deal with problems, anything. Then he'd been sent to find a witness, and he thought his way out of a difficult situation, and Royal earned his nickname Ice.

"You are Ice." Cross had beamed. "I don't think Devo could have thought on his feet like that." The girl had slipped through his fingers, but Cross was certain she'd surface sooner or later. But in twenty-five years, that hadn't happened.

Ice never dwelled on his first failure. She was probably dead in a gutter, he thought now, brushing away any regret. Thinking about the one who'd gotten away made Ice renew his vow to find Chevy by whatever means necessary.

If the partnership with Cross had changed his life — and he'd been all over the world with Cross and his man Digger, who'd become his mentor — it was Cyrus Beck who had given Ice purpose. By the time Cross got tripped up by kiddie porn, Ice was freelancing. He'd learned how to speak fluent Spanish, and he'd become a master at procuring women and girls for Cross's vast network. Cross had even created a new identity for Ice, complete with a forged driver's license and a bank account.

Cross's arrest and subsequent death had rocked him hard. Ice couldn't figure out how the canny Cross had let it slip that he had so much kiddie porn for the Feds to find. He believed someone had betrayed

Cross, and it made him furious. At first, he'd wanted to find the leak, deal with the person who'd betrayed Cross. But then the Boss killed himself, and for a brief time, Ice was adrift.

Then Cyrus stepped in and saved Ice from aimlessness. Cyrus had been there the night Royal earned his chops and called Ice ever since, and Royal liked that.

He liked thinking of himself as cold as Ice. Nothing bothered him, and nothing could touch him. He believed he was smarter than any cop, especially a Fed.

His phone dinged with a text. Ice punched in his code and saw that Cyrus had texted him a brief message.

FBI Agent Bass recently traveled to Medford, southern Oregon, went private, so my bet is he's hidden the girl there somewhere. Suggest you check it out.

Ice knew that Bass was the agent who'd made catching Cyrus his personal crusade. At one point Cyrus had played around with the idea of having Ice take Bass out, but at the last minute backed off. As Ice reread the text, he thought maybe Cyrus had made a mistake. Bass was like a pit bull, hanging on to Cyrus's leg, desperate to take him down. It would be best to put Bass down first. The thought of killing an FBI agent didn't bother Ice in the least.

He punched southern Oregon into Google and checked out Medford and the surrounding area. Small town, small potatoes. If the girl were there, it'd be a cinch to find her. Another text came through: Maybe Shady Cove?

"Hmm, is that a town?" Ice asked out loud.

He typed, Why there?

Then he put that name into his search and found it. A check of Wikipedia told him that Shady Cove, Oregon, was a dinky place, population just over three thousand. A recent news article from another nearby small town, Rogue's Hollow, indicated the area had been devastated by a fire just days ago.

We've searched hotels in Medford, Ashland, can't find any indication Bass stayed either of those places. Grants Pass is another possibility, but this Cove place, it looks like a place they think we'd ignore, came the answer from Cyrus.

Ice thought about that. Cyrus might be right. In any case, the town would have Barney Fife–type cops, he bet. Yeah, if the girl were there, he'd find her.

It would be child's play.

12

Several days passed before Tess could review the thumb drive Alonzo Bass had left her. She'd wanted to get to it sooner, but there had been so much to do after the fire, she'd had to sideline it.

After all evacuation orders were lifted, she'd been busy with organizing fire cleanup and helping the families who'd lost everything in the fire. The threat of shifting weather added urgency to her task. Cold and rain — a lot of rain — were forecast soon, and they had to hurry to prevent landslides from destroying more in the burn area. The city council raided an emergency fund to help with the cleanup. The new mayor, Pete Horning, decided on what he saw as the most cost-effective way to proceed with the job. His thinking was that this was a transition time for seasonal workers. Summer work was winding down and winter work had not yet fired up. He felt there would be plenty of people eager and available to help for a week to ten days.

Tess was wary of the idea for a lot of reasons, but it was the first time in her tenure as police chief that she saw unanimous agreement on the part of the city council. And an ad in the paper asking for temporary help, promising a little better than minimum wage, had brought in a surprisingly large number of applicants. The city council would oversee the program, reviewing applications and hiring people to start ASAP. Rogue's Hollow employed one maintenance person and he was on vacation. The county stepped in to help with the program, offering a man from their public works to supervise the team, along with a work van, a trailer, and tools.

The cooler weather assisted the final dousing of fire hot spots, but as the rain started to fall, there was even more urgency to the cleanup work. Déjà vu, Tess thought, reminded of what typically happened in California — summer fires, then winter landslides. Places where the loss of vegetation might lead to those landslides needed to be dealt with. A lot of the work would be filling and placing sandbags; some of it would be mulching, shoring up bare spots.

One property that required assistance was

Arthur Goding's. Though his home and outbuildings were spared from the flames, the historic logging camp behind his house had been completely destroyed by the fire, along with a lot of brush in the canyon. Denuded hillsides could funnel a deluge of muddy water straight onto his property.

Tess and Mayor Horning toured all of the properties that needed help in order to make a priority list for the crew to follow. The day they visited Goding's home, a light rain, slightly more than a mist, was falling, foreshadowing that more was promised soon.

"Be happy your house is safe," Tess offered. "After all, with all the ATVs in your garage, that would have been quite a loss."

"And you're first on the list for a work crew to come through and help with the canyon," Horning told him.

"Thanks, I appreciate that. I'll help too, of course. I can fill a sandbag as well as the next guy."

Monday, with the council in full hire mode and nothing left for Tess to do in regard to the fire, she ducked into her office after shaking water off her raincoat and settled in to review the information from Bass. He started out with an unfortunately familiar story, as far as Tess was concerned.

Over the years Tess had come across many young women whose names could be interchanged with any of the girls rescued by the raid in Arizona.

Victim was recruited at sixteen by a good-looking guy who claimed to care for her. At that time she was unhappy at home. He spent a few months grooming her, wooing her in a way, before the real purpose he had for her became clear. Since the day she willingly went with him, she's been sold over and over again for sex from one end of this country to the other. Usually at big sporting events — the Super Bowl, World Series. Poor kid doesn't know which end is up.

As for Chevy . . .

Victim one was taken out of the stable of girls and brought to the boss. For two years she enjoyed a position at the top, was flown around the world in a private jet, and was treated as a favorite sex slave.

Tess grimaced as she read the narrative about the bust in Mesa. Some of the girls who were rescued actually fought the cops, such was the nature of their brainwashing.

She thought about Chevy and her angry attitude. Would the girl continue to cooperate?

Tess was nervous about the case in general and Chevy specifically.

In Mesa, Beck turned the tables on Agent Bass. He made a preemptive court appearance to answer the charges before the warrant could be served. Tess watched snippets of the press conference online. Beck's sanctimonious lawyer claimed the charges were trumped up by his client's political enemies. The claims were all baseless, blah, blah, blah. And the preemption did the trick. Despite the fact that the charges were all serious felonies, Beck's apparent willingness to cooperate was enough to convince the judge, and Beck was released on two million dollars bail with an ankle monitor. He couldn't get out of surrendering his passport, though. But Tess knew there had to be a leak for him to be able to preempt Bass like that. The man should be in jail, not on monitored release.

She spoke to Bass briefly. He was stunned but not down for the count. They were still working on breaking the encryption of all the files on the tablet stolen by Chevy. Once they did that, it might tell them a more horrifying story and get Beck remanded.

She'd heard in news reports that Beck's

attorney decried the whole operation as a witch hunt. He was screaming about his client's rights being violated and threatening all kinds of motions to get everything thrown out of court. Part of what he claimed was that the entire search was a violation of his client's privacy and his constitutional right to be protected from unreasonable search and seizure because Chevy stole it. This was a predictable move, but it was anyone's guess if he'd be successful. Bass didn't think so.

"This guy is scum and he will fall, iPad or no iPad."

Tess hoped he was right. After reading through everything on the drive, she realized that Bass had been chasing Cyrus Beck for the majority of his career. Obsession?

In any big case, there was a fine line between obsession and dogged determination. From everything Tess read, she saw Bass as meticulous and careful. He dotted all the i's and crossed all the t's.

You can never have too much evidence, she thought. Sometimes a preponderance of evidence helped avoid a trial because the bad guys would accept a plea. Tess never liked the idea of lessening charges for any reason, but nowadays juries were unpredictable. They watched too much TV and wanted everything wrapped up with a neat and clear DNA bow.

She wondered about Chevy, if she'd be a credible witness. Tess hadn't talked to her, but Oliver had. It was a good thing that Bass had approved Oliver being let in on the secret. The girl asked to talk to someone, "like a priest or a counselor," after almost insisting that she be let go, that she didn't want to testify against Beck, who she was certain still loved her. Oliver defused the crisis. He had a way of talking that made people stop and think.

"She's wounded and angry," Oliver told Tess after the episode. "Sadly, she thinks she's in love with Beck, and she's having doubts about stealing the tablet. She hopes Beck will forgive her for that. But her emotions are a seesaw. It's good she's hidden and can't contact him. I'm afraid she'd go back to him if she could."

"Will she stay in the shelter?"

Oliver held his hands out.

"It wouldn't surprise me if she tried to leave. I hope Takano is prepared for that," Tess said.

Oliver nodded. "Stockholm syndrome. I'm sure you've dealt with that."

"I have," Tess agreed. Too many women stayed with abusive men for reasons often complicated and twisted with unhealthy emotions.

Tess knew that in domestic violence and human trafficking, a sick side effect was that women believed themselves to be in love with their abusers. In the case where her father had been murdered, the woman had been put in the hospital five times by her boyfriend. That was before a law was passed to allow the state to prosecute when the victim was unwilling. Not that it mattered in her father's case; the woman refused to prosecute every single time.

Considering Chevy and her predicament funneled Tess's thoughts to Livie Harp. Was Harp so antisocial and secretive because of a toxic relationship? Then there was the TV-inspired reason: she was a witness in the federal witness protection program.

Tess doubted that theory, just like Steve Logan had, as being not really plausible. The only other options that made sense to Tess were that she was a true prepper or that she was a fugitive from justice. And if she was a fugitive, she'd hidden everything well. Tess had spent a day trying to find out anything she could about Harp. There was nothing. Even the house was not in her name, but in the name of a corporation. Livie Harp had an Oregon driver's license and three vehicles registered to her, and a one-page bare-bones website touting her skills in combating cybercrime, and that was it.

Curiosity was strong in Tess, and the enigma of Livie Harp tested all her self-control. She'd searched for information on the woman only through public means. She was not about to violate the law and conduct a law enforcement search when, to her knowledge, Harp had done nothing illegal. Harp wanted to be off the grid and was as successful as anyone Tess had ever been acquainted with. Without probable cause to articulate a need to know, Tess would have to be satisfied with leaving the mystery alone.

13

After a day of online searching, Ice had found nothing to confirm beyond any doubt that his target was located in Shady Cove, Oregon. Cyrus had law enforcement on his payroll, Ice knew, but they either didn't know exactly where the girl was or were not coughing up any more information because of the heat. And there was heat.

Ice had considerable hacking skills, but wherever the Feds were hiding Chevy, he couldn't find it on the web. Yet Ice's gut told him it was a good lead, so in spite of the uncertainty, he packed up his belongings and prepared to head to the Northwest. He stole a nice BMW motorcycle, then some clean license plates and pulled up his destination on GPS.

Cyrus had been cocky about still being free when Royal had first spoken to him. Yeah, he was free, but the charges were big-time. Once the Feds opened the iPad . . .

well, Ice for one wanted to be somewhere else. The arrest and subsequent bail of Cyrus Beck was front-page news, and there was a frenzy in the cable news arena — it was almost wall-to-wall coverage.

Ice smiled when he saw the rent-a-mobs show up to protest against Cyrus's prosecution with signs claiming it was a government conspiracy and a setup. Several signs even blamed people who didn't believe in global warming for setting Cyrus up. He knew that Cyrus had a pipeline to under-the-radar agencies who could produce mobs at the drop of a hat.

As amusing as Ice thought the protests were, he'd told Cyrus to leave the country and forget the mess here. There were plenty of nice places to live that had no extradition agreements.

"I won't let a little nothing high school dropout chase me out of my own country. Find her, Ice. Find her."

Ice would, he promised.

He rolled into Shady Cove, Oregon, in a little over six hours and rented a small hotel room at a place called the Maple Leaf. Ice considered the place Hicksville and knew that when he found the girl, he'd have no trouble overcoming any resistance. He had little respect for cops and even less for small-town Barney Fifes.

But after watching and listening to local gossip for a couple of days, doubt crept in that he'd found his target. He'd heard no chatter about her at all, and that bugged him. There would be a wisp of a trail if she were hidden somewhere here — and a sign of federal presence, he was sure — but there was nothing but local hicks and tourist traffic.

Still, his gut instincts told him he was on the right track. And with no other locations popping up on his radar, no other whispers about where the girl was, and Cyrus's sources completely dried up because of the indictment, he wanted to be thorough. In any event, he knew it would be easy to blend in for a week or so. Especially when he saw the ad for temporary help needed at a town not too far down the road on the other side of the river.

He found Rogue's Hollow without any trouble. They were hiring anyone breathing to help with cleanup after a big fire that had destroyed a lot of forest. He showed up in town and applied. And was hired almost immediately. He decided to smile a lot, work hard, and listen.

14

Oliver felt as though he'd never get the smell of burnt wood and houses out of his nostrils. All four families who lost their houses wanted to rebuild. The work crews had just begun and were doing a good job so far, clearing debris and filling and placing sandbags. Arthur Goding's place, first on the list, was now ready for the rain. Whenever he had time, Oliver assisted. Now, with storm clouds forecast to bring a lot of rain, he'd just finished helping on the Coopers' lot.

The Coopers were problematic. They had only minimal insurance on their hundred-year-old house and barely enough money to make it day to day. Oliver and his board of elders had agreed to let them stay in a mobile home the church owned in Blackberry Hollow, Rogue's Hollow's trailer park, and used for just such emergencies. But it wasn't a long-term solution. Part of the problem was Garrett and his inability to hold a steady job. While Garrett did watch their three children and that saved on child care, he'd never worked regularly for the entire time Oliver had known the couple. And Janie's job as a cashier at Walmart wasn't quite enough to support the family. Oliver had known Janie's mother well and been at her bedside the day she died. She'd worried then that Garrett would never be a good breadwinner and she feared for Janie.

Her last words were a request that Oliver look after Janie. Oliver had promised he would do his best. The promise weighed on him. He'd meant it, but now, four years later, he feared he was failing.

Once cleaned up and headed to his office, he noticed Janie in the church clothes closet, where all the clothing donations were stored. She was going through children's clothing. Noting the torn and worn jeans and sweatshirt she was wearing, Oliver hoped she'd also look for something for herself. Another reason Janie tugged at his heart was that she'd named her youngest daughter Anna, after Oliver's deceased wife.

"Hi, Janie, how are things going?"

She looked up, eyes rimmed with exhaustion. "Oh, hi, Pastor Mac. We're okay, I guess. It's just hard. Helping the kids to understand why everything is gone —" Her voice broke, and he put a hand on her shoulder.

The hardship of the last few days seemed to make Janie, a small, pale woman to begin with, even smaller, and his heart went out to her.

"We're here for you, Janie. You know that."

She sniffled, wiped her nose with a crumpled Kleenex she had in her hand. "Thank you. I do know that. And we have a place to live for the winter. I'm very grateful for all your help." Janie managed a smile, and that touched Oliver.

He noticed the bags of clothing she'd gathered so far. "Can I help you with anything?"

"Well, yeah. I need to get these things home and then head to work. Do you think you could give me a ride?"

"Of course. Is Garrett at home watching the kids?"

A shadow crossed her face. "He dropped me off and then went to the library in Shady Cove to use the Internet. He had business to take care of. Before the fire, he was trying to earn money by selling stuff on eBay, but now . . ." She bit her bottom lip for a second. "Kayla is watching the kids for me."

Oliver worked to keep his expression

neutral. Business to take care of for a guy who didn't work? eBay? Now he was further stretching the family budget by forcing the hire of a babysitter. Oliver had tried to get Garrett on the work crew, but he'd disdainfully said no. "I'm not the manual labor type," he'd sneered.

Oliver let it go and nodded. "Well, let's put these things in the car."

The Coopers had been in Oliver's office for counseling right after Janie's mother died and they found themselves in possession of her home and belongings. He recalled that Garrett wanted to sell the place and buy something bigger and newer. At the time, he'd been working, driving a logging truck. Janie was adamantly against moving; after all, the house had been in her family for a hundred years, and it was paid off.

Eventually she'd won, but Oliver wondered if she'd paid a steep price. Shortly after that conversation, Garrett had crashed his logging truck, and though he wasn't hurt, he was fired when the crash was deemed his fault. Since then he'd been a stay-at-home dad, but something in Oliver told him that the young man was immature and paying his wife back for not giving in to his demands. And Oliver feared the claim of "selling things on eBay" was cover for wasting time playing computer games.

Bottom line, Janie had done the right thing. If they'd taken on a large mortgage like Garrett had wanted, they'd be in worse shape, and that was saying a lot considering they'd just lost everything to a fire.

Janie and Garrett's situation brought Tess and one of her rules to mind: "Always trust your gut." Oliver's gut told him that the Coopers' marriage was tenuous. He'd doubted it would survive before the fire, and now . . . He hated the doom he saw foreshadowed. But unless Garrett grew up and behaved like a husband and father, Oliver feared Janie would soon be a member of the single mothers' ministry.

Not if I can help it. The Coopers were at the top of his prayer list, and Oliver would strive in prayer for them, certain only the Lord could save the shaky marriage.

"Have you had any problems with your insurance company, Janie?" Oliver asked after they'd loaded her stuff into the trunk of his car and started out of the church parking lot for the short drive to the trailer park.

"No, not really. I have a living expense check to deposit today on my way to work. It will help us replace the computer, my phone, and a few other electronic devices. The house . . . I think we were underinsured."

"Happens to a lot of people."

"Hopefully we'll be able to afford a mobile. I'd like to clear the lot, then find a used one to put there. It won't be the same as that old house, but it will be a roof over our heads."

"That sounds like a good plan. I might have a lead on a used mobile, a double-wide."

She turned toward him, eyes full of hope. "Oh, Pastor Mac, that would be a godsend."

"It may take a week or two for me to get a solid answer, but I'll get on it. In the meantime, when you're ready, I'll start organizing something to help you clear the lot and prepare everything for a new home."

"Thank you so much." She beamed.

He pulled into the carport, noting that Garrett was not back. After he helped her get everything into the house and spent a few minutes with the kids, each under eight years old, he saw Janie's face tighten with stress as she talked on the phone, presumably to Garrett.

"Something wrong?" he asked when she hung up.

"I'm going to be late to work and all I'm

getting is Garrett's voice mail."

Oliver glanced to Kayla and then back to Janie. "I can take you to work if Kayla doesn't mind staying with the kids a bit longer."

"Oh, Pastor Mac, I can't put you out like that."

"It's not putting me out. I have to be in Medford anyway. I have a meeting at the jail. Walmart is on the way. Can you get a ride home at the end of your shift?"

She looked at the clock and then out the window, no sign of Garrett. "Yeah, a couple of people I work with live in Trail, and they can give me a ride home. I just don't understand where Garrett is. He knows that I have to get to work."

"I don't mind taking you."

She chewed on her bottom lip. "Let me change. Maybe he'll be here by the time I'm ready."

Oliver nodded and sat with Kayla in the living room as Janie grabbed the bag of clothes she'd picked up from the church and went to a bedroom in the back of the home to change.

"Okay with you, Kayla, to stay a little longer?"

"I'll call my mom; she'll probably come over too. It's okay. I like these kids; they're well behaved and easy to entertain."

Oliver had to agree. The two older boys were on the floor surrounded by toys he knew had been donated, playing happily. The youngest, a little over a year, and the only girl, fifteen-year-old Kayla held on her hip like a pro.

A few minutes later, Janie emerged dressed for work. "I'll try Garrett one more time," she said when her attention was directed outside as they all heard Garrett's truck pull up.

"He's home." Janie opened the front door as Garrett hopped out, leaving the truck running.

"You ready?" he snarled and then stopped short when he saw Oliver. "What are you doing here?"

"He brought me home from the church. Remember you were supposed to pick me up there? I got stuff for the kids and some clothes for you as well."

Garrett's brow furrowed, and Oliver wondered why he was so angry.

"I had things to do," he snapped. "I didn't forget. Now let's get going. Do we need to take the kids?"

"I can stay till you get back," Kayla offered.

Garrett grunted and stomped back to the truck.

Janie offered an apologetic glance. "Thanks, Pastor Mac, for everything."

"Sure. Will you be okay?"

"Oh yeah. He's just mad at himself for forgetting."

Outside, the car horn blasted, and Janie hurried to get into the truck.

As they pulled out of the lot, Kayla stood next to Oliver. "That guy is always mad."

"He ever give you any trouble?"

"No, but he's never happy. I texted my mom. She's coming to stay with me until he gets back."

"Good," Oliver said as he frowned after the truck. What was up with Garrett Cooper?

15

Oliver's next meeting with Don Cherry was tempered by the fact that it was likely going to be his last. Federal authorities were ready to move him, and it could happen any day.

"How do you feel about the move?" Oliver asked as they settled into their routine of conversation before Bible study.

He held his hands out, palms up. "What's to feel? It's gonna happen. I have to remember that the Lord goes with me wherever I go, no matter what."

"Glad to hear you say that." Oliver was happy with the transformation he'd seen in Don Cherry. It was genuine — the man read his Bible, prayed, but most of all his demeanor was convincing. The hard, menacing man Oliver had met months ago was different. He was polite and respectful to all law enforcement personnel. More than one had mentioned to Oliver that they didn't mind Cherry at all; they liked having him around because he was easy to deal with and never gave them trouble. That was what true faith was supposed to do: transform people.

"Thank you, padre, for all that you've done for me."

"I can't take all the credit — you know that — but you can thank me by keeping up with your studies and letting me know what's next on your journey."

"I will. I have something I've never had before. Peace. I know I'll be okay, no matter what."

"Amen."

Oliver opened his Bible for their last Bible study, thankful that he'd been privileged to walk this journey with Don Cherry.

Tess checked the clock as she walked into her house. A quarter to six. She'd wanted to make it home earlier, but like always, something popped up at the station that delayed her.

One week into the cleanup, and one of the guys on the crew had been fired when he was discovered looting. One of the burned-out houses had a shed that survived, and the man pried open the lock and removed some small tools. Bender caught him while doing an impromptu drive-by. The man was fired and cited because there was no room in the jail to keep him, but the incident made Tess regret she hadn't forced the issue of background checks for the temp crew. But the manual labor was necessary because of the topography of the Hollow, bordered as it was by steep mountains on one side and the Rogue River on the other. She'd been guardedly happy that Mayor Horning stepped up and designated funds for it.

"We've money to cover the cleanup; hopefully two weeks will do it," Pete had said. "It's just grunt work. We can't afford extensive background checks for grunt work."

On one hand, she knew he was right, and they had run want/warrant checks on everyone. Other than a couple of suspended licenses, everyone was clean. But some shady-looking guys had been hired for the work crew, and the one just fired was obviously an opportunist.

The incident made her take a hard look at the rest of the crew. Only one gave her pause, and she wondered if it was just because of his name, James Smith. When she worked patrol, that was a throwaway name if someone didn't want to be identified. It was the most common man's name in the country and it always sent up red flags, so she wasn't sure if it was the name or his demeanor. He didn't strike her as a down-and-out in-need-of-any-kind-of-work guy. There was an edge about him. Yet when she spoke to the supervisor, he got high marks. "One of my hardest workers," he'd said.

Tess let it go, recognizing that there were thousands of men legitimately named Jim Smith. His California driver's license was valid after all, and she was a little too on edge because of the arrest.

Maybe the problem has been solved, she thought as she turned on the oven and set a loaf of French bread inside to warm up. Then she quickly shed her clothes and jumped into the shower.

Oliver would be here in fifteen minutes. Luckily, dinner was ready, simmering in the Crock-Pot since she'd put it together this morning, and the house was filled with the mouthwatering aroma of beef stew. She forced her mind to shift gears and consider the pleasant evening ahead she had planned with Oliver. Weekly dinners together, either at her house or his, followed by a Bible study, had become standard. No one was more surprised than Tess that a pastor could so completely fill her mind and heart.

While she'd stepped away from faith after

her father's death and come to view pastors and people of faith as one-dimensional, deluded, and boring, Oliver had shattered all her preconceived notions. He was so alive, interesting, clear about his beliefs, and solidly three-dimensional. They connected on so many levels, shared many interests, and completely enjoyed one another's company. Tess finally felt as though she were coming out from under the shadow of her failed marriage and the betrayal that caused it.

Humming to herself, she finished her shower and changed into comfortable clothes with five minutes to spare. Fluffing out her hair, she decided to let it air-dry and hurried to the kitchen to check on dinner.

As she lifted the Crock-Pot lid, she could see that the stew was nicely finished, and with bread browning, everything smelled awesome. She set the table, pouring glasses of mineral water that they both enjoyed, and stepped back just as Oliver's knock sounded on the front door.

Oliver waited, smiling at the fact that this dating thing still made him nervous. He'd never thought after Anna's death there would be room for anyone else in his life, much less his heart, but Tess had crashed in with both feet without even trying and he was over the moon. And there was no reason for nerves because everything about dating and being with Tess was so easy. There was no pretense about her — in fact often she was baldly blunt about things, but Oliver loved that about her. There was no guessing, just a relationship that bloomed and blossomed brighter with each passing day.

The door opened, and Tess smiled at him, hair damp, obviously just out of the shower. So small and petite, wearing a soft cotton blouse and black jeans, looking as if she needed to be protected when he knew firsthand she could more than take care of herself.

"You're late."

Oliver's heart fluttered in his chest. "Five minutes. I heard what happened and figured you'd need some extra time." He handed her the flowers he'd brought as he stepped inside — cliché, yes. He often felt he wanted to give Tess the world, but he'd have to settle for the prettiest flowers he could find on any given day. "Smells great in here."

"Thank you." She took the bouquet, stepped forward on tiptoes, and kissed him on the cheek. "They're beautiful." She stepped back, green eyes warm and sparkling. Such a deep, bottomless green, he could drown there.

Oliver smiled back, throat dry, again wondering at the fact that lightning had struck twice for him.

"Hope you're hungry," she said, turning.

"I'm famished." He followed her into the kitchen, where she put the flowers in a vase and filled it with water. "I was sorry to hear about that worker being arrested. Those guys are here to help, and instead someone tries to compound the misery."

Oliver had spent some time with the temporary help and found most of them to be hardworking and civic-minded. He knew he shouldn't be surprised by what happened, but he was.

"Sorry; this is where I get cynical," Tess said, motioning for him to take a seat. "Disasters bring out the best and the worst in people. I don't have to tell you that I was lukewarm about the mass hiring of strangers."

"They aren't all strangers; several live in the Hollow," Oliver said with a sigh. "And I always saw it as a community ready to help."

Tess shot him a "you sure are naive" look, green eyes shining with mischief, before filling a bowl with wonderfully fragrant stew and setting it in front of him. Then she opened the oven and pulled out a loaf of French bread, slicing it, placing it in a basket on the table.

She sat down with her own bowl of stew and nodded for Oliver to say grace. He reached across the table, gripping her hand, loving the warmth there. He closed his eyes. "Thank you, Lord, for the blessings you give daily, the food we're about to receive, and the hands that prepared it."

He opened his eyes, glad to be gazing on Tess again. "It was a blessing that Pete allocated the funds. Landslides and mudflows would have compounded the damage from the fire," he said as he helped himself to a slice of steaming bread.

"I know that. The work crew was a necessary evil. I'm just glad they're almost finished."

"Not a moment too soon. Big, cold storm is forecast in a couple of days." He tasted the stew. "Ah, this is wonderful. I've been blessed by a lot of home cooking —"

"Playing the poor pastor card?" she teased.

He loved the playful sparkle in her eyes. "Of course. I'm not ashamed. If people want to bless me, I graciously accept. But this stew is the best I've had in a long time."

"Thanks. Talk like that will get you a

second helping of dessert. I tried my hand at blackberry pie, made with fresh-picked berries from my own property."

"Mmm, that's my favorite."

They settled into a familiar routine, enjoying the meal and discussing events of the day.

"Besides the thief, any other issues I should be aware of?" Oliver asked.

"You mean have I heard anything more from Bass?" She shook her head. "The fight is in the courts; Beck's attorneys are doing everything they can to get the charges thrown out. How is Chevy?"

"She's quiet. Which worries me more than angry tantrums. It's almost as if she's plotting. Still seeing Dr. Peel, but quiet."

In the one controversial event surrounding Chevy so far, Oliver himself had spoken to Bass about her mental state and forced the issue of counseling. He knew Emma Peel, a trauma counselor and member of his congregation, and he wanted to let her in on the situation and bring her to speak to Chevy.

Bass had been vehemently against it. "The more people know she's there, the more likely the wrong person will discover her."

But Oliver persisted. He feared for the girl's mental state and was adamant, and

Tess had backed him up. "If you don't try to help her," she'd told Bass, "if you just use her for the trial and toss her away, you're no better than Beck. Many women rescued from trafficking situations face a long, hard road ahead to regain a normal life. The dehumanizing practice of slavery messes with their heads."

In the end, Bass ran a check on Peel and then allowed it. Oliver told the woman about the situation and she volunteered to help. So far, Dr. Peel and Chevy seemed to be a good fit.

Oliver hated to think about what Chevy had been through, what the past three years had done to her physically, emotionally, and spiritually.

"For a young person, she has been through so much," he said. "It worries me that she never talks about her parents or family or life before Beck."

"From what I read, she doesn't have any family to speak of. She had a horrible home life, actually left with Beck of her own volition."

"Yes, but you and I both know what a manipulator he is. She doesn't want to contact anyone from her past, which is okay with Bass right now, but what happens when the very public trial starts?"

"Cross that bridge when we come to it. But speaking of family, there's a lot of chatter around town about a certain couple —"

"Janie and Garrett Cooper?" Oliver winced. He'd bent over backward trying to help the pair, but nothing seemed to make a difference.

"Yeah, not so much her, but that Garrett is a hothead."

"He hasn't always been this bad, but I guess the stress of losing the house sent him around the bend."

"Most people are likely to cut him some slack, but . . ." She shrugged and Oliver knew what she meant. Their fighting was often public and loud. Tess went on. "Right now, it's a gossip problem. My fear is that it will soon become a police problem."

Oliver held her gaze. "If it does come to that, arresting Garrett won't solve the problem."

"It will if he hurts her or tries to. I have zero tolerance for domestic violence."

"I do too. It's just that I've known those two since they were kids. My prayer is that they stop fighting with one another and come together, not just for themselves but for those kids."

"I'd like to see that too, but maybe in this case, prayer isn't enough."

Oliver considered her words. The sentiment he knew came from the fact that she'd seen so much evil at work in people's lives in her line of work. Oliver too had seen evil and viciousness, but he'd also seen healing and battles won by being fought on his knees.

"Ah, and you know me — prayer is the first best answer for everything. Though you might not agree, I saw it work with Don Cherry, and he was a much harder case than Garrett Cooper."

For him, prayer was always the answer — the first step at least, and at best the tonic that solved the problem. Would he ever be able to get Tess to see it that way too?

Tess bit her lower lip, and Oliver feared that she'd be cynical about Cherry. But she threw him a curve.

"What about someone like Cyrus Beck?"

"What do you mean?"

"Do you pray for him?"

"Wouldn't you say he needs prayer?"

"I'd say that his victims need prayer."

Oliver remembered Cherry's words about justice and mercy. Tess was all about justice, but Oliver didn't believe you could have one without the other.

"Like all of us, Beck is a sinner — I would never deny that. But he's no less deserving of salvation. So, yes, I do pray for him."

Tess sighed. "I know that's the way I should feel, but I don't. He's pure evil. Oliver, he's been victimizing women for twenty-five years. You truly believe there's something redeemable there?"

He reached across the table again and squeezed her hand. "There is no matter of degree to sin. All of us have our own baggage. Let me ask you this: If Cyrus Beck were the victim of a homicide here in Rogue's Hollow, would you be less inclined to find his killer than, say, if a law-abiding resident were murdered?"

She frowned. "Aw, that's not fair. Murder is murder."

"Even if someone like Beck is the victim?"

She rolled her eyes. "You got me. Even Beck. Even if some vigilante killed him thinking they were dispensing justice. I would work just as hard to put his killer behind bars. But it would be for the *law,* for true justice, not for *him.*"

"But there is a principle there, I think. Everyone matters under the law, or nobody matters. If under man's law, everyone matters, how much more to God does everyone matter? God's offer of grace is made to everyone. Not everyone accepts it, but nonetheless, the offer is free to all and covers all." He released her hand and leaned back, watching her features soften.

"You believe Don Cherry is really a changed man? That he accepted the grace God offered?" she asked.

"I do. I've seen the change in the man, real change. He's not faking."

"Well, then I have to say that maybe there is a small —" she held up her thumb and forefinger, very close together — "very small chance for Beck. Cherry was certainly a surprise to me — I'll give you that. He turned state's evidence on the most vicious prison-slash-street gang there is, so unless he has a death wish . . ." She held her hands up. "You got me; he's a true answer to prayer."

"Miracles all around for you to admit that, I'd say."

Tess laughed.

Oliver sipped his water and prayed, for Tess and Garrett and Janie and the children, that a solution and true healing would come to the situation.

16

Sunday service marked the first Sunday when all the extraneous equipment was gone from the church parking lot — the trailers and fifth wheels and everything else that had been staged there for the fire emergency. The baptisms that had been planned the day everything exploded had been rescheduled. It felt like a normal Sunday. But Oliver had a lot more on his mind than a truly normal Sunday, and it was hard to focus on one topic. He didn't want to be random; he wanted to tie everything together.

He was proud and inspired at how the community had come together for the emergency, he was gratified for Don Cherry, and he was very happy to see Tess seated in the front row. It wasn't the first time she'd been in church; she'd been attending regularly since the shoot-out. But Oliver had left dinner at her house knowing that he loved

Tess. The knowledge had hit him like a thunderbolt when he'd kissed her good night. He hadn't told her yet but knew that he would soon, and the anticipation was sweet.

The text he'd finally settled on for the message was in 1 Corinthians, and it dealt with the body of Christ working together in love. It applied to how the Hollow had come together, to his work and effort with a criminal like Don Cherry, and to how he felt about Tess. Last year had been so dark when he lost Anna. Now there was light in his world again.

The routine of Sunday service had become welcome and comfortable to Tess. She'd come to know many in the congregation, and she enjoyed listening to Oliver. His voice sang more with his Scottish background when he preached than at any other time, and it was mesmerizing. She knew the first time she sat to listen that this was one reason why his church was so popular. The other was the way he made the Bible come alive. Tess had been away from the Bible for so long, it had taken time to learn her way around. Oliver always had them turning pages.

But sometimes, as she sat in the sanctuary, a niggling self-doubt would grab her. Did she really belong with a man like Oliver? His priority was his congregation. Was that something she could live with?

Her best friend from Long Beach had helped the self-doubt grow. On the phone Tess had asked Jeannie for her honest opinion. Jeannie had met Oliver and liked him personally, but she doubted the match was viable. *"Cops and nurses, cops and teachers, even cops and dispatchers, but not cops and preachers — they just don't mix."* To Jeannie, cops had to be too hard and pastors had to be too soft.

The honesty stung, but Tess was glad she had friends who would be honest. But the stronger her feelings for Oliver grew, the stronger the niggling doubts became.

Tess was on her way out of the sanctuary when she ran into Oliver's friend Jethro. He was also the head of the prayer ministry and a familiar fixture at the church. Tess's first impression of Oliver when she met him was that he looked more like a rugged mountain man than a pastor. With Jethro, he looked more like an outlaw biker than someone who would lead a prayer ministry. His long gray hair was usually free flowing, but today he had it braided, the tail hitting just past his collar.

"Hiya, Chief, how are you today?"

"Doing good, Jethro. Glad the fire is out and things are back to normal."

"Me too. Hey, can I ask you a question, law enforcement related?"

"Sure, go ahead."

"Have you been following that human trafficking story, the one about Cyrus Beck?"

"I have, pretty closely too. Oliver told me you knew Beck's father."

Jethro shook his head, expression sad. "I did. He was one of the finest men I served with. Breaks my heart about his son. Do you figure everything they're saying about him is true?"

"From what I've read, they have a really strong case."

He gave her a somber look. "Like I said, it breaks my heart. Cyrus was a spoiled rotten kid, but I never thought he'd become . . . Well, what he's accused of is wicked."

"I agree."

"I don't envy police, what you people have to deal with. I'll tell you, I wish I could get the chance to speak with Cyrus. Haven't seen him since he was seventeen or eighteen. But for his father's sake, I wish I could talk some sense into him."

"I don't know, Jethro. Part of me thinks

he's beyond hope."

"No one is beyond hope, not until they reach room temperature."

He walked on and left Tess to think about that. Jethro's statement echoed Oliver's, and she thought about their dinner. In spite of his use of murder and the law to parallel grace and redemption, Tess could not wrap her mind around Beck being redeemable. To her, Cyrus Beck was past saving, unredeemable. Was that a lack of faith, another nail in her relationship with Oliver?

17

Monday morning, Tess heard the call crackle over the radio, and before Bender responded, she got up to go help.

"Boy-2, copy a call at Blackberry Hollow, space 24. Disturbance, loud voices, possible domestic violence. We have three CPs on this call. Handle code 3."

She recognized the address in the trailer park and knew that the space number was where the Coopers were staying. Aside from the conversation she'd had with Oliver the week before, she'd heard from several people that things were tense between the pair. Her friend Casey Reno had even expressed concern about letting her daughter babysit for the couple.

"I almost want to say no," she'd said the other day. *"But I feel sorry for Janie. She works so hard and Garrett has never been a help."*

"You don't think Kayla is in danger, do you?"

175

"No, no. I don't think Garrett would hurt her. But she doesn't need to hear the fights and the language."

Tess had left lunch frowning about the Coopers and hoping none of the fights got physical.

Then Oliver doubled down about the situation with his comments at dinner. Garrett Cooper was a hothead and not pulling his weight. On one hand, Oliver sounded like he wanted Tess to intervene and on the other that he believed prayer would solve the problem.

"He's immature, and I sense a lot of anger. He uses Janie to vent."

"Doesn't necessarily mean he gets physical."

"Emotional abuse can be every bit as dangerous as physical abuse."

"While I agree, it's harder to prove for a cop."

"I lift that family up in prayer every day. Their eyes need to be open to the fact that they have three children to raise and nurture. The fighting and division have to stop."

She knew Oliver believed prayer was the answer to every problem, every situation. And she'd read enough of her father's comments in his Bible to know he'd felt the same way. Just like the idea that there was hope for everybody. Tess wasn't there yet.

Prayer was a nice topping, but to her way of thinking, it wasn't the whole pie. They hadn't yet finished that conversation, and she wondered what would happen when they did.

In any event, the conversation they did have about the Coopers echoed in her mind as she started her car. Bender responded, but he was actually farther away than Tess. Officer Gabe Bender, Boy-2, was more than capable of handling the call. But it was Tess's discretion whether or not to respond, and she was curious about the situation, so she continued on, activating her lights and sirens and reaching the entrance to the park in less than ten minutes.

Blackberry Hollow was the only trailer park in Rogue's Hollow. It was not a large park, and it was mostly seniors on fixed incomes, but Tess knew there were a couple of problem trailers. Her officers had made arrests for drugs and disturbing the peace in the park several times. There was, however, a park manager who took his job seriously, and she saw Henry Polk standing outside his unit, the first park space, when she pulled into the lot.

Tess shut down the siren and came to a stop as Henry walked up to her window, waving to catch her attention.

"Hi, Chief, thanks for getting here so fast. But Garrett took off right after I made the phone call. He's gone."

"What made you call?"

"Oh, it was horrible. He just went off. I was taking some wood to a space three doors down and I could hear it. Profanity, things breaking. The only good thing is I understand that the kids weren't home; they're either in school or at someone else's house. If you ask me, that young man is wound just a tad too tight."

"I'll check it out." Tess radioed Bender that she was on scene and asked him to look for Garrett's truck. Tess hadn't passed him on her way in, so there were only a couple places he could be if he left just after Henry called. One good thing about a small town — there really was no place to hide.

She continued on to space 24.

After she parked and got out of her SUV, Tess noticed a pile of firewood off to the right of the door. It wasn't stacked; it looked like it had been dumped there by someone in a hurry. As she walked up the steps to the front door, she could hear sobbing inside.

Tess knocked. "Janie, it's Chief O'Rourke. Can I come in?"

There was some shuffling and then faintly,

Janie's voice. "Just a minute."

Tess stepped back and after a minute Janie opened the door. Her face was red, her eyes bloodshot, but Tess didn't see any obvious injuries.

"What's going on, Janie? Are you okay?"

She sniffled and nodded. "Yeah, just a disagreement, that's all."

"It sounds like more than a disagreement. Three people called, worried about your safety."

Janie let out a heavy sigh and leaned against the doorframe, looking weary beyond her years. "Chief, we fight a lot, I'm sorry to say. Where we used to live we had privacy. No one heard us. Here —" she waved a hand — "everyone hears everything."

"Do you mind if I come in and look around?"

Janie hesitated but eventually stepped back, and Tess walked into a living room that looked as if it had just been ransacked. A lamp and a chair were broken, there was glass on the floor, and one couch cushion was even shredded.

"He did all this?"

"He said no. But it was like this when I got home from getting the boys to school and baby Anna to a friend's house. It's my day off and I had some chores planned. Anyway, the kids sure didn't do it. He did break a couple of vases when I confronted him. What am I going to tell Pastor Mac?"

Before Tess could respond, she was interrupted by a radio call from Bender, who'd found Garrett at one of the two places he could have been. He was in the parking lot of the Stairsteps, a waterfall attraction.

"Do we have a crime?" Gabe asked.

"Stand by," Tess said into her radio. "Janie, did Garrett hit you?"

She shook her head. "No, but he broke a lot of things in the house, things we'll probably have to pay for, and he said some horrible, hurtful things . . ."

"What was the fight about?"

"Besides all of this? What it usually is — money. He took all the insurance money I just deposited, and he won't tell me what he did with it. Chief, we need that money for daily living expenses. When I got mad, he got madder and accused me of not understanding —" Her voice broke.

To Bender, Tess said, "Apparently we have destruction of property. Detain him. Take him to the church to see if Oliver wants to press charges. He destroyed the living room in the mobile. I'll photograph the damage and meet you at the church."

Janie's eyes got wide. "Chief, no! He didn't hit me."

"But he did destroy church property. Pastor Mac will have to decide."

"I don't want him to go to jail." More tears rolled down her cheeks.

Tess didn't think Oliver would prosecute, but she wanted to put some fear into Garrett. It might work, it might not, but it was one card she could play.

"I'll ask Pastor Mac to take that into consideration." Tess's attention went back to her radio.

"What about the truck?" Bender asked, referring to the Coopers' pickup.

"Do you want to retrieve the truck?" Tess asked Janie.

"I'll need it — it's our only transportation."

"I'll bring Janie up to get the vehicle."

"10-4. I'll see you at the church."

"What time were you going to pick up your daughter?" Tess asked Janie as she held her phone up and photographed the destruction inside.

"I'd planned on picking her up after the boys get out of school. I thought Garrett and I could do it together and then have a family day in White City, maybe end up at a pizza place."

Tess gave her a minute. After taking several photos, she turned back to Janie, who seemed to have pulled herself together. "Grab your spare keys and I'll take you to pick up the truck."

She nodded, and Tess went back to her SUV. Out of the corner of her eye, she caught a man watching her, standing at the corner of a single wide, on the street side of the park. She didn't recognize him at first, but there was something familiar about him. He wore a baseball cap, a camouflaged parka — though it wasn't that cold — and he ducked behind the trailer as soon as their eyes met.

Her neck tingled. Was that Ken Blakely? The more she thought about it, the more she was certain it was Blakely. True, the apartment complex where Blakely lived wasn't that far from the mobile home park, and he could be out for a walk. Still, she wondered why he was here.

He was someone who set all her alarms off. Yeah, she didn't doubt that he was the poacher, but he was as cagey as anyone she'd ever met. Win Yarrow had his work cut out for him catching Blakely in the act. She almost wished she had a reason to question the guy. But just because he was watching her didn't mean he was up to no good.

She didn't know everyone in the park, and maybe Blakely had a friend here. And it wasn't unusual for people to watch police activity out of curiosity, especially people like Blakely.

She had her hands full with Janie and Garrett in any event.

Janie stepped out of the trailer, locked the door, and got into the patrol car. Tess forgot about the man as she questioned Janie further about her relationship with Garrett and they drove to the Stairsteps to pick up the truck.

18

"Would it really help anything to prosecute Garrett?" Oliver asked after Tess showed him photos of the destruction and he'd tried to speak to a sullen Garrett Cooper. The man wouldn't say anything. Janie had taken the truck back home.

"It's up to you, Oliver. You know there's no room in the jail. We'll book him, they will cite him out, but at least he'll have a court date to think about before the next fight."

"Yeah, but the loss is all monetary, and that is likely to hurt Janie and the kids more than it would bother Garrett."

"I can't disagree with that."

Oliver sighed. "I want to help this family. Let me see if I can get Garrett to talk about what the real problem is."

"Have at it."

Tess walked over to where Bender was leaning against his patrol pickup. "Pastor

Mac wants to talk to him."

Bender nodded, and he and Tess ambled over to her SUV while Oliver opened the truck door to talk to Garrett.

"Did he have anything to say to you when you found him?" Tess asked.

"Nah." Gabe scratched his forehead. "To be honest, he seemed scared more than anything. Not scared of me, but scared of something."

"Hmm." Tess cast a glance toward Oliver. He appeared to be listening intently, so maybe he'd get some answers.

"Garrett, I'm here as a friend. I don't want to send you to jail. Janie and the kids need you. But can you tell me why you busted up the trailer?"

Garrett wouldn't look at him and for a minute was silent. Oliver almost gave up, but Garrett finally spoke up.

"I didn't do that. I was out getting some wood for the stove. Mr. Polk had some — you can ask him. I didn't lock the door because I knew I wouldn't be long. I got back home and the place was trashed."

"Why didn't you say so? If the trailer was burglarized, the police need to know."

He banged his head against the door. "Don't want the police to know."

"But why? They're ready to send you to jail for something you say you didn't do."

He hit the doorframe with the side of his head and moaned. "Ahh, it's all wrong! It's all wrong!"

"What's wrong, Garrett? Tell me. I want to help."

"I tell you, you tell the cops."

Oliver frowned. "If you know who the burglar is —"

"It's not that. It's . . ." He finally met Oliver's gaze, and tears streamed down his cheeks. "I made a mistake, a big one. And the fire ruined everything."

"If it's a mistake, then maybe we can fix it. Tell me what you did."

"You can't tell the cops. I'm begging you: don't tell the cops."

Oliver knew he couldn't violate a confidence, at least not an emotional plea like this. "If I can keep your secret, I will. But, Garrett, I'm not going to hide something from the chief that is serious or may lead to someone being hurt."

Garrett sniffled. "It's killing me. I have to tell you."

Oliver waited.

After a couple shuddering breaths, Garrett composed himself. "I did a favor for someone. He asked me to keep some things for him. I hid them in our cellar. In our old house. I didn't know they were all going to burn up in the fire."

"Of course you couldn't know that. Surely this fellow must understand —"

"He doesn't. He wants money for the stuff, money I don't have."

"That's why you took the insurance money."

Garrett nodded. "But it's a drop in the bucket. He needs more than I have."

"Do you want to tell me who this guy is?"

"Won't help."

"He might listen to me if I ask him to be patient."

Garrett gave a derisive chuckle. "Not likely. I just don't know what to do."

"I want to help you — I do — but you'll have to give me more information."

"Well, I can't. So I guess I'm just stuck."

Oliver climbed out of the car looking for all the world to Tess like a man on the horns of a dilemma.

"Well," she asked, "what shall we do with young Mr. Cooper?"

"I'm sorry, Tess. I can't see prosecuting him for the damage in the mobile. It won't get anything fixed, and it will only stress the Coopers more."

"Absolutely true," she said, studying him. There was more, she was certain, but he wasn't saying. "I can have Gabe drive him home with a stern warning."

He nodded. "I think that will be best. I can only pray that Garrett and Janie find a way to be strong together rather than always butting heads."

"I hope that too, for both their sakes."

19

Ice didn't mind the physical labor; after all, it was cold here in southern Oregon — colder than what he was used to, anyway — and working hard kept him warm.

What he did mind was the soot and ash. Sometimes when he got back to his tiny hotel room, he felt as if he could never get all the black gunk off. Because his personal vehicle was a motorcycle, when it was too cold, he stayed in his room. That he was getting cabin fever was an understatement.

He'd been in southern Oregon for a week and a half. All that time he'd kept his ear to the ground, riding around on his motorcycle to check out the lay of the land, yet he'd heard no whisper of a federal witness being sheltered in the area.

The only notable happening so far was that he'd had the chance to size up the local law enforcement. Some moron on the work crew got himself arrested for looting.

Stealing some stupid screwdrivers of all things. Ice had watched it all with interest. The male cop seemed competent. The woman cop, the chief, Ice had ignored. He knew he had nothing to fear from a woman. Even one with a gun. The guy seemed savvy, but Ice would bet money that he could best him. Still, he decided it wouldn't come to that. He'd find the girl, take care of business, and be gone before the local yokels knew what hit them.

It was troubling that he'd heard not the slightest rumbling about the girl. Even while at the market where the work crew stopped every morning for coffee and Red Bull, and sometimes later for lunch, he'd not heard anything. It was frustrating, especially since he still had a strong feeling that he was on the right track.

Wednesday morning he had to meditate to center himself after a phone call from Cyrus.

"Ice, I'm paying you for results! I've got the Feds breathing down my neck."

"Hey, I'm on it. I'm sure the girl is close. I'll find her."

"I'm sending help."

Royal bit his tongue. The man was hysterical, and being this emotional would only cause problems.

"I work best alone," he said through gritted teeth. *"You know that."*

"There's strength in numbers. Gage is coming your way." He disconnected, leaving Ice fuming.

Gage was one of Cyrus's on-call musclemen. More brawn than brain as far as Ice was concerned. He wanted to scream that Gage was all wrong on every level. An ex–basketball player, he'd stick out like a sore thumb here simply because of his height. And he wasn't that mobile, either; a bum knee gave him a limited range. Cyrus always counted on Gage's size and bad attitude to intimidate problem people. Ice had no respect for the man. If you talked the talk, you had to walk the walk, and Gage could only do that with people who were stupid and slow.

Ice glanced at the clock. He needed to get ready; the van that picked him up each morning to take him to Rogue's Hollow would be there any minute.

Inhale, exhale. Ignore Gage. Inhale —

There it was — the cashier at the market came to mind. The woman had flirted with him several times when he'd been in her lane. He'd flirted back once or twice for something to do. He hadn't intended to take it any further; after all, she was too old for

Cyrus or any of their customers, and Ice didn't need any companionship. Still, with the meditation clearing his thoughts, he could see that as unappealing as she was age-wise, she'd be in a good position to hear gossip because local market cashiers see everyone in town.

Why hadn't he thought of this sooner?

"You're not from around here. I'd recognize you if you were," she'd said, smiling and popping her gum. *"Bet you work harder than all these other guys."*

"New here, yeah. Looking for reasons to stick around," he'd said with a wink.

"Glad to hear it." She'd blushed and some of the other guys pushed him along.

He kicked himself now for not digging deeper into what that local woman might know. He vowed to do better the next time he came into contact with her.

Ice got his chance later that day when the work crew pulled into the market for lunch. There were two cashiers, and even though the line was longer, he stood in the flirty one's line. Peering over the shoulder of the person in front of him, Ice saw that the woman's name tag said *Tami*.

He greeted her with one of his best smiles when it was his turn to be checked out.

"Afternoon, Tami, how's your day going?"

She looked up at him, face brightening. "Well, hello. It's going okay. Better now. How about you? They must be working you hard." She held up one of his cans of Red Bull before running it across the scanner. "Looks like you need some energy."

"Yeah, don't like coffee." He made sure his smile accentuated his left side dimple. "Name's Jim, by the way. Jim Smith. Should have introduced myself a while ago."

She grinned broadly now, eyes bright. "Better late than never." His snacks were next. "Where're you from? You're part of the work crew, right?"

"Uh-huh. I travel around a lot, kind of a handyman. Haven't found a place I'd like to settle in yet." He glanced behind him. There was a woman reading the *Enquirer* and not paying attention, so he loitered.

"Really? That sounds exciting. Seeing new places and stuff. Furthest away I've been is Disneyland in Southern California."

He nodded. "That's far and sounds like fun. Sometimes traveling is exciting, but it can get lonely. So I like to stay busy. That's why I'm here."

"We're grateful for all of you here working, helping. Be careful; we've got some rugged terrain to deal with here in the Hollow."

"Always careful, Tami." He leaned forward and handed her his money. "Always."

She took his money but held it over the register. "Good. I'd hate to see you get hurt. Thanks again for helping."

"My pleasure." He gave her a knowing wink. "What time are you off?"

She blushed. "Six."

"If I stop by tonight, might I be able to buy you a drink?"

"Sure, I'd like that. I'd like to hear about your traveling life."

He leaned close and lowered his voice seductively. "I've got lots of stories."

"I want to hear them all."

Ice promised to see her later, grabbed his purchases, and left the market. Not all of his coworkers were finished shopping, so he popped a Red Bull and scanned the parking lot as had become his habit. He always searched for the out-of-place car, one that would indicate a federal presence.

He saw lots of pickups, several with boats hitched to them, though to Ice, it was too cold to be out on a boat. There was a Rogue's Hollow police car at the far end, by the burger hut. He sauntered to where he could see the cop. Never hurt to be clear on where the enemy was. She was sitting at a table with a man Ice had seen helping at one of the burned-out houses. He'd heard that the man was the local head Bible-thumper.

He walked back and leaned against the van, thinking about the best tack to take with Tami on their "date." He was in a hurry, didn't see any reason to pussyfoot around the issue. Since she was talky, he'd probably find out right away what he needed to know. Force might not be necessary, but he was ready either way.

Just then a vehicle came screaming into the lot. Ice stood up straight, peering intently as the vehicle came to a stop in a parking space three cars down on the other side of the lot from where he stood. Unmistakable, it was a Fed car. The driver jumped out, a small Asian woman wearing jeans and a flannel shirt. With a sidearm. She looked as if she'd lost something, something important. And she had Ice's full attention.

20

"She's acting as if she finally settled down," Oliver said as he picked up his iced tea. He and Tess were enjoying lunch from Max's Grill in the market parking lot. At sixty-five degrees there was a fall chill to the air, but that was set to change. He wasn't sure how much longer lunch outside would be an option. Clouds were moving in, the temp was dropping, and tomorrow would be a totally different day than today.

He followed Tess's gaze to the river and knew that she hadn't heard him. He couldn't blame her; Midas Creek roaring into the Rogue River was a captivating sight.

"Earth to Tess."

"What?" She faced him. "Sorry, but doesn't that water look awesome?"

He chuckled. "It does. So do you. But if I spent all day looking at you the way I'd like, I'd never get anything done."

She darkened a shade as he knew she

would, something he loved about Tess. She really had no idea how pretty she was and easily blushed when complimented. He wanted so much to tell her that he loved her, but the time hadn't been right.

"Okay, Romeo, what was it you wanted to talk to me about?"

"Chevy. I think she's a bigger problem than we thought."

"How so?"

"Acting settled, but not really being settled. She's trying to play Bronwyn. Which hasn't gone very far, but Agent Takano is a different story. She's not paying close attention because she doesn't want to be here. It's affecting her job a bit."

Tess blew out a breath. "I was afraid of that. What do you think her endgame is? Chevy, I mean. Will she refuse to testify?"

"That I can't say. She's built a protective wall around her emotions, not surprising. But I truly think we're dealing with an eighteen-year-old going on thirty with the emotional makeup of a thirteen-year-old."

"What about Counselor Peel? What's her take?"

"She thinks Bass is pushing the girl too hard too soon. Think of what she's been through in the last three years of her life. Now, overnight, she'll be a credible witness in a high-profile criminal case? Against a guy like Beck?"

Tess sighed. "I can't say you don't make sense. I've tried to keep my distance from the girl, Faith's Place, and Takano because the trial is not my rodeo. And Beck is still stonewalling. His lawyers are filing motion after motion, trying to delay or derail the case. In my opinion it was a mistake for the judge to release him on bail, even with an ankle monitor. Chevy and Takano might have to be here a while longer. If I —"

Squealing tires sounded, and Tess looked over his shoulder, her attention drawn to the market parking lot.

Oliver turned to see what had interrupted her train of thought and saw a car come to an abrupt stop and FBI agent Mia Takano jump out.

"Speak of the devil," Tess said as she stood. "What is she doing here and where is the fire?"

"I take it you're going to go ask?"

Tess nodded, leaving her half-finished lunch on the table. Oliver followed, realizing that he was just as curious as Tess was. Takano was supposed to be low-key. Her entrance to the market parking lot just now was anything but.

Takano was looking all around the lot as

she walked toward the entrance of the market. She must have caught sight of Tess because she stopped, changed direction, and hurried toward her.

"What's the problem, Agent Takano?" Tess spoke in a formal cop tone that told Oliver she was not happy with the agent.

"She's gone."

Tess stopped, and Oliver felt his pulse surge as he wondered if he'd really heard what he just thought he'd heard.

"What do you mean?" Tess asked.

"That girl. I was on the phone, Nye was out, and Bronwyn was dealing with a minor animal emergency. She slipped past everyone. She's gone."

Tess stared at Takano. She'd known the woman was not happy with her assignment. But a lapse like this was inexcusable. The girl was supposed to be kept safe and secure. Where would she go?

"How long ago did she leave?"

Takano shook her head. "I don't know. I went to get her for lunch and she wasn't in her room."

"She left on foot? She couldn't have gotten far."

"I know; that's why I came here. I thought maybe she'd come to the market." She grabbed a fistful of her hair. "Oh, man, I've messed up. My head was not in the game."

"Let's check inside the market," Oliver suggested, his calming voice meant to settle Takano, Tess was certain.

Tess nodded and walked past Mia. And nearly ran into Chevy.

The girl had a bag of groceries in one arm, was staring down at a pay-as-you-go cell phone in the other.

"Hey." Tess reached for the free arm, afraid the girl would flee. Keeping her voice low, tone even, Tess said, "What on earth? What do you think you're doing?"

Chevy tensed; then her brows lowered in anger. "Shopping. Am I under arrest? I thought I was free. Didn't you cops free me?" She tried to jerk away, and Tess was painfully aware that everyone was watching. Chevy was now the center of attention, exactly what she shouldn't be.

Before Tess could speak, Oliver stepped up. "Chevy, we were worried about you." He spoke in a soothing voice, a low tone Tess had come to love for its calm, sure strength. It was also commanding in a way — it made people listen. "All of us are simply concerned about you."

The girl's attention shifted from Tess to Oliver and she relaxed.

"I know you are," she said to Oliver. "But these other two are jailers. I just wanted to get out, get some fresh air, find current things to read, not feel like a prisoner."

Tess released the girl's arm and Oliver moved in beside her. "I had no idea that was so important to you. How about we talk about this elsewhere?" He gestured toward Takano's car.

For a second, Tess thought the girl would resist.

"If you're going to drag me back, I'll go back with you, not with them."

"Good, fine." Oliver looked to Tess and she nodded.

"You know the phone is out of the question, right?" Tess asked, holding out her hand, wondering if the girl would hand it over.

"It cost me thirty bucks."

"Chevy, I heard Agent Takano explain the rules to you. A phone is a clear no-no," Oliver said. "Give the chief the phone. She'll either pay you back or return the phone to you when all this is over."

Chevy huffed and jammed the phone toward Tess. "Fine then."

"Thanks," Oliver said; then he led Chevy toward where his car was parked.

Tess looked around at all the people

watching and prayed there wasn't anyone in the group who would do something — intentionally or not — to bring Chevy any harm. Then she turned to Takano.

Through gritted teeth, she said, "This is a major mess — you know that, don't you?"

"I do, and I'm sorry." At least she was contrite. "I'm not going to let this happen again."

Tess watched Chevy get into the car with Oliver.

The cat was out of the bag now; damage control was all they could hope for.

"Let's go back to the shelter and try to figure this out," Tess said to Takano and headed for her car.

21

Ice couldn't believe his good fortune and stood, openmouthed, careful to stay out of sight, watching the confrontation with the cop, the Fed, and the pastor. He knew the girl was Chevy; he'd recognize her anywhere. He just had to be certain she didn't recognize him — at least, not yet. And he kicked himself. She was in the store and he'd missed it! *I was too worried about the cashier,* he thought.

"Jim, saddle up — we're ready to go," his supervisor called out.

"Huh?" Ice didn't want to tear his eyes away.

"Stop gawking at the cop. Work calls." The guy pointed at the van.

"Uh, sure thing," Ice said. He walked slowly to the van, trying to watch but not be so obvious. He forced his way to a window seat, ignoring his coworker's whining. He focused on the little drama, hoping somehow he'd be able to see where Chevy went.

Ice lucked out. As the van's driver waited for everyone to get in, Chevy walked off with the pastor. He watched her get into his car. Then, while the van paused for traffic on the highway to clear, the sedan that the pastor and Chevy got into started to move.

The van pulled out of the lot. To Ice's surprise, the pastor's car eventually followed. He was able to keep tabs on them in the rearview mirror. But as the van continued up the road to the burn area, the other car turned left, on a road Ice had never been down because nothing had burned over there. He needed to find out what was down that road.

The drink he planned to buy for Tami would have to loosen the woman's tongue. But now Ice knew he was in the right place. His spirits soared. There was no need at all for Gage; Ice had things well in control.

Besides, he thought, *the people around here are stupid; they're no threat to me. Neither is one little Fed or an entire backwoods police department.*

Tami better have something useful to tell him because he wanted to wrap this up before Gage arrived and messed everything up.

Ice crushed his can and placed it in the recycle bag. He would find her — he was certain. And he'd end the threat to his friend Cyrus. Then disappear with his new wealth.

22

"Chief, I am so sorry." A mortified Bronwyn greeted Tess and brought her into the house. "Our security is more concerned with keeping people from getting in, not people getting out. But there's no excuse. Chevy never should have been able to walk away."

"I understand, and I don't really blame you." Tess cast a glance to the living room, where Oliver, Mia, Chevy, and Dr. Peel were skyping with Agent Bass. It was heated at times, with Chevy acting thirteen and petulant. She kept insisting that she was just as much a prisoner here as she was in Mesa. If she'd truly been rescued, why didn't she really have freedom?

"Takano should have been more involved with her from the get-go. Chevy is her responsibility," Tess said.

"In my home she's my responsibility," Bronwyn countered. "Do you think Bass will move her?"

"He should. Her cover was just blown to smithereens. But I don't think he has any place to move her to."

Tess was the one who had called Bass to tell him what happened.

"My hands are tied. We're waiting on the next legal maneuver. Right now, Beck appears to be stalling. I'll know more after the next pretrial hearing." Bass didn't sound as confident as he had the last time Tess spoke to him.

"If I were paranoid," she told Bronwyn, "I'd think Beck's tactics are a purposeful stall so that he can locate Chevy and have her taken out of the picture."

"And her walking out like she did . . ."

"Broadcast that she was here in Rogue's Hollow," Tess finished Bronwyn's thought. She glanced to the living room as the conversation shifted. Mia closed the laptop, and she and Dr. Peel bracketed Chevy as a deep, quiet conversation began among the three.

Oliver got up from the couch and joined Tess and Bronwyn. "Agent Bass is not happy." He shrugged. "But Chevy has a point. She's young; it's difficult to have her movements so restricted after making an escape from what was, essentially, slavery."

He held Tess's gaze. She knew he'd fall on the side of forgiving the girl for jeopardizing her situation. Tess was less sympathetic.

"If her movements are restricted, it's for her own good." It was black-and-white to Tess: Beck was evil at all levels. Chevy needed to see that and lie low until she could testify. She wasn't only jeopardizing herself, she was jeopardizing the entire case against Beck. Isaac Pink came to mind. *Is this what cost him his life? An ungrateful witness who by her actions brought killers to his house?*

"She's young — you can't expect this to be easy."

"If she wants to live to be old, she'll need to buckle down and listen to the people who are trying to help her."

Oliver placed a hand on her shoulder. "You sound like Agent Bass."

"Hmmph."

He looked back toward Chevy, who finally seemed to be listening to Dr. Peel.

Tess took a deep breath. She knew how tangled court stuff could get. She was sure Beck's first move would be to try to get all the evidence thrown out. If that happened, there would be no need to keep Chevy here and no need for the FBI to continue with her protection. She was eighteen; she'd be on her own.

"Her cover could be completely blown here. The case might already be lost." Tess spoke her pessimistic thoughts out loud.

"I don't want to see that any more than you do, but would getting rid of Chevy really get Beck anywhere? Agent Bass has the tablet."

Tess chewed on a thumbnail and considered the question. She thought about the many investigative hours Bass had spent — how difficult it had been to get solid evidence against Beck. What would convince juries these days should be clear, but it was often hard to peg.

"Besides the chain of evidence, Chevy puts a personal face on the results of Beck's evil. It will be much easier for his defense attorneys to attack the iPad and how it was recovered if Chevy isn't around. Then they'll attack the agents and the methods they used, diverting everyone's attention away from the human trafficking. Putting the cops on trial is standard operating procedure."

"But isn't the iPad hard evidence?"

"In a logical world, yes. I've just seen so many games played by defense attorneys. . . . Juries are human, and today, sometimes easily conned."

"Cynicism does not become you."

"Ah, but it's a broken world. A certain pastor I know says that all the time." Tess grinned at Oliver, who returned her smile.

"Sounds like a wise man. But in his wisdom, he probably still believes in the legal system to eventually triumph."

The one good thing that came from Chevy's escape attempt was that Mia Takano appeared more committed to her job.

"I realize it's a little late," Takano said, "but I'm paying closer attention now. I don't want anything to happen to Chevy or the case." She apologized to Tess for freaking out and screaming into the market parking lot.

Chevy was still froggy and apparently still under the illusion that Cyrus Beck was somewhat of a good guy. When Tess got up to leave, Dr. Peel stopped her and asked that she speak to Chevy.

"You've seen what happens to young women victimized by monsters like Beck — just tell her what you know."

This was something Tess dreaded because in her experience, there was nothing worse than a petulant female teen who thought she knew everything. But Tess was a team player.

"I don't want another lecture," the girl said, studying her fingernails instead of looking at Tess.

Tess sat across from the girl. "I don't want to give a lecture. Just want to give you my perspective."

The girl took a noisy, bored breath.

"I'm a cop. Cyrus Beck is a criminal. You are a victim. You have the power here. You can put Beck in jail. But make no mistake: he'll do everything in his power to keep you from testifying, including kill you if he gets the chance."

"You don't know him."

"There you're wrong. I do know him. He's a man who victimizes people weaker than himself to satisfy his own appetites. He never cared for you, Chevy. He used you. There's a big difference."

23

Not certain if anyone got through to the girl, Tess headed back to the station, still bothered by the very public incident. The idea of protective custody was to protect, and in Chevy's case to hide, a subject from bad people.

Oliver thought she was being overly paranoid. Was she?

Tess settled behind her desk and woke up the computer. She tapped on the keyboard and decided that no, she wasn't being overly paranoid. The rumors Bronwyn had shared about Beck still lingered in the back of her mind. He was a man with a lot of money. And besides the fact that Bass brought Chevy here because he was afraid Beck would discover the location of a standard safe house, he also believed that Beck had at least one hit man, or enforcer, on his payroll. It went without saying that men who killed for money were without scruples.

Add a lot of money to that and Tess would bet her service weapon there were plenty of people looking for Chevy. And when they found her, they'd kill her and anyone else who got in the way.

But there was no way to know yet if Chevy's little escape had truly compromised her. Of course, waiting for someone to appear on the doorstep looking for her would probably mean it was too late. If Tess were Bass, she'd find a place to move her in any event, even with his hands tied. She opened her e-mail, went through it, and then realized she was hungry. She'd only gotten through half her lunch earlier. She decided to visit the coffee shop, get a cup of the house blend and maybe a cinnamon roll. She got up to leave and nearly ran into Win Yarrow.

"Oh, Agent Yarrow, what can I do for you?"

"I wanted to give you the link to my forest cams and show you how they work. They're motion activated, but you'll have the ability to access the feed on your desktop. I can also pull the feed up on my phone; not sure if you want that ability."

"I'll take a look. By the way, I noticed there haven't been any animals poached lately, have there?"

"None that I've found, not since the fire, anyway. But all the activity in the forest may have forced Blakely to lay low. He's a criminal, but he's not stupid. If he were, I'd have caught him by now."

Tess had to smile. She could hear her father say, *"We don't catch the smart ones."*

She returned to her desk and sat while Yarrow showed her the four trail cams and how she could view or review the feed. A thought crossed her mind that he should be explaining this to Becky Jonkey, her officer with the most computer savvy, but Becky worked nights, and Tess might as well get up to speed on new technology. It took about forty-five minutes for Yarrow to go through all the details. Tess was certain that she understood the whole process but made a note to go over everything with Jonkey as soon as possible.

"Do you have any other suspects?"

Yarrow shook his head. "No one hits my bull's-eye like Ken Blakely," he said as he prepared to leave. "But he fired a shot over the bow. He just filed a formal complaint accusing me of harassing him."

"I'm afraid I saw that coming."

"Yeah, that's why the cams are great. I can watch, and if he shows up on a feed, he's caught, and he'll never know what hit him. I still can't believe that we found nothing at his place."

"He's certainly smart enough to have hidden everything. Maybe that's the key — figure out his hiding place." Briefly Tess remembered the trailer park and Blakely loitering around there. Did it mean anything?

"I'll try, but I can't be obvious, at least not while internal affairs is investigating the complaint. That's why I have high hopes about the forest cams. Thanks for your cooperation."

"Sure. We all want the same thing. I'll spare people to help as I'm able."

Yarrow nodded and almost seemed ready to say something else, but he didn't. He left the office. Tess was glad his visits lacked the edge they used to have. He hadn't been nearly as brusque since the fire, and that was welcome.

Tess continued on to the Hollow Grind, where she enjoyed an infusion of caffeine and sugar, and was on her way back to the station when her phone rang. It was Agent Bass. She answered, wondering if he'd found a new place for Chevy.

"I just don't have any place else to put her right now." He sounded harried and preoccupied. "What's your opinion? Was there any damage done?"

"That's impossible to tell. But people are talking. I was just at the coffee shop, and two people asked me about the incident. They figured out that she came from Faith's Place. I'm sorry, but if it were up to me, I'd move her."

"I was afraid you'd say that."

"Is there any movement with the case?" Tess asked.

"Beck's still trying to get all the search warrants invalidated, the charges dropped."

"They always try stuff like that."

"Yeah, he might have a loophole. Remember I told you this all started with a flight attendant pointing out a man traveling with two girls she thought looked hinky?"

"I do."

"There might have been a Miranda violation there on the part of an air marshal. Beck's lawyer is screaming that the search warrants were obtained using fruit of the poisonous tree and therefore they need to be thrown out, along with all the evidence, and his client released from any monitoring."

"Wow." Tess felt anger surge. It was so very important for all law enforcement officers to follow procedure to the letter. She felt sick to her stomach about the thought that a mistake at the beginning, when officers really didn't have a complete idea about what they had, could destroy what looked like a solid, serious case.

"When will you go before a judge on the situation?"

"Soon, I hope. So far, Beck's lawyers have been slowing things down, but with this new gambit, we may hear in a couple of days. In the meantime, I'll see if I can move Chevy. . . . I'm just not hopeful."

24

Gage had not yet arrived. According to the latest communication from Cyrus, he was taking care of some last-minute details. Ice didn't care. He had high hopes that he would wrap up this assignment long before Gage got in a car and headed north.

Ice was pinning everything on his upcoming "date" with the cashier. They'd made arrangements to meet when Tami got off work. Ice arrived late, wanting to avoid any introductions to coworkers if possible. It was hard to wait because he was pumped and wanted to complete his mission. Now that he knew beyond all doubt that Chevy was there, she was as good as his. He just needed to find her hidey-hole.

As part of the cleanup work crew, he was usually picked up at his hotel every morning. When he was out and about on his own, he rode his stolen motorcycle. He had clean plates on it and knew cops would only figure it out if they looked closely to match the VIN. He would never give them an excuse to look that closely. The bike was likely to impress Tami, help her get over any miff at him being late, he hoped.

He was right. She appeared to be frowning when he pulled into the parking lot, but her face brightened when she saw him step off the bike.

"Wow, what a pretty bike," she said, eyes raking over the machine. "Can I have a ride?"

"Love to, Tami, but I only have one helmet. Can't take the chance. I trust my driving, but . . ." He tilted his head and gave her his best "I care about you" look.

"Still, maybe if I borrow a helmet sometime?"

"You bet."

There was one bar in Rogue's Hollow, a small locals' place called The Stump. Tami wanted to go there, but Ice pulled the six-pack he'd bought in Shady Cove off the back of his bike.

"How about we go to some place more private." Ice gave her his most seductive smile, but she hesitated.

"I hardly know you." She tried to sound reticent, but Ice read her body language and she was anything but. "We should go to some place public."

He turned on the charm, knowing from experience that this girl was lonely and wanted to be with him. This was what he did — he found the lonely and conned them.

"Come on, I don't want to compete with any other guys for your attention."

She blushed but still needed convincing.

Ice gently rubbed her shoulder. "How about this? You pick the spot and you drive — that way you're in control. I just want a private visit with a pretty girl since I spend all day with smelly guys. No hands, I promise." He grinned, and she blushed deeper and laughed.

"Well . . . okay. I guess we can go up to the Stairsteps. That's a public place and a little private, especially after dark."

"Awesome." He grinned and moved his bike out of sight.

She had a small two-door beater car. Ice popped his first beer before they reached the destination she'd picked. He opened up the conversation asking what she knew about the girl who made the scene in the market parking lot earlier.

"Oh yeah, wasn't that crazy? People were talking about that all day. Most of them think she ran away from the women's shelter."

Women's shelter. Bingo. Ice had to fight to keep his composure. He had Chevy now.

"Women's shelter — you mean like for homeless women?" he asked, playing dumb, sipping his beer, acting slightly interested.

She parked the car at the far end of the Stairsteps parking lot. Ice opened a beer and handed it to her.

"No, we have a shelter in town for battered women." She took a quick drink. "I had a friend who stayed there for a few days. Her husband smacked her around." She undid her seat belt and moved closer.

Ice did likewise, throwing his arm over her shoulder. She smelled pleasantly of freshly applied floral perfume.

"Strange that the girl would run away from a place that's supposed to keep her safe," he said. "It must be close to the market. I didn't see that she had a car."

"It's maybe one and a half or two miles away, over on Oakwood Court. The place also rescues horses. I know the lady who runs it, Bronwyn. She's nice, has a neat British accent." She sipped her beer.

His mind whirring on the information about the shelter, Ice chatted, keeping his tone easy, asking her about herself and pretending to listen and care. By the time she'd finished her second beer, he knew he had all he needed and was overwhelmed with a sense of urgency to do some recon at the shelter. There was a second reason for urgency: it was likely the Feds would move the girl now since it was obvious she'd blown her cover.

"You haven't told me anything about you, Jim. What's up with you? I want to hear about your travels." Tami prodded him in the ribs and smiled broadly.

"Um." Ice forced his thoughts back to Tami. He needed to deal with her directly; she was now a loose end. But first he wanted to know a little about the police force. "I'm thinking that I like Rogue's Hollow a lot better than many of the places I've been," he said, brushing his lips across her forehead. "Besides you, what else in this place is interesting, exciting?"

She giggled and pulled her head up to look at him, scrunching her face. "This Podunk town? I'm glad I have a job, but there's nothing to do here."

"You can always travel. But as far as living, this place is pretty safe, huh? That cop in the market parking lot seemed to be on the ball."

"Hmm, that was the chief. There was a

big shoot-out a few months ago. She handled it, took down a big drug dealer, so I guess she's good. There's hardly any crime in the Hollow, no gangs. It's boring. But you could say it's safe."

Tami kept talking, sharing the story of her friend and the mean husband, how the cops dealt with him, but Ice wasn't listening anymore.

He was planning.

"Hey, you listening?" Tami shifted and looked at him.

Ice changed gears and smiled. He'd decided how to deal with Tami. The chatty woman had served her purpose. Now what would be the best way to do that and not leave any evidence? Water had worked for Ice in the past. Yeah, the girl had picked a good spot.

"You feel like a little walk, maybe to check out the falls?"

"It's dark and cold out there."

"I'll keep you warm. I'd just like to see you under the stars. It's a little cloudy, but there are bound to be a few stars up there." He brushed her lips with his and felt her lean into him.

After a heavier kiss, he pulled back and opened his door. She followed suit, and as they met at the front of the car, he pulled her close and they walked together to the viewing platform.

"Beautiful night, beautiful girl . . . I must be in heaven," he whispered, his voice crooning right into her ear to be heard over the loudly rushing water. But it was freezing; the temp had dropped precipitously since the sun went down and he tried hard not to shiver. She continued to lean into him and didn't notice the change in his demeanor until they reached the railing and he pulled back.

Her brows scrunched together. "Hold me, Jim. It's cold."

As she turned toward him, putting her back against the railing, Ice drew the small .38 from his waistband. Shock registered on her face, but she had nowhere to go. It was over quickly, no muss, no fuss, and no emotion, just cold calculation. Ice, baby.

Ice shoved the gun in his waistband again and jogged to the car, thinking about what he'd touched. To be safe, he wiped down all the main surfaces carefully, knowing that time at this task was well spent. He also threw away all the beer cans, full as well as empty. Though he was positive the cops here were clueless, he wouldn't leave any evidence behind.

Once he finished, he hurried away from

the car and the parking lot, jogging easily back to where he'd left his bike.

25

The worst part of being chief of police was all the paperwork, Tess decided as she yawned over the pile of work she'd brought home with her. Clearly, she'd violated her own rule #11: "EOW is EOW — leave work at work." As a beat cop, when she needed to document every little thing, often the paperwork was overwhelming. Now the need to document had multiplied for Tess as she had to review not only her day but everyone else's as well.

It was late when she finished and laid down her pen. She stood and stretched, considering watching some TV but immediately dismissing the idea. She was tired; time for bed. A knock on the door woke her up. No one she knew ever called this late, and she was on alert.

From a side table she grabbed her .380, an off-duty weapon that she liked to keep handy. After all, a man had been murdered on her porch not too long ago, so Tess felt her caution was justified.

She approached the side of the door, flipped on the porch light. "Who is it?"

"It's Livie Harp."

Tess recognized the voice, but shock replaced her caution. Peering through the curtain, she saw that it was, indeed, the mystery woman. She opened the door.

"Sorry for the surprise visit, but I wanted to talk to you privately. This seemed like the best time and place."

For a second Tess wasn't sure what to say. She swallowed and stepped aside. "Well, okay then. Come on in."

Harp entered. She was dressed all in black; from her cargo pants and mock turtleneck sweater to the gloves and boots, she reminded Tess of a commando.

"What can I help you with?"

"I've come to offer you my help." She fixed a steely gaze on Tess.

Tess motioned for her to have a seat. "What do you think I need help with?"

"I'll stand." Harp glared at Tess, or right through her, Tess thought. She was wound up, and Tess didn't have to wait long to find out why. "I know you're sheltering a human trafficking victim."

Tess held her tongue and refused to be

shaken. After the incident at the market, why should she be? Earlier she'd already imagined that everyone now knew where Chevy was.

She cleared her throat. "What do you mean, me personally?"

Irritation washed across Harp's features. "I'm not stupid, Chief. And I won't beat around the bush. I know about Faith's Place. I'm glad the house exists, but it's not a secret. And I've been following the recent news stories about the arrest of Cyrus Beck. When I heard there was a witness, I went out of my way to try and find her, in order to make certain she was safe."

"If you're here because of what happened at the market today —"

"Market?" Harp frowned, clearly unaware of the market fiasco. "I'm here to try to save a girl's life."

"Wait. Let's say you're right, and there is a witness at Faith's Place. Why do you believe it's up to you to keep her safe?"

"I know a thing or two about predators. Cyrus Beck is the worst type. He has money and the air of respectability that conceals his perversity. And since his crimes supposedly occurred in Arizona, but the witness is being hidden here, I believe that says the FBI sees Beck as a threat, a serious one. To survive, the girl has to hide and hide well. I'm willing to help. It's a cause I can get behind."

Tess regarded Harp with an appraising eye. The woman was fired up and passionate. But Tess needed clarity, facts, not emotion. "You're going to have to explain. That's a little vague."

"A full explanation might just send me to jail."

Tess rocked back a bit. "Unless I know exactly why you think you can help me, I have nothing to discuss with you."

"I'm giving you a valid warning, Chief, and you should listen. The girl you've hidden . . . well, her life depends on it. That should be enough."

Tess held her hands out. "I barely know you. In fact, I've tried to find out about you and can find nothing. Why should I trust you?"

Harp's eyes bored into Tess. "Beck is a monster. He hires monsters. And if I could find Roberta, so could he."

Roberta. Harp even knew her name. Floored by Harp's claim and trying to process how she could possibly have found Chevy even though she had no clue about what happened at the market earlier today, Tess wanted to demand the woman tell her.

But this could all be a ruse; the woman could be trying to get Tess to reveal something.

"Okay, I'll play along. Say you're correct; your solution is . . . ?"

"Let her come and stay with me. I can keep her safe. I am completely off the grid. You've seen my place. No one will find her if she stays with me. And I can protect her if they do. Anyone steps foot on my property, I know exactly where and when. I know how to deal with threats to my safety."

"We're going in circles here. I'm not conceding that there is a girl here. But if there were, I wouldn't trust her to someone I know nothing about."

"Chief, if I tell you everything I know, and why I know it, I need your word that you will not arrest me on the spot."

"I can't make an agreement like that."

"We're at an impasse."

"We are, and I'm not going to blink."

After a long, tense moment, Harp did blink and strode to the door, stopping with her hand on the knob. "I'm serious, Chief. Maybe you have no reason to trust me, but you can pick up the phone and let the people at Faith's Place know that anyone with a little computer savvy could find out they're sheltering a witness there. Please tell them to be extra vigilant. Cyrus Beck is evil personified."

She opened the door and was gone. Leaving Tess wide-awake and feeling as if she'd just been through a washing machine spin cycle.

26

Oliver listened to Tess tell him the story of the late-night visitor. Six thirty in the morning and they were eating breakfast at the Hollow Grind, a rare and pleasant way for them to start the day.

"I'm amazed that she came to talk to you. She came to talk to me once shortly after she moved into her mystery mansion."

"What did she want to talk about?"

"She had Bible questions. As I recall, she wanted some proof the Bible is true. And she wanted an explanation for all the evil in the world."

"Oh, she had easy questions, huh?" Tess grinned at him.

"We talked; I invited her to church." He shrugged. "I've only seen her briefly once or twice since then, and she doesn't seem interested in talking to anyone. How are you going to handle this?"

"I called Agent Bass right after I called

Bronwyn and Nye and asked them if everyone was okay. Things have calmed down since the market fiasco. But it worries me more than I can say. Harp knew the girl was there, knew her name. The whole episode spooked me a bit."

She sipped her coffee and picked at her breakfast. Oliver could tell she hadn't gotten much sleep.

"Bass has no idea how anyone could find Chevy via the computer. There is no record of her anywhere on a public domain. She's in a secure law enforcement system, and that's not public. He was rattled about that and the market incident, but a text I got from him this morning said he wants her to stay put anyway. He's completely tied up in the court proceedings and extremely worried that part or all of the evidence will be excluded. If he is able, he will find out exactly who Livie Harp is."

The angst in her voice got to him. Oliver reached out and put his hand over hers. "Tess, you've done everything humanly possible to keep that girl safe. And Bronwyn and Nye are capable as well. I wish I knew more about Livie Harp and what would possess her to come to you like that."

Tess gripped his hand; her hands were always warm, and Oliver loved the firm touch of her hand in his.

"She said she knew about predators, that she recognized how dangerous Cyrus Beck could be. She also said that if she told me her whole story, I'd arrest her on the spot. All night I ruminated over that remark, wondering now if she's hiding because she's wanted somewhere."

"That idea was kicked around when she first came here."

Tess sighed. "I can't find anything to indicate that she's wanted. But it all struck an echo of a memory with me. Bass brought up a cold case when he talked to me about Chevy."

"And?"

She told him a horrific story about Isaac Pink and a prostitute named Heather Harrison. Oliver felt cold, slapped at the brutality of the tale.

"Are you thinking maybe she could be Heather Harrison?"

"That's not possible, right?" Tess rolled her eyes. "It's too fantastic, a completely crazy idea. Harrison was an eighteen-year-old prostitute when she disappeared. She is most likely long dead. But I need to digest all of this."

The shop door chimed as it opened, and she looked toward the entrance. Oliver turned and followed her gaze. Officer Bender came toward them. His expression told Oliver something bad had happened.

"Sorry to bother you, Chief, but we've got a missing woman."

"Who?" Oliver and Tess spoke in unison. Sheepishly, Oliver gave Tess the floor.

"Who is it?"

"Tami Vasquez, works at the market."

Tess frowned and nodded. "Yeah, I know her. What's happened?"

"Hopefully it's nothing, but she didn't show up for work today, and she was scheduled to open up. And earlier this morning, Jonkey made a note about seeing her car abandoned at the Stairsteps lot. The store called Tami's mom, who hasn't heard from her either. She filed a missing report."

Tess sat back, and Oliver saw the worry cross her face ever so briefly before she composed herself and her expression became all cop. His thoughts lingered on the Isaac Pink story. At times he wished she could be talked out of her profession — so much pain and hardness there. But it was who she was, and she was good at it, very good at it.

"I'll go with you. Thanks for breakfast, Oliver." She stood, and so did Oliver.

"Of course. Please let me know what you

find. Tami is a fixture at the market."

Tess said she would, and she and Bender left the shop.

As Oliver was busing his table, his gaze met the decidedly disapproving expression of one of his parishioners. He smiled, and Alana looked away. Sighing, he wondered if he should nip this in the bud. He'd heard from the Rogue telegraph that several women in the congregation were not happy with his relationship with Tess. They were all women who'd been with the church since its very beginning. They liked Tess . . . they just didn't think she was a good match for him.

"Her work is antithetical to your work. It's dangerous," Addie Getz — councilwoman, parishioner, and friend — told Oliver one day. *"And these women are very protective of their pastor."*

He decided to step over and talk to Alana about the issue, but his phone buzzed. The text was from Jethro and it was about Tami. Her mother was at the church asking for prayer. He threw the remnants of his and Tess's breakfasts in the trash and left the shop, concern lingering over what exactly he could do to assuage Alana's fears.

"No sign of a struggle — or theft, for that

matter," Bender said when he and Tess reached the car.

Tess noted that it was at the far end of the lot, as if the place had been crowded when Tami picked the spot, or she wanted a semiprivate space. It wasn't all alone as it had been in the early morning hours when Jonkey had noted its presence; now there were a few tourists on the overlook for the Stairsteps, despite the cold weather. A front had moved in last night, and it had rained a little then. Morning temps had hovered around thirty-eight. Now, with the sun covered by a thick veil of dark clouds, the temp had dropped probably a few degrees since daybreak. Intermittent sprinkles were appearing on the pavement.

Overnight parking was prohibited here. Jonkey had run the car but not cited it because she knew who it belonged to. Tess read the notes her overnight officer had left. She'd looked the car over, called Tami's roommate, and was told Tami was out on a date and that she believed the car would be removed by the morning. So Jonkey had left a note for day shift to follow up, which Bender had done when he got the report about Tami not showing up to work.

"On a date?" Tess looked at Bender, who shrugged.

"Her mom hadn't spoken to Tami for a couple of days, so she knew nothing about a date."

"Any idea who the date was with?"

He shook his head. "Her roommate also works at the market. I'll be talking to her."

Tess carefully surveyed the area around the car. There was no indication that a crime had occurred here. She shifted her gaze to the inside of the car. Likewise, it appeared neat, nothing out of place. She donned gloves and pulled on the door, which was unlocked. Tami's purse was on the backseat.

"It's obvious she had a passenger. When I'm by myself," Tess said as she grabbed the purse, "I have my purse on the seat next to me. I only put it in the back when I have a passenger." She set the purse on the hood and began to look through it. Nothing in it stood out; it was a normal assortment of things a woman might carry in her purse. The wallet contained twelve dollars in cash, an ID, and a debit card.

Tess turned to Bender. "I have my kit with me. I'll dust for prints before I call Forest to come tow it. You go ahead and follow up at the market."

He nodded and left.

After she readied her kit, she stood and

surveyed the few people on the overlook. They were bundled up against the wind that had just picked up, and none were concerned with what she was doing.

Not feeling the cold, Tess bent to the task at hand, but it wasn't long before she noticed something unusual. The car had been wiped clean; every surface where she was likely to pull a print was clean as a whistle. A line of clean above the dirt was noticeable on the passenger door. Steering wheel, dash, mirrors, all spotless.

A sick feeling began to form in the pit of her stomach. Unless Tami left in someone else's car and was playing hooky from work, something bad had happened to her — something very bad.

27

Tess finished with Tami's car as an icy rain began to fall. It was early for this type of cold storm, and Tess wondered if it fore-shadowed a long, harsh winter. She did a cursory walk-through of the parking lot and viewing area while waiting for Forest Wild, local automotive shop owner, to arrive and tow the car to his facility. Tess saw no reason to put a hold on the automobile, so Forest would keep it until Tami's mother could pick it up.

Tess had spoken to Tami from time to time, like everyone in town had. She was the normal day cashier at the only market in Rogue's Hollow. She'd been divorced once, so the first place they'd look would be the ex. Tami had no kids and lived not far from her mother, behind the station in a small house she shared with a roommate. She always walked to work in the sum-mertime. She was a likable, if a little talkative, woman.

Before she would even voice the idea that foul play might be involved, a question bounced around in Tess's head: Who would want to hurt her?

She chewed on that question and her lower lip as she drove to the market. Bender was writing on his notepad as she parked. He'd finished by the time she walked to where he stood.

"The other cashier at the market told me that Tami's date was with one of the guys on the cleanup crew," Bender said.

Irritation spiked inside, and Tess frowned. "The cleanup crew again? At the rate they're going, they're likely to have done more harm than good."

"I hear you. No one got a name on the guy, but two of the other women who work at the market said the guy was older but hot. I've got a call in to the supervisor who was overseeing the cleanup. They'd be here by now if they were working today. Their work is almost finished. Pete's talked about ending the detail early."

Tess nodded. Pete had told her that the most devastated and at-risk properties were as good as they could make them. If a big storm hit, he didn't foresee anything catastrophic happening. So the work detail was ending, and she'd have to get her mind back onto Tami and off things she had no power over at all.

"As I recall, she was divorced. Any bad blood with the ex?"

Bender shook his head. "Divorce was about three years ago. I know Frank, the ex; he lives in White City with his new wife. He's happy as a clam, not the type to get physical. But to be thorough, I asked Jackson County Sheriff's to run by his house and talk to him."

"Okay, so it sounds as if we really need to look into the work crew. Did anyone see her leave with this 'hot guy'?"

"No, all I got was that he might have been riding a motorcycle. You know the night crew at the market is light. Everyone was busy with their work when Tami left with her date. I'll keep asking."

Tess went back to her car. She pulled up the work crew roster on her car computer. She'd put the list into a file after the incident with the theft. When she'd run all the names for wants and warrants, she learned a couple men and one of the women had prior records — they were homeless, so they had the associated convictions: loitering, drug possession, littering, suspended license — but nothing violent or serious. Two had out-of-state licenses, one from California and one from Washington, bordering states, so that wasn't a big deal.

"I've been impressed with their work," Pete had said. *"They got a lot of hard work done before the weather turned bad. I think the one you arrested was an aberration. He gave in to easy temptation."*

Tess had visited the crew once or twice, and she struggled to remember if any of them stood out as "hot." She was chagrined that she hadn't paid closer attention. But then, hot was a matter of taste. To her, Oliver was completely hot. Would Tami and her coworkers see him that way?

She sat in her car for a few minutes as the rain *tat-tatted* down. She grabbed her phone and called Steve Logan and filled him in on the situation.

"Ah, I know Tami. She's a talker but all heart. And I hate to tell you, but earlier, around 3:30 a.m., medics picked up a Jane Doe at the Shady Cove boat ramp."

Tess sucked in a breath, taking a second to process this information. "The boat ramp — that's what, ten miles downriver? That can't be Tami."

"I'm reading the call now. It looked as if she came out of the river, was hanging on at the ramp. She had a lot of superficial

243

injuries, but they did find a pulse and transported her to the hospital."

Tess's heart dropped as she considered the possibilities. If this was Tami, could the current have taken her down Midas Creek into the Rogue River near Shady Cove? And could she really have survived the trip?

"What are the odds of Tami going in the water here, ending up there, and still being alive?" she asked.

"Not good. Look, this Jane Doe had no ID. I'll head out now, go to the hospital and check on her. I know Tami. I should be able to give you a yea or a nay."

Tess thanked him and hung up as her queasy feeling turned to anger. If there was a monster on that work crew, she'd find him. Monsters deserved to be in cages.

Thoughts of Alana's snub fled from Oliver's mind when he saw Rosita Vasquez. While Tami only attended sporadically, Rosita was a member of his congregation, always at church.

"Pastor Mac! Tami didn't come home last night. That's not like her. She's a good girl; she always comes home. I've called all of her friends, but no one has seen her."

Oliver placed an arm around the woman and pulled her close. She was trembling with fear and anxiety, and he did his best to calm her. Off to one side of the sanctuary there was a small prayer room. He looked over Rosita's shoulder at Jethro.

Jethro met his gaze with a knowing nod. "I called on the prayer team. A couple of them are already in the prayer room."

"Rosita, let's go to prayer. You know I believe that's where we should take every issue, large or small."

"Yes." She dabbed at her eyes with a Kleenex. "I believe that too. I'm praying for a miracle."

Oliver, Rosita, and the other members of the prayer team prayed for several minutes. And then Rosita wanted to talk. She chatted about Tami, what a good girl she was, but that she was lonely. Rosita was clearly afraid that her daughter had somehow gotten involved with a bad man.

Oliver listened, still praying quietly that Tess would come to the door with good news, that it was all a misunderstanding and Tami was safe. He left to go to his office when several other members of the prayer team arrived, and he knew Rosita was in good hands.

Fifteen minutes later Steve called Tess back. He talked in a low voice, and from the sounds on the phone, Tess could tell he was in the hospital.

"You won't believe this. It is Tami, and she's still hanging on."

"What?" Tess froze. This was wonderful news — would it stay that way?

"Yeah, and get this — the doctors were about to notify us. She's been shot at least twice."

"What?"

"Besides that insult, she's severely hypothermic. I barely recognized her. She's beat up from being in the water, her lips are blue . . . One of the doctors thinks that being in the cold water may have slowed her blood loss. She's listed as critical." Steve sighed. "It'll be amazing if she pulls through."

"Yes, it would be. Please keep me up to speed. I'll go tell Oliver."

Tess hung up, energized and angry at the same time. She rubbed her hands together, praying for Tami to pull through and for the break she needed to catch a bad guy.

Oliver was going to text Tess when he saw her SUV pull into the lot. He perked up as soon as she stepped out of the car. She had news, and it didn't look as if it would be bad. He met her in the parking lot.

"Tami?"

"Tami is alive. Deputies found her in the river down by the Shady Cove boat launch."

"In the river?" Horrified, Oliver felt his body go numb, thoughts swirling about what this meant. He doubted with every fiber of his soul that Tami went into the river voluntarily.

Tess nodded. "It looks as if she was shot and shoved into the river. Steve said she's listed as critical."

"Shot?" Anger coursed through Oliver and pushed away the horror. "Could she tell Steve who did it? And how on earth is she still alive?"

Tess shook her head. "I don't know. All I know is what Steve told me. Deputies responded to a Jane Doe. Tami had no identification on her, but Steve went to the hospital to check on her personally. According to Steve, she's in bad shape but alive."

"A miracle," Oliver said, hope and amazement mixing. "Rosita prayed for a miracle."

Tess didn't disagree. For Tami to have survived from somewhere around 6 p.m. to 3:30 a.m. in the frigid river with a bullet wound, it would have to be a miracle.

"Rosita is in the prayer room. I'll let her know and take her to the hospital."

"I'll go with you," Tess said. "After we tell

her what happened, maybe she'll have an idea about who might have done this."

28

Ice paced like a caged animal in his small hotel room. After he'd taken care of the checker, he'd hotfooted it back to where his bike was stashed. Good thing about a small town, the sidewalks folded up early. He'd not noticed anyone in the area when he hopped on the bike. He chugged carefully up the road he'd seen the Fed take, and it wasn't long before he found what he was certain was the shelter. He probably would have found it even without the cashier. The place was gated, and tight security in a small town was a dead giveaway that something was different.

Parking the bike, Ice carefully took a walk along the fence line. It was good security; in the dark it wasn't easy to tell if he could breach it. Because the exterior of the dwelling was well lit, he was able to view most of the structures on the property and recognized that getting in was not going to be easy. The fence around the property was climbable, but that would be time-consuming. The only way to get in quickly was through the front gate, but how? It wasn't like he could just drive up and ask for admittance. And he was on a motorcycle — that was more problematic.

It was then that this spitting, icy rain had started. He'd pulled his hood up and headed back to his hotel. He'd intended to pack his stuff, finish the job at dawn, and then be gone. But this freezing, icy, on-and-off rain had stopped him. He was used to working in climes where the weather didn't restrict him like this. Being on the bike in this weather would be treacherous. On the way back to the hotel, he'd almost lost control in a slide on the slick roadway.

A nagging anxiety about exactly how he'd kill the girl and get out of the state unde-tected weighed down on him. He was hav-ing trouble formulating a plan. Ice realized that it had been a mistake to get rid of the cashier so quickly. He could have used another couple of days for reconnaissance.

Fear that the girl would be moved and the pressure of Gage coming had forced his hand, and the more Ice thought about it, the angrier he got. He knew Cyrus was nervous — this was the closest anyone had gotten to him — but Ice never should have let pressure influence the way he did his job.

While he paced, he tried to figure out how to get out of the hole he found himself in. His burner phone buzzed with a text and he picked it up. It was from the work crew supervisor. They were delaying the work start this morning because of the icy conditions.

Ice responded with a thumbs-up emoji and tossed the phone back on the bed. A small bit of good news. He had no intention of returning to work. This would just mean a few extra hours before they'd notice "Jim Smith" was gone.

His other phone vibrated with a text, and Ice cursed. Gage had arrived — he must have flown — and Ice was out of time. He took several deep breaths to center himself. It didn't take long for him to calm down. Gage would have a plan, and Ice would go with the flow. If that didn't work, it would be on Gage, not Ice.

He texted Gage the name of his hotel. Twenty minutes later the big man knocked on the door.

"You find her?" he asked.

"Yeah. She's holed up in a women's shelter nearby."

"Feds?"

"Only one that I've seen. But the place is locked down tight. Not sure yet how we can get in."

Gage grinned. "I am." He pulled a wallet out of his pocket and handed it to Ice.

Ice took it. Inside was a US marshal ID card, the real deal from what he could tell. It had the name Joseph Turner under Gage's picture.

"I got the creds, man. I'll drive up there and take her right from under their noses."

"They're not going to just give her to you."

"Oh yeah, they will." He retrieved some more papers. Ice looked them over. They were as authentic as any he'd ever seen, court orders that Roberta Impala was to be released to US Marshal Joseph Turner ASAP.

Ice was impressed, but he kept his expression blank. "How do you want to play it?"

"I say we drive over there now. I'll head straight for the front door. If it goes smooth and they hand over the girl, we beat feet out of here. There's a private jet waiting for us at the airport."

"And if they don't just hand her over?"

"Well, it's scorched earth — you know that." He tapped the ballistic vest he was wearing. "We go in hot. I don't think the cops here are anything to worry about." He arched an eyebrow, and Ice shook his head.

Gage continued. "I've got the hardware in the car. You're my backup. Any hitches for me, you'll know what to do."

Ice studied Gage. He stood six feet nine inches tall and probably weighed three hundred pounds. He'd done some boxing and worked as a bouncer before Cyrus hired him. He was a scrapper, but he didn't read people very well. He could at least serve as a distraction, though. He'd get Ice through that first gate. Maybe the fake order would work, maybe it wouldn't. But scorched earth covered a lot of ground, and things could get ugly if the one Fed put up any kind of resistance.

In spite of the simplistic plan, Ice found himself smiling. Yes, this could work. It wasn't the first time someone would be stepping in front of him. The point person usually took the first bullet.

He nodded. "Okay, let me tell you about this shelter."

Ice explained everything he knew. He drew a crude map of what he had seen on his brief recon trip, then dressed in his best jeans, set aside his work boots for a pair of shoes, put on the body armor Gage had brought for him, and armed himself. Ice normally hated anything that restricted his movement, but the vest could come in handy.

Gage had also brought an assortment of weapons, and since this might be a scorched-earth situation, Ice put away his favorite weapon, his shiny .357 revolver. He picked up a couple of 9mm automatics that Gage had brought because the clips each held fifteen rounds. He hadn't loaded the clips, so none of his prints would be on the casings. He put one in a belt holster and the other in a shoulder holster. Then, for security, he put his little .38 revolver in an ankle holster. Lastly, he jammed a box of extra ammo in his pocket. He wasn't wearing a suit, but with his close-cropped hair and a close shave, he was certain he'd pass as an agent.

When they were ready, he took his belongings and climbed into Gage's rental car. It was a nice ride, a top-of-the-line Dodge Charger. He'd seen Fed cars like this, so that was a good thing. But for Ice the biggest perk of this ride was that it would make a good getaway car, impervious to the cold and spitting rain. Despite the dark day and storm clouds, Ice put on a pair of mirrored sunglasses.

Gage drove leisurely, and when they reached the gate to the shelter a little after

8:15 a.m., he punched the intercom button, placed his fake ID up to the small monitor.

Ice straightened his sunglasses and held his breath, knowing that they'd only get one shot at this.

29

It was a guardedly somber day at the church, and in the town as a whole. Tami was well-known and liked. And word spread rapidly about what had happened. The Rogue telegraph was on overdrive. In her year plus working in Rogue's Hollow, Tess felt crime here more personally than she ever had in Long Beach. Someone, usually someone Tess knew, always knew the victim. Crime, especially violent crime, hit home.

Tess knew that it hit Oliver particularly hard as she watched him console Tami's mother at the church. Sadly, the woman could tell her nothing about who Tami might have been with.

Tess planned to follow them to the hospital, but when it became apparent that Rosita really didn't know any more about her daughter's "date," she decided that she could do more in town, trying to find the culprit.

"I understand, and I agree," Oliver told Tess. "I'll call you if there is any news."

"Thanks." Tess reached out and gripped his arm. "I'll find the person who did this — I promise."

He nodded. "I know you will." He touched her hand briefly before heading for his car.

Several people from the prayer team followed Oliver and Rosita to the hospital. Tess watched them go, wishing she felt as comfortable with the prayer team and other members of Oliver's church as she thought she should be. That niggling worry hit again. She'd realized early on that Oliver was the whole package — he was as dedicated to his church as she was to her job. Sometimes fear struck. Could the two of them really forge a life together when their two professions often seemed intent on pulling them apart?

"Do you really think you're any good for him?"

"What?" She turned, frowning. An older woman Tess knew in passing — Alana was her name — had come up behind her. Alana was a longtime church member, from before Oliver was hired, and part of the meals ministry that had kept Oliver fed after Anna's death.

"Pastor Mac. He deserves a woman completely dedicated to him, to his calling. You can never be that woman."

Taken aback, Tess remembered Oliver mentioning once or twice that a lot of the older women in his congregation were very protective of him. Was that what this was?

"Pardon me, but I don't think that's any of your business." Tess swallowed and fought to keep the edge out of her voice. She left the woman standing in front of the sanctuary and went back to her car.

Alana had stabbed at the very real fear Tess felt and worked to bury and ignore. A man like Oliver did deserve someone totally devoted to him, with nothing else distracting her. Someone like the woman he'd lost. Someone like Anna.

Tess knew she could never be Anna. Could she truly be good for Oliver?

Tess was good at compartmentalizing, and she stuffed the encounter with Alana down deep when she returned to the station. She hadn't been in her office long when there was a knock on the door.

"Hey, how are things going?" Steve Logan asked.

"Crazy." She detailed for him her part of the investigation concerning Tami so far. "We think she went in the water at the Stairsteps."

Steve whistled. "Wow, and she survived the Stairsteps, then the creek, then the river all the way through Shady Cove?" He stopped to consider this, and it struck Tess hard as well. Tami being alive was a true miracle.

He continued filling her in on Tami's condition. "She's on the edge, had obviously been knocked around by the current. Besides having two bullet holes, her face, hands, and legs were scraped up, so she probably grabbed at bushes along the bank in several different places before she came to the launch ramp."

Tess gritted her teeth, the thought of Tami being shot twice causing her anger to ramp up. She'd have to return to the Stairsteps, do a better search. Though she'd looked around the area, they hadn't known Tami had been shot and had not searched specifically for shell casings. Did they miss discarded brass?

"Did she say anything about the shooter?"

"No, but according to the medics who brought her in, at first she was mumbling — delirious, I guess you'd say. She was repeating lessons from water survival courses."

"You're kidding."

He shook his head. "I took the same

259

classes. You live near a river like the Rogue, you need to learn safety. She kept repeating, 'Feet forward, head up, try for the side.' If that's what she was doing all night, then it probably is what saved her life. I imagine that also enabled her to stop herself at the boat ramp."

Tess remembered those commands from when she'd taken a rafting trip. If you fell out of the raft, it was important to turn your body so your feet were pointed downriver, and to try to keep your head out of the water to breathe.

"Amazing" was all Tess could say.

"Yeah, she's tougher than I thought. I bet she pulls through."

"We're sure praying for that."

"I put a deputy on her door, didn't think you could spare the manpower."

"Thanks, Steve, I appreciate that. Do you have any idea what kind of weapon was used?"

"Small caliber. My guess is a .22 or .38. You recover any casings?"

"I'll need to give the area a better look. That she'd been shot had not occurred to me earlier."

"Let me know. I've asked the doctor to preserve any slugs if he's able to recover them. I'll call if anything else comes up."

Tess walked him to the station door, thankful that Tami was alive and praying she'd lead them to her assailant. In the meantime, she left Bender to try to contact the supervisor of the work crew while she went back to the Stairsteps to look for brass. It was raining lightly; her mother would call it a drizzle. An icy drizzle. And it was cold, which thankfully meant the few tourists had been chased away.

She first rechecked the area where the car had been parked and then walked to the viewing platform, all the while thinking about the cold, harsh journey Tami took downriver. Tess had rafted the Rogue from the fish hatchery below Lost Creek Lake to the very boat ramp where Tami had been found. It bothered her beyond belief that anyone would shoot a person and shove them in the water, much less a harmless, innocent woman.

She wished a shooting had occurred to her earlier. But this was Rogue's Hollow, not Long Beach. What could Tami have done to anyone that would provoke a shooting?

The viewing platform was off to the side of Midas Creek. Only the far edge was close to the water, and even then, Tami would have to have practically been thrown from the platform to hit the creek and go over the falls. That would have been enough trauma to be fatal, without being shot twice.

As she looked over the railing at the stair-stepping waterfalls, a troubling thought creased her brow. Did this violence have anything to do with Chevy, or was it just another matter of an opportunistic work crew member?

Tess hated coincidences, and this one bothered her as she returned to the station. She and Bender went to work accounting for all the members of the work crew. Bender had had no luck raising the supervisor of the work detail on the phone, so they drove to his house in White City. The weather grew increasingly worse; freezing rain turned to hail. They found the supervisor hungover and grouchy.

"We're working a half day today," he said. "Hoping it will warm up a bit after noon."

Tess told him why they were there.

"My guys have worked their tails off for nearly two weeks and you want to pin a shooting on one of them?"

"If one of them is guilty, yes. Did you see any of them spend a lot of time with the cashier at the Hollow market?"

He sighed and leaned against the door-frame. "Nah, no one more than another."

"Any of them seem off to you?" Bender asked.

"No. Like I've said repeatedly, they are all hard workers. I was surprised about the thief."

They pressed him a little more, but he had nothing to say. Tess knew he'd been angry after the theft arrest. He'd felt that Bender had accused him of not watching his people carefully enough.

"He couldn't have been less helpful," Tess said as she and Bender walked back to their cars. "Let's split this list up. We have to get all these guys interviewed."

"Agreed."

Splitting the list gave them each six names. Tess committed the names to memory and pulled up the addresses.

30

Ice checked his watch. They'd been at the gate for ten minutes and he was getting antsy. There was a tense back-and-forth at the shelter's gate, but Gage stayed cool and kept his marshal ID front and center. Finally the gate swung open and Ice felt himself relax. He was in a go-with-the-flow mode, and a keep-a-sharp-eye-out-for-any-opening level of alert.

"After I park and get out, stand by the car and look official."

Ice stared at Gage. "I'm not a moron. Just sell the fake order."

"Oh, I'll sell it. Once I get the girl, we need to be outta here fast."

Ice clenched his teeth. He didn't need Gage acting as if he were some new guy out on his first job.

"Let's do a sound check," he said.

They each had earpieces so Ice could hear everything that happened at the door. He put a hand to his ear.

"Check as we kick butt," Gage whispered.

Ice held a thumb up. "Loud and clear."

Gage pulled to the front of the shelter, positioning the car in a spot on the circular drive so they could drive straight away and not waste any time when they needed to leave. He grabbed Royal's sleeve. "You know what to do."

Ice bit back something snarky. "I sure do." All he'd have to do was wait and watch. It was all on Gage, really. If it went smoothly for him, then as soon as they had the girl, they'd hop in the car and hit the gas. If things went wrong . . . well, they had the firepower to just take her. If anything unplanned happened, Ice would move in fast and shoot anyone who got in his way.

Gage shoved the car into park but left it running as he opened the driver's door. Ice climbed out of the car, irritated at the cold rain that was falling, hoping not to be in the elements for long. He took a position at the back door, ready to open it for Chevy, try-ing to mimic a posture he'd seen cops on TV take. He stood tall, hands clasped in front of him. The Asian woman Royal had seen the other day exited the front door and met Gage on the porch.

Gage greeted her. "Morning, ma'am, do

you run this place?"

"No, I'm Agent Takano, FBI." She held up ID. "What do you mean you're here for Roberta? I'm waiting for a call back from Agent Bass."

"Agent Bass should have already called you. The marshal's office is taking over Roberta's protection — we should have had that detail from the beginning. I have all the paperwork."

There was a rustling of papers. Gage handed Takano the fake court order. She took it and looked everything over. For a minute, Royal thought Gage's ruse was going to work. But then Takano balked.

"Agent Bass should be calling me back any minute."

Gage moved toward the door, blocking Royal's view of the agent. "I don't have time to wait for that. You can see that everything is clear and legal —"

The agent backed up a step but must have held her ground because Gage stopped moving forward.

"I'm not going to turn the girl over to anyone at the snap of a finger. I need more confirmation."

"According to a judge, this paperwork is all the confirmation you need. Now, where is the girl?"

Uh-oh. Ice tensed. Gage was pushing too hard. He had to sell the con, finesse it, not pound it home. Ice wished now that he was the one at the door. This required a smoothness that Gage surely lacked. It was going all wrong, and he gripped the butt of his weapon, considering his options.

The woman wouldn't give an inch. "Bass should —"

"This is a court order from a judge. No little peon FBI agent is going to countermand it."

The agent held up her phone. "You can back off. I'm not letting you get anywhere near Roberta."

Ice, concerned now, stepped forward, opening his coat, the hand on his weapon tight. He was ready to jump in the fray. If they only had to go through one Fed, it'd be easy. After all, he had no problem with scorched earth, but unease niggled. He knew they hadn't done enough reconnaissance. Maybe this place wasn't as poorly defended as it looked. Suppose there was more than one agent?

"I want the girl now! You aren't stopping me." Gage was losing it.

"You're not getting —"

Slap!

The crack of a hand against skin screamed

in his ear and he saw the agent jerk sideways, phone flying from her grip. Then Gage grabbed her arm, lifted her as if she were a rag doll, and flung her over the railing and into the yard. She hit with a blunt *oomph,* shocking Ice and causing him to hesitate as he looked her way, hand still on his gun but gun still in its holster. He knew it was time for all in, but a queasy feeling about this situation suddenly paralyzed him.

Gage cursed, and Ice turned his attention back to the front door. The big man yanked on the door; it must have been locked. Gage drew his weapon. Then he stepped back and brought his foot up, smashing the front door open.

It was Ice's turn to curse and to snap out of it. Hesitation gone, replaced by adrenaline and anger, he yanked his auto from the holster and moved forward to help Gage. Then it went all wrong.

Boom! Boom! Boom! The unmistakable sound of a shotgun rent the air. The blasts were deafening in his earpiece, and Royal yanked it out, instinctively ducking and looking for cover. Gage seemed to step backward, stagger, and then fall in the doorway.

"There's another one — another one," a woman's voice yelled.

Ice was about two feet from the porch when a figure appeared in the doorway behind the body of poor, dead Gage, and he had the terrifying experience of having a shotgun pointed right at him.

"Drop it!" the agent on the ground screamed from his left, and suddenly Ice found two guns aimed at him.

The shotgun boomed again, and because he was turned slightly, Ice took the blast a little off center. The body armor saved him, but he lost his footing and went down on one knee, struggling for his breath and blinking with the pain. Stunned and disoriented, he fought to get back on his feet and raise his gun and kill the woman in the doorway when she cracked the shotgun open to reload.

The hit had knocked the wind out of him. He fired two shaky rounds in her direction, but his aim was off, and the shots went high, smacking some horns above the door and sending them clattering to the porch next to Gage. The woman with the shotgun ducked back. Now he moved, thinking only about survival. He needed to get back to the car and out of the line of fire.

On wobbly legs he turned toward the car, only to face another weapon. The Fed on the ground fired twice at him, a bullet whistling by his face, missing but impacting the car. Royal jerked away.

He brought his gun up to shoot the Fed, but from the corner of his eye, he saw that the woman with the shotgun had finished reloading and was in the doorway taking a bead on him again.

Scrambling, he lurched to the only cover close, a horse statue off to his right.

The woman with the shotgun fired, hitting the wooden horse square and sending bits of wood into Ice's face. A sharp pain in his shoulder told him one of the pellets had made its mark outside the body armor. For the first time he could remember, Ice felt cold, hard fear course through him. All he could think was *I have to get away.*

Another shotgun round smacked into the horse — it wouldn't shield him for long. Shotgun Annie jumped over Gage's body and was pursuing him. Ice leaped away, firing his handgun blind, but making her duck, and sprinting toward the side of the house, his only chance to escape. Breath barely back, he dived behind cover with another shotgun blast raining down on him, pellets smacking the corner of the house.

When Ice had hit the ground and turned, he realized his mistake in cutting right. The women had effectively cut off any hope of escaping to the car. He peered around the corner of the house and fired blind as the shotgun barked again.

"Ahh," he screamed as buckshot tore through the edge of the building and into the side of his face and arm. They now stung like the pain in his shoulder.

He could hear the woman racking more rounds into the shotgun. He barely held on to his gun before turning and sprinting to the back of the property, into the forest, away from the crazy woman and her shotgun. When the shotgun went off again, he was out of range of the pellets.

"I'm getting my rifle," he heard the woman yell. *"You're dead meat!"*

Ice didn't look back. He needed to get out of harm's way and regroup.

31

Tess was in Shady Cove, had just pulled into the parking lot of the Maple Leaf, the hotel Jim Smith listed as his residence, when the radio sounded with an emergency tone. She stopped in front of the office, tense and alert.

Shots fired.

And she recognized the address — Faith's Place. It was now after 8:30 a.m. The drive back would take her at least ten minutes.

Work crew forgotten, she shifted her vehicle into reverse, flipping on her lights and sirens, tires squealing as she merged back onto Highway 62. She heard a sheriff's deputy, the one assigned to Shady Cove, also indicate that he was en route to assist, but he was farther away than she was.

This had to be about Chevy. Tess now regretted agreeing to keep the sheriff in the dark. It was kind of like the kid taking the car without his parents' permission. It's not a problem if he manages to return the car without anyone noticing, but if he crashes the car, then he's in trouble. Tess felt like that kid, and while her first prayer was that everyone at Faith's Place was okay, she knew this would be a jurisdictional nightmare.

Lights and sirens blazing all the way from Shady Cove to Rogue's Hollow, Tess amped up the radio volume, waiting for any update.

"One shooter is down; one fled to the rear of the property."

"Are any of the residents of the house injured?" Tess asked.

"Unclear at this time."

"Did someone at the house return fire?" Tess asked. It was then that she found herself behind Bender, also traveling code 3.

"Affirmative," came the reply from dispatch. *"Calling party reports that they fired in self-defense."*

Bender had reached the front gate and it swung open. She guessed someone in the house saw him and opened it.

She killed her siren as she drove through the gate close behind Bender. There was an unfamiliar dark sedan in the drive. Bender parked in front of it, and Tess kept going to block the back.

Off to the right, at the corner of the house, Tess saw a crouching figure, and she realized it was Livie Harp with a hunting rifle, up and ready, as if she had someone in her sights behind the house.

"You take the house," she called to Bender. "I'm going to see what's going on over here." She drew her duty weapon and jogged to Harp. "Is the shooter back there?" she asked.

Harp turned. "He took off up through the forest. I lost sight of him, but I wanted to make sure he didn't double back. He was hit — center mass, I think — at least once, by a shotgun. It stunned him but didn't knock him down, so he has to be wearing body armor. And I think I winged him after that." She stepped back but didn't completely lower the rifle.

The sheriff's deputy had joined them. "What type of rounds were in the shotgun? Buckshot?" he asked Harp.

"Double-aught buck."

"He'll have a good bruise," the deputy said, "maybe some cracked ribs, even with body armor."

Tess considered this. Double-aught buck contained nine pellets, .33 caliber rounds, and she'd seen body armor tests conducted at the range. At ten yards there was no penetration through the vest, but she doubted it felt very good. In any event, she believed that an armed, injured man could be doubly dangerous.

"We need to get after him," Harp insisted. She was ramped up like a crackhead.

Tess resisted the urge to be influenced by Harp's energy and run headlong after the shooter. "Where can he go? This property butts up to BLM forest; there's nowhere for him to go, but there are a lot of places for him to hide in ambush. We need an organized search. And I have to figure out what happened here. What kind of weapon did he have?"

"A handgun, automatic." Harp blew out a breath, lowered the rifle, and brought a hand to her brow.

Tess hesitated, not wanting to leave Harp alone, but needing to be sure they were no longer in danger from the gunman. The deputy must have sensed her indecision because he offered before she could ask.

"I've got this," he said. "I'll do a visual survey of what I can, make sure the shooter is in the wind. But if he cuts south, he could reach the road."

Tess stepped aside so he could have her position at the corner of the house. She moved to deal with Harp, holstering her weapon. She'd already considered the area they'd need to cover for the search. Right now, the bad guy had options, and they needed to eliminate all of them.

"Thanks. I'll have my people cover the road to the south. Ms. Harp, the deputy can watch here; come with me." Tess regarded the woman. She needed to get inside the house, regroup with Bender, but Harp was a powder keg.

For a minute, Tess didn't think the woman would comply, as amped up on anger and adrenaline as she was. But she relaxed and stepped back, grip relaxing on the rifle. Tess held her hand out and Harp gave her the weapon. Tess wondered about the shotgun but wanted Harp unwound before she broached the subject.

"Do you want to tell me what happened?" Tess asked as they walked toward the house.

"I'll let Mia tell you. I need to calm down." She'd begun to tremble, and in spite of the weather, sweat dripped down the side of her face.

They stopped by the horse carving, and Tess saw the divots and splintering from buckshot, which she knew didn't come from the rifle. Harp read her mind.

"I didn't fire the rifle. I got it after he ran away. I just wanted to make sure he didn't get back to the house," Harp said, looking pale and unsure now.

"You're not in any trouble," Tess said, now afraid that the woman was going to faint. "Why don't you sit?" She helped Harp to sit at the base of the statue. "Where is the shotgun?"

"In my car. He hurt Mia." Harp wiped sweat from her brow and leaned against the horse. "I'll be okay in a few minutes."

Tess knelt next to her. "You sure? You're white as a sheet."

Harp managed a weak smile. "Never been shot at before."

"You're in one piece, so I'd say you did okay. Why don't you wait here until you feel better?"

Tess watched her for a minute, until color began returning to her face, and then continued toward the house, climbing up on the porch. There was something in the doorway. At first she thought it was a piece of furniture, but when she reached the top step, she saw it was the body of a very large man. She could see Bender inside the house, in the open doorway.

"I went around and came in through the kitchen."

Tess did the same. Harp's vehicle was parked in back. The back hatch was open and she saw a shotgun. She touched it — still warm from being fired. She retrieved it, noting that there was a lot of ammunition in the back of the SUV as well. Harp was prepared for war. Did she know ahead of time about the threat to Faith's Place? Tess pondered that question for a couple of seconds before heading for the house. When she entered the living room from the kitchen, she noted that Bender was on the radio asking for paramedics. "Are the medics for Takano?" she asked.

A harried Bronwyn met her gaze. "Yes, Mia needs to see medics."

"No, not an emergency." Mia, seated on the couch, weakly waved a hand. "I'm fine."

Tess could see the agent was injured. One side of her face looked swollen and she had a bloody rag in her hand. Her right shoulder also leaned at an awkward angle.

"Your shoulder is dislocated," Bronwyn said. "I'm glad Officer Bender asked for medics."

Tess nodded to Bender. "Thanks." She held the rifle and shotgun out toward Bender. "Can you secure these in your vehicle?"

He took the guns from Tess, but she stopped him from leaving immediately.

"We're going to need more help. I'll

contact Sergeant Logan and see if we can get a dog out here. I want you to notify Curtis to help provide containment and see if Victor Camus is available."

"We need a perimeter," Bender said. "Is that where you want me to put Curtis?"

"Yes, south I think. You know the area better than I do. If the guy headed straight to the back of the property, he's likely to get lost in the woods. We want to avoid letting him slip out somewhere else."

He nodded. "We might need Del Jeffers as well."

"Call in whoever and whatever you need."

"I'll tape everything off outside as well." He exited the house through the back door to avoid stepping over the big man.

"Is Livie okay?" Mia asked as Tess approached. She could see that the agent's shoulder looked painfully out of place. "He ran to the back of the property."

"Yes, she's okay. We'll start a search for the second gunman as soon as we can do so safely."

Tess pulled out her phone to call Steve but needed a better idea of just what had occurred.

"What exactly happened?" She looked from Bronwyn to Takano.

"He came here saying that he was from

the marshal's office and he was going to take Chevy," Takano said. She nodded toward the dead man.

"What?"

"That's what I said. But he had ID, so we let him in the gate —"

"Where is Chevy?"

"She's in the media room with Nye. She's shaken but fine," Bronwyn said, and Tess returned her attention to Takano.

"Like I said, he had an ID and paperwork that looked like the real deal," Takano said. "You can see the ID; it fell in front of him."

Tess walked to where the body lay. It was more outside than in, and it blocked the door completely. She noted the gun beside him — looked like a .45 — and there, next to it, was what appeared to be a wallet ID. It had fallen open, and she knelt down to look at it, not wanting to move anything until Steve arrived. She could see a picture and a name, Joseph Turner. She couldn't tell if the picture matched the face of the dead man. If it did, and it was a real ID, someone in Faith's Place had killed a federal agent.

"It seemed so off that the marshals would suddenly step in like this," Takano continued. "I called Bass but got his voice mail. I told the guy I had to wait for a call back.

We got into it and then he slapped me, grabbed my arm, and threw me off the porch."

"Where's the paperwork?" Tess asked.

"I think it's under him," Bronwyn said.

"And the second guy, did he have identification as well?"

"No, he never said anything. He stood by the car. I saw him start forward after I got thrown off the porch — that's when the big guy kicked the door in." She winced and repositioned herself. "After I got thrown, I had a hard time drawing my weapon with my off hand."

Bronwyn picked up the story. "When the door got kicked in, we were ready. I think the first two shotgun blasts hit his chest, but nothing happened. He must have a vest on. But the next one hit him in the face. He went down hard."

Tess could see some pockmarks around the door that indicated a shotgun blast loaded with double-aught buck, besides the fact that the dead guy's face was destroyed. The doorframe was also a mess, corroborating Bronwyn's statement that the door had been kicked in. And the long horns, usually over the door, were now on the porch, next to the body.

"Did you shoot him?"

"No. I was in the kitchen. I had my handgun ready in case the shotgun didn't stop him."

Tess turned to Takano.

Takano shook her head. "I was in the yard, trying to get a clear shot on the second guy."

Tess frowned. "Harp shot him?"

She appeared in the doorway. "Yes, I shot him. It was self-defense. We'd all be dead if he'd gotten in the house."

32

Ice ran for all he was worth. His chest was burning, and every breath was hard and agonizing, but he had to get to safety. He wasn't used to being shot at — he'd always done the shooting.

It was all Gage's fault. Cursing the big man under his breath, he slogged through the terrain. The ground was muddy, and it was cold, hard going. He forced himself through some thick underbrush, sliding in shoes that were probably ruined. The icy rain still falling on and off didn't help his mood or his progress. But he kept going. The key to avoiding capture was to get as far away from the crime as quickly as possible.

When he hit the back fence, he stopped for a breath. He didn't hear pursuit, but his ears were still ringing from the gunfire, and his ego stung from the fact he'd been chased away by a woman. Breathing hard from the restriction of the body armor, he holstered his weapon, now wet with blood that dripped down his arm. Figured he'd get hit in areas the vest didn't cover. He didn't think he was hurt bad, though the side of his face stung from where a pellet had sliced across his cheek, and his upper arm and shoulder smarted from where a couple more had found their mark.

He cursed Gage again and opened and closed his hands several times, trying to steady himself and determine how badly he was hurt. He should have told Gage that he didn't need him, no matter what Cyrus thought. In all the years Ice had been at this, he'd never been the prey. And he didn't like it.

He brought a hand to his face and it came back bloody. He took off his jacket and dabbed his face with his shirtsleeve. Looking at his shoulder, he saw the blood was already drying up. He palpated the wound, wincing, but determining that while it smarted, he still had full function. His chest was another matter. It felt as though he'd been hit by a jackhammer. He ran his hands over the divots in the vest made by the buckshot. Every breath hurt. Maybe a rib or two was cracked, but he could breathe, so he figured he'd live.

Ice put his jacket back on and decided to leave the vest on. He turned his attention to the fence in front of him. It was chain link, with nasty points on top. As he gripped it, pain stabbed his shoulder. Gritting his teeth, he determined to ignore the pain and get as far away from this place as he could. He lifted a foot up to climb the fence.

"Looks like you're in a bit of a pickle."

Ice let go and jumped back from the fence, drawing his handgun.

A bearded man on the other side of the fence, dressed in camouflage gear, leaning against a tree, stared back at him from behind a raised hunting rifle.

"Easy, friend, I'm on your side . . . I think. I'll put my gun down if you do the same."

Ice didn't lower his weapon and he didn't have the energy to dive for cover. "Where did you come from? What are you doing here?"

"I was doing a little hunting. I heard gunfire, wondered if someone else got something. Heard you crashing through the forest. You're lucky you didn't get mistaken for a bear." He held his weapon out in a nonthreatening way. "I'll put this down. Show me a little good faith and put yours down."

"Why should I trust you?"

"I've got something in my pack you can use, but only if you put that gun away. You have other options?"

Ice considered the question for a moment. Of course he had no other options. He holstered his gun. "Why do you want to help me?"

The guy shrugged and tilted his head toward the shelter. "Me and the shelter have a history. What just happened? Were you trying to break your lady out?"

"Something like that," Ice said, breathing now calmed to normal, trying to figure this guy out, wondering how he could use his help, then get rid of him.

"Then I'd like to help. I think you're in trouble, and I kind of like trouble myself. Women are the root of all that troubles a man." He set the rifle down and took off a backpack. From the pack he pulled out a small pair of wire clippers. In a quick minute, he'd cut a hole in the fence big enough for Ice to get through.

Ice squeezed through, grimacing at the pain in his chest but working to ignore it. "Thanks, man."

"Sure. We better move." He took a bottle out, opened it, and spread a foul-smelling liquid everywhere.

Ice stepped back, nose scrunched. "Whoa,

what is that?"

"Something to throw the dogs off if they bring them out." He finished, secured the bottle, put it back in his pack. "You're free, on your own," he said and turned to leave.

"Wait, I need to get out of here, to the airport."

Camo Man looked at him. "Let's walk, get away from the property line."

He started walking and Ice followed. He said nothing, explained nothing, but Ice recognized he was out of his comfort zone and needed to trust someone, even briefly. And Camo Man was obviously in his element. First there was a thin trail; then there wasn't, but he seemed to know where he was going. Then a trail reappeared, and they could walk side by side.

Finally Camo Dude spoke again. "The airport? That'll be tricky."

"I'll pay you."

"How much?"

"Five grand to get me out of here and to the airport."

He stopped and stared at Ice. "You have it on you?"

"Not all of it."

"How much you got on you?"

Ice reached for his wallet. His wounds had stopped bleeding, but they still stung. He

grimaced as he pulled the wallet out of his pocket. He had twenty-five hundred-dollar bills.

"Two grand. Is that enough for a down payment?" He held out twenty bills.

Camo Dude took them, looked them over, then grinned. "That'll be just fine. I had something else to do, but it can wait. For five grand, it can wait. We got a bit of a walk ahead — you good for that?"

"Just get me to the airport."

He nodded and turned slightly, picked up his pace, and Ice followed.

33

Tess was not lacking a sense of urgency. It took all of her self-control not to rush out and chase the gunman who'd fled to the back of the Scaleses' property. But even after a year living here, she was in no way an expert at forest searches. She wanted to catch the man without getting anyone hurt — or killed. Already guilt was building. *I never should have let Bass shelter Chevy here. I've put the whole town in jeopardy. I broke my own rule — I should have trusted my gut.*

After she recovered from the shock of being shot at, Livie Harp was dead set against doing any waiting, and she was a living, breathing characterization of what Tess felt inside.

"We need to start searching now," Harp said. She'd been pacing in the kitchen since she came back inside the house. "I saw him head toward the back of the property. It's fenced back there. We can corner him and catch him."

Tense, Tess said, "Cornered means more dangerous. We need a coordinated, orderly, and safe search. I'm not sending people out willy-nilly to get shot by a man who could be lying in wait." It had taken Steve an hour to get here, but he'd brought three deputies with him so Tess would not need to stretch RHPD any tighter.

"There's no rush because there's nowhere for him to go," Bender added. "We've got Del Jeffers out on the road, Curtis on the far corner of the property, we're here. The only direction left is into the forest, and from there even on a trail, it's fifteen miles to the nearest paved road." He left with a map of the property to wait with the deputy outside the house for the search dog.

"Right." Steve Logan nodded in agreement. "If this guy is hurt like you say, he's not getting through the forest quickly unless he's Superman. The search dog should be here shortly."

Steve had arrived just after the Rogue's Hollow officers Tess had called in were positioned at their places on the perimeter. Crime scenes and perimeters took time, and it was going on eleven thirty. Besides waiting for the search dog from Jackson County

Search and Rescue, they were also waiting for Victor Camus, local hunting guide.

But Steve's arrival was not without its own tension.

He'd pulled Tess aside when he got to the scene. "What do you mean Faith's Place has been harboring a federal witness?"

"Steve, I'm sorry. Agent Bass wanted as few people in the loop as possible. I made a judgment call."

"Tess, I don't know that it was your call to make. Bronwyn and Nye could lose their county license over this."

Tess hadn't considered this. "Can we talk about this after the search?"

He nodded, clearly unhappy.

Now Tess left Livie in the kitchen and walked to where Steve was finishing up an interview with Takano. The agent's pain level appeared more controlled since the medics had stabilized her shoulder to prepare her for transport.

Tess considered the totality of the situation and realized how much she missed Oliver, his counsel, his calming presence. She had let him know what was happening with a brief overview, but he opted to stay at the hospital.

"Rosita needs me here. Tami is really on the edge. Doctors are warming her up slowly, but

it still could go either way."

The twinge of irritation she felt was like the rub of a large, sharp pebble caught in her instep, and it kept jabbing her. He'd chosen to stay with someone else rather than come to her aid. Part of her knew she was being childish, even petty, but with everything swirling around, the knowledge of how much she'd come to depend on Oliver weighed on her.

"Do you really think you're any good for him?"

It was his profession; she'd never be his priority. Caught by surprise at how much the reality of that truth hurt, she almost sucked in a breath. She looked up and saw Steve watching her.

"Don't worry about it."

"Huh?" She realized she was frowning and chastised herself for letting this personal issue interfere with her game face. "What do you mean?"

"About this," he said, waving a hand around the room. "If the situation were reversed, I'd probably have done the same thing, not told you about the witness. I'll work on the sheriff, explain to him that I agree it was necessary."

Tess sighed, relieved beyond belief that no one could read her thoughts. "Thanks."

"But we still need to decide who's handling what."

Tess realized he was giving her first choice. "I agree. How about you handle the crime scene here at the house? I'll oversee the search for the suspect. Would that work?"

She watched him consider the task. He looked at the dead guy in the doorway, then to Mia Takano on a gurney, and then to Livie Harp, pacing in the kitchen. The only other involved people, Nye and Chevy, were still in the media room. Dr. Peel was on her way. Bronwyn didn't want Chevy out in the living room as long as the body was in the doorway. Apparently Chevy had been in the room when the big man came to the door. She witnessed the attack on Takano through the front window before being dragged to the media room by Nye. While she hadn't seen the actual shooting of the big guy, she was rattled by all the gunfire and the attempt to take her by force.

"Okay. I'll need to talk to Bronwyn and Harp."

Harp stepped out of the kitchen. "Talk away, but be quick about it. We need to get searching."

"Why were you here?" Steve asked.

"I came to help shore up their security," Harp said. "I knew Chevy was in danger."

"I, for one, am glad she was here," Bron-wyn added. "I'm not sure I would have acted quick enough after Mia went down."

"She was a big help," Takano chimed in. Medics were taking her out through the kitchen so as not to have to go over the dead guy in the doorway. They paused to let her finish. "She knew right away that something was off with those two guys on the intercom. Told Nye to be ready to get Chevy into the media room. Then she kept that big guy from getting any farther than the front door." The medics continued on their way out with the wounded agent.

"Ms. Harp?"

"I told Chief O'Rourke I was worried about the girl. I found out she was hiding here by digging around the web. I was certain Cyrus Beck would find her as well."

Steve glanced at Tess.

"She came by my house to warn me last night. But I thought Bass would maybe move the girl and it would no longer be my problem." She'd quickly explained about the incident at the market.

Steve nodded, returned his attention to Harp. "How did you find her?"

"I'm good with computers. It's how I make my living."

"You're a hacker," Tess said, realizing now

how Harp found Chevy.

Harp shrugged. "I'm a World Wide Web expert."

Tess considered Harp and the crime scene the deputies would handle. The woman was amped up again. It was obvious she'd fired her weapon to protect herself and everyone else in the house. But while everything pointed to self-defense, Tess knew the need for a thorough investigation had not lessened at all. She'd collected Harp's shotgun, reminiscent of the shotguns Tess had been issued in Long Beach, with a folding stock. And the woman had turned over the hunting rifle and a handgun that she'd also brought to the shelter. It was clear she'd been expecting trouble at Faith's Place. What else had she hacked? As for all the ammunition, she said that she'd just wanted to be prepared.

Steve went on to ask Harp to describe what happened, to walk him through how many times Harp had fired her weapon and how the dead guy became dead.

According to Harp, she'd fired a total of eight shotgun rounds, three into the dead guy and five at the guy who fled.

"I'm sure I hit him close to dead-on, from about thirty-five feet away. And then again with a couple of pellets. He might not be hurt bad, but he's hurt."

"Did you get a good look at him?"

"Not his face, no. He's tall, taller than me for sure, and he was wearing jeans and a brown leather jacket. He had a handgun and I think he fired at us at least three times, maybe four."

Tess wished Harp had gotten a better look at the man, but a clothing description was helpful. Her attention was drawn outside as more personnel arrived, including a search and rescue dog and Victor Camus.

"Everyone is here for the search," she told Steve. "We'll get going ASAP. I'm switching radio channels."

He nodded and switched his radio to the channel she selected. This would allow them to communicate without disrupting or being disrupted by routine radio traffic.

"Good hunting," Steve said. "Be careful."

"Thank you, will do." Tess nodded to Steve.

Livie Harp started for the door as well, but Steve stopped her. "Hang on. Where do you think you're going?"

"Joining the search."

"No," Tess and Steve spoke simultaneously.

Tess nodded sheepishly and let Steve handle it while she continued outside to get the search going. She heard him explain to Harp that the search was a law enforcement issue. Besides the fact that she'd just shot and killed a man and needed to give a recorded statement, her place was not on the search team.

Harp's answer was lost to her hearing as Gabe Bender approached.

"I filled everyone in," Gabe told her. He pointed to the side of the house. "We're over here, discussing the terrain. And we found some blood, so the guy is hit. No way to know how badly he's hurt."

Tess zipped her jacket and pulled up her collar as they walked to where Victor stood. The deputy with the dog joined them. It was cold and spitting ice on and off. Altogether a miserable day for a search in the forest.

Victor studied a map with the dog handler while the dog jerked energetically on his lead. Two more deputies joined them, and Tess had her whole team assembled now.

"What do you think, Victor?"

"It's almost noon. We have daylight for a few more hours. The guy is bleeding, but he's got the advantage. We could walk into an ambush."

"I agree, but he's armed and dangerous. We can't just wait for him to surface somewhere. He's a clear and present danger."

"I'm not suggesting we don't search. I'm just saying we need to be cautious."

Tess noted that Victor was wearing body armor. Though a civilian, he was a member of Jackson County Search and Rescue, so he had a lot of police equipment.

The deputies agreed.

"I'll keep my dog leashed. He's got a scent, but with this weather . . ." The dog handler shrugged. "We should get going ASAP."

"Agreed." Tess nodded.

Victor pointed out landmarks on the map such as where the property line ended. The entire acreage was fenced — unusual, but a must for Bronwyn because of animals she rescued. Though the plan was that they stay in eye contact, everyone needed to be on the same page about the property layout. No one could get ahead of the dog because that would destroy the scent.

Once everyone was clear, Tess turned to the dog handler. "We'll follow you." She directed the two deputies to the left and wanted Bender on her right, with Victor and the dog handler in the middle.

They started out with promise, spread out as best they could. The dog hit on a scent right away. And they quickly found more blood. The suspect had rubbed against a tree trunk and the rain hadn't been hard enough to wash it off.

But then they found the hole in the fence.

"Look at this," Victor said. "That is a clean cut."

"Hmmm." Tess studied the chain link. "Either he had help, or he came prepared."

"What is that smell?" Bender asked.

"Smells like death," Victor noted.

The dog handler had squeezed through the fence after his dog, who had its nose to the ground but was not moving forward.

"He poured something on the ground here, trying to confuse the dog."

"Will it work?" Tess asked as she scrunched herself through the hole.

"For a few minutes, maybe. Some guys use pepper spray to confuse the dogs." He paused, checking the area. "Let's get away from where it's concentrated, and we'll pick the trail up again."

They did pick up the trail again as the rain let up. But after nearly two hours, they hit a logging road and the dog began running in circles.

"He's gone," the handler said. "Got in a car or something."

Tess looked around. Here it was open. The lack of tree canopy allowed for a direct drenching of rain, and because of that, if there had been a vehicle here, the tracks were gone. But then Victor spoke up.

"Or something," he commented as he squatted by some brush. "There was a small vehicle here, maybe an ATV. Your man took off that way, possibly toward Butte Falls, or he doubled back to the Hollow."

"Would that make sense?"

"Not sure, just telling you what I see."

Tess frowned. "I don't believe this guy was that prepared with an ATV hidden in the bushes. He had help — he had to have."

The deputies agreed.

Tess grabbed her radio, wet, cold, defeated, and drowning in guilt. All she could do was let everyone know that the shooter had escaped their perimeter. He was armed and dangerous, but where on earth could he go?

34

By the time Tess and the searchers returned to Faith's Place, the coroner had removed the body in the doorway and Steve had the false paperwork that the man had brought with him spread out on the counter.

And Oliver was there.

Before Tess could take a look at the fake court order, he stepped forward with a cup of steaming coffee in his hand. Tess realized that she must look like a half-drowned dog. She brought a hand up to smooth down her hair.

Until Tess looked at Oliver's face and saw the worry in his eyes, she hadn't realized how cold, wet, and tired she was. The earlier irritation she'd felt when he'd put her in second place faded as she took a welcome, warming drink of coffee.

"Thank you," she said, grasping the cup in both hands. She took a sip before explaining to Logan how they'd lost the trail. "We put out all the alerts possible for the guy, but without a better description . . ."

"Harp came here meaning business," Oliver said. "The guy is lucky he got away."

"I don't think he'll get far," Steve said. "If Harp did hit him dead center with a round of double-aught buck, he'll be hurting. It will only get worse as time goes on. I'll send out an alert to all emergency rooms as well."

"Thanks, Steve." Tess was a little chagrined that she'd not thought of that angle. She drank some more coffee and turned to Oliver, remembering Tami and the odd feeling she'd had earlier that the two situations were related.

"How is Tami?"

Oliver shook his head. "She was stable enough for surgery and came through that okay. They're classifying her condition now as serious but stable."

"Was she able to tell you anything?"

"She hasn't regained consciousness. Rosita promised to tell the deputy if Tami wakes up and is able to talk."

He gave Tess one of his looks, a penetrating one that made her feel as if he could see right down into her soul. There was more there than worry — Tess also saw irritation.

"What's the matter?"

He lowered his voice to a whisper. "Why

do you always put yourself in jeopardy?"

"What are you talking about?"

"The fire, now this search . . . you always put yourself at the tip of the spear."

Rocked back a bit, she said, "I'm doing my job."

He gave her an impatient look. "You can delegate; you're in charge."

Tess stared at him, wondering if this was the same man she'd been falling in love with over the past couple of months.

"I don't want to have this discussion right now."

"Of course not." He ran a hand over his face and seemed to try to change gears. "I'm sorry. I don't mean to distract you. You're obviously upset. What's got you so wound up?"

She took a deep breath, knowing that they would have to have a serious conversation soon if Oliver expected her to ever do her job from the sidelines.

"Besides Tami's shooting? It's this incident here. Two vicious shootings in Rogue's Hollow in a twenty-four-hour period? I don't believe in coincidences."

"But what does Tami have to do with Faith's Place?"

"It's Beck — he's desperate," Livie Harp said.

Everyone turned their attention to Harp. Tess noted that she'd calmed down quite a bit from her level of agitation before, when Tess was readying to leave on the search. Now she wasn't pacing and was looking at the paperwork with Steve.

"How can you be so certain?" Tess asked while, internally, she feared Harp was right. "I'd really like to hear a clarification on your relationship with Beck," Tess said.

"No relationship. I just know the type."

"But it's so personal with you."

Harp looked around the room and folded her arms, leaned back against the wall. "I said it before, I'll say it again: He's got money and he thinks he's above the law. I'd bet my eyeteeth that whoever came here to get Chevy also shot the woman you're concerned about."

"I don't believe in coincidences either," Steve said, "but how would shooting Tami and tossing her off a bridge help Beck? I have to say I don't think the incidents are related."

"I believe there's a connection — we just haven't found it yet," Tess said, brain burning with the realization that she was responsible for Tami as well. She stepped to where she could look at the paperwork Steve was studying.

"No wonder Agent Takano hesitated," he said. "I've seen a lot of court orders, and this one would have fooled me."

Everything looked legal to Tess, right down to the time stamp.

"So brazen. I can't believe they thought they would just walk out of here with Chevy," Oliver said.

"That's Beck, brazen and shameless." Harp walked back into the kitchen and Oliver followed. Tess heard him ask her if she was okay after shooting a man. That was a good question. Harp was shaken earlier, but now she seemed awfully calm and collected about having just taken someone's life. True, it was obvious self-defense, and Tess had more than enough personal experience with that kind of difficult judgment call. But she had seen trained police officers break down and have difficulty with the realization they took a life, even though it was in the line of duty.

There was more to Harp, and Tess knew that after this was all over, she was going to have to find out what that was.

Right now, she couldn't concentrate on Harp, but maybe Oliver could get what she couldn't. She turned her attention to Steve. "Were you able to ID the dead guy?"

"No, but he wasn't Joseph Turner, though

there is a federal agent by that name. An ex-agent. He's retired and living in New Jersey."

"Did Chevy get a look at the guy's ID picture? Maybe she'll know who he is."

Steve stared at Tess. "Wow, I have a confession to make — the thought of bringing her into this never crossed my mind. How fragile is she?"

Tess called out to Oliver.

He stepped back into the living room. "She's shook up. Nye basically yanked her into the media room, but she heard the door kicked in, then the shots fired. Dr. Peel is with her, along with Bronwyn. I'll check."

He walked toward the back of the house.

"By the way," Steve said, "Agent Bass called while you were gone. He's sending an agent here to help with everything, but he can't come himself."

"I would have thought he'd hop right up here."

"He sounded stressed. I don't think the court battle is going the way he wants it to."

"I hope he's just being overly paranoid. What about the car?"

"Rental, by a corporation. Still trying to get to the bottom of that." He cocked his head toward a pile of stuff by the door. "Got that out of the trunk."

Just then Dr. Peel came down the hallway with Chevy right behind her. The girl looked cowed to Tess, as if she'd been deflated. And she looked young. She had on a long-sleeved shirt but had pulled the sleeve down over her right hand and brought her hand to her mouth and was chewing on the cuff.

"Chevy, I have a photo for you to look at," Steve said. "You may know the man, you may not. Just take a look, okay?"

Chevy's attention was on the doorway where Nye was working on repairing the damage. He'd already cleaned up the blood.

"Chevy?" Steve prompted again.

She turned to him and nodded. He handed her the ID card in an evidence bag. She held it close to her face and squinted, then made a face and handed it back to Steve. "That's Gage."

"You know him?"

"I saw him a lot. He was mean to girls. Cyrus used him for security."

Tess sucked in a breath. This was huge. The room was so quiet, you could hear a pin drop.

After a moment, Tess asked. "Do you know his last name?"

She shook her head. "He was just Gage. Cyrus liked giving nicknames to people. Where's the other guy?"

"He got away," Tess said. When Chevy paled, she added, "But we're looking hard for him."

"The other guy is probably Ice."

"Ice?"

"Yeah, he's like a lieutenant for Cyrus. He's the one who brought me to Cyrus. I didn't tell Agent Bass about him." Tears started to fall.

Oliver stepped forward and put a hand on the girl's shoulder. "It's all right. None of these people in this room will let anyone hurt you."

"It's not that. It's . . . Well, I didn't tell Agent Bass because . . . I thought Cyrus still loved me. That we could go back to the way things were before . . ." She sniffled, and Steve gave her a Kleenex.

"What didn't you tell Bass?" Tess asked.

"Ice. He's the one Cyrus calls when he wants people to disappear. If he's the other guy, then that means Cyrus sent him after me." She choked on a sob. "Cyrus really doesn't love me." She dissolved into tears on Oliver's shoulder.

Tess shot a glance at Steve. She could tell he was thinking the same thing she was. If this Ice was the second gunman and Chevy could give them a good description, they might be on their way to identifying him.

Another associate of Cyrus Beck implicated in the incident today could help Bass and his case.

35

Ice scowled into the spitting rain, freezing and trying to keep his teeth from chattering. Besides, shivering sent pain through his body from the bottom of his feet to the top of his head. His newfound friend had stashed a sharp little Polaris RZR utility vehicle in the bushes. They'd hopped on and were heading out of the forest, so on one hand he was thankful to be taken out of harm's way. But on the other hand, Ice hated trusting his safety to a stranger. There was no way this guy was going to get five thousand dollars.

He lost track of time as they traveled along a rutted road. The farther he got from danger, the angrier he became. He vowed never to trust his well-being to anyone else ever again. From now on, he was solo, and he would stay that way. And along with the fact that he hated feeling disoriented and lost, it felt like his face was frozen solid by the time the rain stopped and they cut off the main path and down, eventually reaching what looked like a trailer park.

Camo Guy drove the RZR behind a little shed and killed the motor. He turned to Ice. "You can go inside that mobile and get warm and dry. I have to pick up my truck; then we'll head to the airport."

Ice nodded, not trusting his frozen mouth to form intelligible speech. He followed Camo Man to the door of a mobile home, waited as the man unlocked the door, opened it, and motioned Ice inside.

"Shower is in the back. Help yourself to anything you need. If anyone knocks on the door, don't answer. This place ain't mine, but I got permission to use it." He stepped back out the door, pulling it closed behind him.

Ice looked around the mobile he found himself in. It was sparse and looked fifteen years out-of-date in terms of furnishings, but it was warm, dry, and his face began to thaw. He sat at the small kitchen table, wincing as pain stabbed when he tried to raise his stiff, cold shoulder. His chest had mellowed to a dull ache. But deep breaths were difficult. He pulled his phone out of his pocket and froze. All his other belongings were in his backpack — burner phone,

311

money, favorite gun — and now the police had them.

He closed his eyes, leaned back, and cursed. Nothing could identify him specifically — he knew that — so it wasn't a horrible loss, just irritating and so uncalled for. Anger coursed through his veins, first at Gage and then at those stupid women. He vowed to himself that he would return and kill them all, no matter what Cyrus said or did. The two who chased him away he'd kill for free. He opened and closed his fingers several times before he trusted them to text Cyrus.

Gage dead, court order rejected.

An answer came immediately. Where are you?

Safe for now, trying to get to the airport.

Hang tight. I may have some news soon.

It's hot for me here. You have a plane at the airport?

If you need a place to lay low, yes, private jet is hangared at the Rogue Valley airport. Digger will get you anything you need. But keep phone close.

Ice sat back. He wanted to get out of this hick place and back to a big, thriving, warm city. But he'd hide in the plane until stuff calmed down if he had to. He was surprised that Digger was here. Originally completely loyal to Boss Cross, the guy became Cyrus's personal man, kind of a valet, shortly after Cross died. Since then, Cyrus rarely went anywhere without Digger. Since Cyrus still had the monitoring anklet on, Royal knew he couldn't be here. Sending Digger was like being here himself. He also knew that if Digger was in charge here now, Royal would have to accord him the same respect he'd accord Cyrus. That was just how it was. It was the weirdest relationship Royal had ever seen.

Ice had to get to the airport, and he planned to do that without the Camo Man. True, he'd made a mistake getting rid of the cashier too early, but this bearded mountain man was an entirely different situation. It meant nothing to Royal that the guy had saved his life. He knew nothing about the guy and had no plans to sit down and chat about life with him.

He slowly shed his jacket and body armor, grimacing as he took stock of his wounds. In the small bathroom of the mobile he found some antiseptic and bandages for the open wounds. The slash across his cheek was bad — it would leave a scar. Another reason he vowed to go back and hunt those women down. His chest was already a dark-purple bruise, and as he pressed around with his fingertips, he found some very sensitive spots — cracked ribs, most likely. Gingerly he rinsed off in the small shower and cleaned the injuries that were superficial. The warm water felt like heaven, but he knew he had to hurry.

When he finished in the shower, he rummaged through the closet for some clean clothes. He found a shirt and a pair of jeans that fit, which surprised him because the Camo Man was much shorter and stockier. There was also a nice pair of boots and a warm jacket that fit. He helped himself to that as well since his jacket was ruined by pellets, blood, and mud. Whoever did own this place was about his size. About time things started working in his favor. He froze when there was a knock on the door.

Remembering the warning not to open the door, Ice drew his weapon and stood still.

"Blakely, I know you're in there."

Pound, pound, pound.

"I'll call the police. I don't care if Ron gave you permission to stay here, there is no subletting allowed in the park."

More pounding.

Ice considered solving the problem once and for all and had begun to move forward slowly when a car pulled up.

"Mr. Polk, I need your help." It was an

old woman's voice. "My water's leaking and I can't turn it off."

He heard a sigh. "I'll be right with you." Then, "Blakely, this isn't the end. If you're not gone when I get back, I'm calling the police."

The man left, and the car drove away. Royal holstered his weapon, agitated now. The last thing he wanted was to be cornered here in a flimsy mobile home. Obviously Camo Man had baggage that Ice didn't need.

He wadded up his dirty, wet clothes and pushed them into the trash. Then he grabbed his new jacket as another vehicle pulled up. Drawing his weapon again, he peered out the window. Camo Man was back in a big, beautiful truck. He could see the guy fumbling with his keys.

Ice looked around the mobile home; he needed a suppressor of some sort. Pillows would work, but he also needed to catch the guy off guard.

The door opened, and the bearded man stepped inside, his gaze going directly to the gun in Ice's hand. "Hey, what's up with that?"

"Some guy was just here, threatening to call the cops." He put the gun back in its holster, wanting Camo Man at ease, planning, always planning.

"Let him — we'll be long gone. You look a heck of a lot better. Are you ready?"

Ice, now warm, dry, and out of harm's way, nodded at the guy, maybe seeing him for the first time. He needed to assess the amount of force he'd have to use. Camo Man was sturdy, compact, thick across the shoulders, with a dark beard covering half his face. His deep-set eyes were focused and mean; he was guarded and dangerous. Ice knew that what he planned to do, he must do quickly. In his injured state, any slight mistake would be fatal.

He nodded and gestured toward the door. "Let's get out of here."

36

Chevy described Ice as tall, older, with blond hair and really blue eyes. As for his appearance, "He changes it all the time. I heard him tell Cyrus once that he was a chameleon — he could adjust to any situation and blend into the background so that no one really notices him, and he can come and go as he pleases."

Emma Peel had taken Oliver's place as support for the girl. To Tess, Chevy looked younger than her years for the first time. She was truly shaken and gripped Peel's hand for support.

"That's how he gets girls," she said, sniffling. "He's got pretty eyes and girls fall for his lines. I did. I really thought he was taking me to a better life. He can be sweet when he wants to be, but . . ."

"But what?" Steve asked.

"I heard rumors while I was with Cyrus. I didn't want to believe them." Chevy studied

317

the teacup she was holding. "There was one girl who got in trouble. . . . She made one of Cyrus's friends mad." She paused and sipped her tea. Dr. Peel had placed a comforting arm around her shoulders.

Her voice was weak and reedy when she continued. "I didn't see it. But I heard that Ice shot her while she was eating breakfast and then wrapped her up in a rug and dumped her in the desert."

Harp snorted with disgust.

Tess, too, felt the disgust. This Ice character was truly evil. Unredeemable. Almost as soon as the thought crossed her mind, Oliver's words came back to her, what he'd said when they discussed Beck. *"Everyone matters under the law, or nobody matters. If under man's law, everyone matters, how much more to God does everyone matter?"* It gave her pause as she considered the vile actions of Ice.

Steve interrupted her musing. "Can you think of anything else that might help us?" he asked.

Chevy chewed on her thumb cuticle for a couple of seconds, then shook her head.

Oliver and Bronwyn called out from the kitchen that they were fixing something to eat. This was welcome news to Tess, whose stomach was making a lot of noise.

Tess put a hand on Chevy's shoulder. "Thanks for your help, Chevy. What you've told us will help a great deal."

Chevy shot her a sheepish look. "Sorry I gave you such a bad time."

"Forgiven and forgotten. Go get something to eat."

Dr. Peel took Chevy into the kitchen.

With Chevy gone, Steve turned his attention to Harp, explaining to her the next steps she needed to take. A formal interview, fingerprints, etc. Tess tuned them out and, sipping her coffee, walked over to look at the items Steve had removed from the rental car. There were a couple of handguns, a MAC-10, an AK-47, a well-used pair of men's boots, and a knapsack.

"Have you gone through this knapsack?" she asked.

Steve turned from his Harp notes. "Not yet. Go ahead."

Tess pulled some gloves from her pocket, picked up the knapsack, and brought it to the counter where Steve and Harp sat. She busied herself with inventorying the bag's contents.

The first few things she removed — a couple of T-shirts, a sweatshirt, and a sooty pair of pants — were not surprising. But toward the bottom, things got more interesting. There was a box of black hair dye for men, a box of Ben Nye theatrical stage makeup, and some .38 caliber ammunition. At the very bottom was the biggest surprise.

"Look at this." She opened the backpack wide. "A .357 if I'm not mistaken." With a gloved hand she held up the shiny chrome revolver. "It's old and beat-up. It resembles the police special my dad used to carry." She squinted, trying to read the serial number. "It looks like he tried to destroy the serial number, but I'm sure it still works. I'm surprised he left the weapon behind."

Harp got up and stepped closer to Tess, peering at the gun. "Your dad is a cop?" she asked.

"He was. He was killed in the line of duty a long time ago. Back in the day, revolvers like this were standard issue."

Briefly, Tess caught a strange expression crossing the woman's face, but her attention was diverted to Steve.

"Dead guy had a .45 but never got off a shot," Steve said. "As for the other guy, we recovered 9mm shell casings in the yard, so he had other weapons. And I don't think he expected to be chased away from here by two armed women. Anything else?"

"Some clothing." She held it up. "This has to belong to Ice. From what I saw of

the dead guy, this would never fit him. There's a lot of cash —" she held up a wad of hundred-dollar bills — "some hair dye and what looks like makeup . . ." She frowned. "And what I bet is a burner phone."

"Hopefully we have all his makeup and he won't be able to change his appearance too drastically. I'll see that all of this gets sent to the lab." He had evidence bags with him and packaged up the fake court order and the contents of the backpack.

Harp left the room, heading down the hall in the direction of the restroom.

Tess stood and stretched, the long day getting to her. "Thanks, Steve, I appreciate all your help." He'd smoothed everything over with Sheriff Belcher, and Tess was grateful. In a small town it was important to nurture and maintain good relationships.

"Just glad everyone here is okay." He looked down the hallway in the direction Harp had gone.

"Missing something?" Tess asked.

"Remind Livie for me about the formal interview and the fingerprinting. I'm heading out. I'll get all this evidence sent to the lab. If we can make a connection, put this Ice character on the work crew, you have copies of all the driver's licenses and IDs,

correct?"

Livie. Briefly Tess wondered if Steve seemed a little too interested in Livie. Did it matter? Other than the fact that she was quite a bit older than him, Tess didn't think so.

"I do. I have a file on my car computer. I'll send it to you."

"Thank you."

Logan left, and Tess finished her coffee, trying to clear her thoughts. Fatigue meant jumbled, out-of-order, murky, and somewhat-random musings, and Tess needed clarity. The tension in her relationship with Oliver was one area she wanted to clarify.

She thought about her brief relationship with Steve. One good thing about dating a cop was that he knew the job, the pressures, the demands, the responsibilities. Oliver would never fully understand her job as chief. He'd proved that by taking her to task about conducting the search.

Maybe if Tess were chief of hundreds instead of seven, she could take the easy way out, but she wasn't. Would that be a rub in her relationship with Oliver forever?

On the other side of the coin, she would never fully understand his job demands and responsibilities.

On cue, Oliver walked in with a plate of sandwiches, Bronwyn on his heels with glasses of tea. He sat next to Tess. "You're exhausted."

Tess blew out a breath, so thankful for the food. "I am. And I'm concerned. There's an armed killer out there somewhere and I need to find him."

"You've done all you can for now. Eat. Try to recharge," Oliver said.

"You don't have to tell me twice." She picked up a ham sandwich and ate half of it before she spoke again.

Harp returned to the living room, walking slowly down the hallway. To Tess, it looked as if she'd been crying. Oliver picked up on it as well.

"Ms. Harp, are you okay?"

"Yeah, it's been a long day." She settled into an easy chair but sat stiffly, not relaxing. "How do you deal with this?"

Oliver frowned. "With what, exactly?"

"Evil men hurting innocent people. And evil that seems never-ending, that goes on for years. Evil men getting away with being evil. I still struggle with this and with God. Why does it just go on?"

"I wish I had a pat answer for you, but I don't," Oliver said. "If I understood God completely, then he wouldn't be God. But if it is any comfort at all, I don't believe that anyone gets away with anything. There will be a reckoning — we may not see it, but it will happen."

"You're just as certain of that as you are that the Bible is true?"

"I am."

Tess watched Harp try to process this, even as she had to process her own thoughts on the matter. After about a minute, she said, "I hope you're right, Pastor. I do. I've not stopped reading the Bible and trying to understand it. The only hope I have is that evil people won't get away with their evil forever." She got up and went into the kitchen.

Oliver turned to Tess. "I'm glad she's still reading, still asking questions."

"She's asking good questions, you know, about evil going on and on, seemingly with impunity. The question of unredeemable — I struggle with that myself."

"I know you do. It's okay to struggle and to even go to God with the struggle. Asking questions will get you answers."

Tess said nothing, wondering if she'd ever be as sure on this subject as he was.

He held Tess's gaze, worry on his brow. "Tess, I —"

The crackle of her radio interrupted him.

It was her call sign, Curtis Pounder calling. He'd stayed on duty after being called in early to help with the perimeter. She frowned, thinking perhaps he was calling about that duty, certain that the perimeter had been broken down since it was obvious the suspect had made it outside the boundaries they'd set.

"Edward-1, I copy. Go ahead."

"Chief, we have a problem — another missing woman."

"What?" Tess said, exhaustion fading.

"Yeah, it's Janie Cooper. She's not answering her phone, seems to have vanished. Gabe is with Garrett at the mobile park. Garrett called Walmart to see if she was there on her day off for some reason. They said that she did have an appointment at the salon, the first one of the day, but she never showed up. But one of her coworkers said her truck is parked in the lot. I'm heading down to Walmart to check out her vehicle and review camera footage."

37

Hearing the radio call made Oliver sick to his stomach. "Not again," he said. A check of the clock said 5 p.m. Would this horrible day ever end?

Tess stood to leave. He could read the angst in her face, and he prayed this call was simply a misunderstanding.

"Wait." Oliver put a hand on her arm. "I'll go with you." He hated the fatigue and tension on her face and wanted to insist that she let someone else handle this but knew she didn't want to hear that.

She acknowledged that she heard him with a head tilt but said nothing.

Oliver wondered what was running through Tess's mind. He thought he saw a little guilt and prayed she didn't blame herself for all that was going on at the moment. He hoped for a minute or two to speak to her privately, clear the air, as he followed Tess to the trailer park, where

Bender was waiting with Garrett Cooper. The man was pacing with his youngest in his arms. He hurried toward Tess when she stepped out of her car.

"Janie's gone! She just disappeared!"

Garrett was as agitated as Oliver had ever seen him. A thought crossed his mind. Had Janie finally given up on Garrett and left him? Almost as quickly as he thought it, Oliver dismissed the notion. Janie would never leave her kids.

"Garrett, tell me what happened," Tess said.

"I don't know what happened!" He stomped his foot like a little boy.

Oliver was ready to grab him and shake him. He was scaring the baby.

Tess must have read his mind because she stepped close and grabbed his arm. "Focus, Garrett. Tell me what happened to Janie."

He tried to glare at her and then nearly collapsed into tears. "We had a fight this morning. She took the kids and left."

Tess released his arm.

He switched the baby to the other side and then wiped his nose with the back of his hand. "I figured she'd come home when she cooled off. But then her friend in White City called me, asking when we were going to pick up the boys."

"Why would she ask you that?"

"Janie asked her to pick them up from school and keep them for a couple of hours. I asked about Anna and her friend didn't know anything about her. At first, I was mad, thinking Janie was trying to teach me a lesson. I figured she had Anna with her, and she'd go pick up the boys and come home after she'd let me stew long enough."

He was on the verge of tears and Oliver could see that his small daughter was picking up on the stress and winding up to cry.

"Garrett, let me have little Anna while you speak to the chief."

He handed the child to Oliver.

"The baby is here now — where was she?" Tess asked.

"That's what freaked me out. Casey came over with Anna about an hour ago, told me that Janie dropped her off this morning, saying she was going to Walmart to have her hair done and she'd be back in a couple of hours." The tears fell. "She never came back for her. Casey called her and got her voice mail. Janie is just plain gone!"

Juggling the little girl, Oliver stepped toward the mobile home, happy to see a smile appear on the baby's face. He could still hear the conversation, and he listened with interest and not a little fear.

"Is there someone she would have gone out — ?"

"No! She was mad, yeah, but she wouldn't have left the baby so long with Casey with no explanation." Garrett kicked the ground and pounded his fists into his thighs with a kind of whimper.

Oliver glanced at Tess, whose face was unreadable.

Then Tess pulled out her cell phone. She turned to Gabe. "I'm going to call Casey and see if she can tell me any more. Watch him?"

Bender nodded.

Tess stepped aside to make the call.

Garrett leaned back against the mobile and wiped his face with his sleeve.

"We'll find her," Gabe said in as soothing a voice as Oliver had ever heard from the man.

Henry Polk walked up, arms folded across his chest, a concerned expression on his face. Oliver nodded to him, but his thoughts were on Garrett.

Oliver remembered Garrett's semi-confession to him earlier this week. He also remembered the numerous fights and the problems the Coopers had had. But would Janie really walk away from her children?

As he watched Tess on the phone, he knew

the answer was no.

Tess finished the call and returned to Oliver's side. "Casey said that Janie was quite agitated when she dropped the baby off. Casey told her she could watch Anna all day if she needed her to because it was her day off from the bookstore. She figured Janie needed some time to herself, thought she was doing her a favor. But when she'd heard nothing from Janie by three, she started calling her, getting voice mail."

"She wouldn't leave the kids."

Tess looked away and said nothing, then walked over to Garrett. "Garrett, the last time I was here, your house was trashed, and you and Janie had a horrible fight. Now you admit that you fought again. Are you sure she didn't just leave, maybe got tired of all the fighting?"

"She wouldn't." His voice broke and Oliver watched him struggle for control. "We fight, but she loves our kids. She'd kick me out before she'd leave them."

Tess looked at Oliver. The cop face was gone, and he could see worry there. Then she turned to Bender. "Curtis should be at Walmart by now. Talk to him for me; ask if there's anything at all out of order there."

Bender nodded and stepped aside, pulling out his phone.

There was a slight shift in Garrett's body language, a tiny bit of tension gone. "Thank you, Chief. Thank you. Find her. Please."

As Oliver watched Tess, he could tell something was bugging her. He knew that most of the time when women disappeared and foul play was suspected, the husband was the prime suspect. But Oliver knew Garrett, and while he was a lazy lout, Oliver doubted the man had it in him to hurt Janie. What was Tess thinking?

"Garrett, I get the distinct impression that you're not telling me something," she said finally.

Oliver did a double take, continually amazed at the sixth sense Tess seemed to have when talking to people. Garrett's semi-confession came to mind again. If Garrett didn't come clean now, Oliver knew he would have to tell Tess what Garrett had told him.

"I'm just worried, Chief — worried that something bad has happened to her."

"Why?"

"Huh?"

"Why? Was she having a problem with someone at work?"

"No."

"Then why are you so certain something bad happened?"

"Random stuff happens! Look at what just happened to Tami."

"There's more to it than that — I can tell. She's been gone all day. And now you call the police? I've been at this too long not to sense that you're hiding something. Did you hurt Janie?"

"No!" Tears rolled down Garrett's face. "I thought she was just staying away to make me suffer."

Oliver interrupted. "Garrett, tell the chief what you told me."

Garrett shot him a frightened look, wiping his face with the palms of his hands. "That was private."

"But it might concern Janie's disappearance. If you want the chief to help, she needs to know everything." Oliver didn't miss the sharp glance Tess shot him.

"If you're withholding something that could help me find your wife, you'd better tell me now."

"I, uh . . ." He looked everywhere but at Tess. "You might arrest me."

"What are you more concerned about, your wife or yourself?"

He closed his eyes and folded his arms, looking for all the world as if he just wanted to withdraw.

Tess turned to Oliver. "What did he tell you?"

"It was after the mobile was trashed. He said he'd hidden something for someone and that it had burned up. Now the person wanted to be paid back for the loss."

"Garrett, tell me what you hid."

"Ah, Chief, if it's him, he'd kill me before Janie." Tears fell freely now. To Oliver, Garrett looked more like a child than the one he held in his arms.

"Who?"

"I hid some stuff for a guy. It was in the cellar of the old house. It all burned up and he blamed me. Wanted me to pay him back and I didn't have the money."

"Who was it?"

"It might not have anything to do with Janie being gone."

"Let me decide that."

Oliver tried to help. "Garrett, the time for secrets is long past."

"Did he tell you who?" Tess asked Oliver.

"No, he never gave me a name."

A long moment passed before Garrett replied. "It was Ken Blakely. . . . I hid three hunting rifles, his laptop, some stuff that he poached, and some cash that he wanted hidden — a lot of cash." He sighed. "He paid me for hiding the stuff; the extra money helped the family. But after it all burned up, he wanted me to pay him back. I had to take some insurance money and buy him a new rifle. But he wants more — $25,000 he says. I don't have that kind of money."

Oliver sucked in a breath. Ken Blakely was a problem, a mean man with no respect for women. If he was responsible for Janie's disappearance, this would not be good.

Ken Blakely.

The name had occurred to Tess, so when Garrett finally said it, she wasn't surprised. She remembered the day she'd thought she'd seen Blakely at the trailer park.

"Is he the one who trashed your mobile?" she asked Garrett.

He nodded. "He thought I was holding out on him. He wanted his money. I don't have it."

"Has he threatened you?"

"Yeah, he has. Me. Not Janie. He wants his money. He says he'll take my truck and sell it for parts. But I don't think he'd do anything to Janie. At least I hope he wouldn't."

"Chief."

Tess turned. Henry Polk wanted her attention.

"What is it?"

"I hate to interrupt, but I wanted to talk to you about Ken Blakely. He's been staying here in the park, even though I told him that we have rules about subletting —"

"Staying here? Where?"

"The other side of the park, space 40, Ron Nelson's place. Ron's in Arizona taking care of a sick relative. Blakely's been there too long — he was just there a little while ago, but he wouldn't answer the door."

"Maybe he's got her there now." Garrett started to leave.

"Now you're saying you believe Blakely would kidnap Janie?"

Garrett threw his hands up. "I don't know what to believe. All I know is that he threatened me. He wanted me to pay him back from the insurance money, but I told him that Janie would never let that happen. I have to go check and see if he's got her."

Tess stopped him. "No, you stay here in case Janie calls and we're worried for no reason. Gabe, anything from Curtis?"

"Truck checks out fine, still locked up. And, Chief?" He glanced toward Garrett.

"Yeah?"

"He called her cell phone. It's on the front seat of the truck."

Garrett moaned, and Tess looked away and clenched a fist. That meant no GPS.

And it seemed nearly impossible for Garrett to have done anything to his wife but leave their only transportation in the Walmart parking lot. Would Ken Blakely really hurt Janie Cooper?

"Curtis is looking through the security video now," Bender finished.

"Thanks. Stay here. I'll go check this other mobile home out." She turned to Polk. "How long ago was he in Nelson's place?"

Polk looked at his watch. "Hour, maybe."

"Space 40 is at the edge of the park, correct?"

Polk nodded. "I'll take you over there."

"I'll find it."

"Well, take the key if you need to look inside. Ron gave me permission to do that." Polk handed her a key with a plastic tag on it. Written on the tag was the name *Nelson*.

"Wait, I'll go with you." Oliver spoke up. He handed the little girl, who had fallen asleep in his arms, gently back to Garrett.

Tess fought the niggle of irritation that flamed up because he'd known this secret of Garrett's and not shared it with her. Was it his obligation to share, or was she taking this personally?

"Stay here, Garrett. I mean it. You have that baby to think of."

Tess glanced at Oliver and got in her SUV

to drive to space 40. He settled into the passenger seat.

"You're angry I didn't share Garrett's secret with you," Oliver said.

Tess started the engine and drew in a breath, then let it out slowly. He could always read her, especially when she didn't want him to. "I shouldn't be."

"Maybe, maybe not. I never thought he'd do anything so stupid as to get involved with Ken Blakely."

"Hmmph" was all Tess could think of to say. Another bit of guilt stabbed. She should have done more to help Yarrow with Blakely.

They approached space 40. There was no vehicle in the small carport. Tess parked in front and got out, attention fully on the mobile and not on Oliver, who'd gotten out and moved to stand next to her.

Blakely had a new truck. Tess had seen him driving it around town in recent weeks. But the truck was nowhere near the space. She knew this end of the park backed up to the forest and could see there was a small shed in the back of the space.

"Wait here," she said to Oliver as she stepped up to try the door. Locked.

She went around the back and headed toward the small storage shed. She could see the front bumper of a vehicle peeking out from behind the shed. She walked to it and saw a utility vehicle, a Polaris RZR, painted in camouflage, something a lot of hunters used. Alarm bells went off. What was it Victor had said when the search for the gunman had ended? *"There was a small vehicle here, maybe an ATV. . . ."*

Tess inspected the machine and found it was wet and muddy. She placed a hand on the motor area. Still a little warm. There was also something on the passenger seat. Blood. But if Blakely was a poacher, it could be animal blood. Then again, it could also be Janie Cooper's blood. Why would Blakely snatch her and keep her alive when she could identify him?

She returned to the front of the mobile, conscious of Oliver's gaze on her.

"What are you thinking?" he asked.

"That I need to get a look inside this mobile." Tess knew she had grounds to enter, even without Polk and his permission. But she was afraid of what she'd find. Worst-case scenario, Janie Cooper could be dead on the floor. She found herself hoping the place was empty.

She climbed up the three steps and knocked on the door. "Hello? Anyone here? This is Chief O'Rourke. I have a key; I'm coming in."

She waited, listening and hearing nothing. Tess turned to Oliver as she unsnapped her weapon. "Stand back, Oliver."

He looked every bit as concerned as she felt, but he stepped back.

Tess slipped the key in the lock and opened the door. Something was in the way and she pushed harder, heart pounding as she stepped up and into the mobile. She saw the legs first, in camouflage pants; then her gaze traveled up to the body that was too stocky to be Janie Cooper.

Tess leaned down and moved the pillows. Ken Blakely's sightless eye stared back up at her, a halo of blood around his head.

38

Ice made it to the airport without any trouble.

He texted Digger, who directed him to the proper entrance and hangar. A shiny Gulfstream waited, half in the hangar and half out.

"Nice ride," Ice whispered to himself, freezing again and vowing that it would be the last time he'd ever be this cold.

Ice had driven Camo Guy's truck to the Maple Leaf in Shady Cove. He half expected cops to be converged on the area, but they weren't. With just a couple of cars in the lot, there was no indication that anybody was onto him. He'd thought to exchange the truck for his motorcycle if he could get to it. It had stopped raining, but it was still cold. He was loath to give up the big, warm, powerful vehicle, but the truck would tie him to Camo Guy. He'd pulled through the lot and parked the truck in the last hotel space, near the restaurant lot next door. He then wiped everything down and left the truck, keys in the console.

Now at the hangar, he climbed off the bike and then up the stairs into the plane. The first thing that caught his eye was the table filled with food — bread, meats, cheeses, and a plate of pastries. Ice's stomach growled, reminding him he'd not had anything to eat for hours. He resisted the urge to grab something, wanting to determine Digger's mood first. Digger always reflected Cyrus. The two were generally joined at the hip.

Digger was seated, watching the news on TV, drinking what Royal guessed was champagne. He turned to Ice and frowned. "What happened to your face?"

Sighing, Ice took a seat across from Digger, his back to the TV, and he explained everything that had happened, making certain Digger understood that the tremendous failure was with Gage. He ended with his escape, never mentioning the Camo Man because he just wasn't relevant anymore. As Camo Man had turned to leave the mobile, Ice took his only chance. His right arm snaked around the shorter man's neck, and he locked in the hold tight by gripping his right hand with his left hand, right bicep and forearm pinching off the carotid arteries, cutting off the blood supply to the guy's brain.

Camo Man had struggled, and Ice was thrown back against the hallway wall. It hurt so much to hold the big, stocky man that tears came to Royal's eyes. But the struggle was over in a few minutes, and Ice dropped the man, unconscious, in the narrow hallway.

Breathing hard, his whole body a study in pain, Ice had grabbed a couple of pillows and put them over Camo Man's head. He fired twice. He then sat back, resting on one knee, wiping his eyes, waiting for the pain to subside, hoping no one had heard the muffled shots.

Wincing from what he was sure was at least one busted rib, Ice had grabbed the dead man's keys, stepping over the body and pausing to look around outside the door. The mobile home park had been quiet when he left.

Digger listened, but from time to time he glanced at the TV and away from Ice. He didn't ask any questions.

When he finished, Ice waited for an outburst, for cursing, anything. But Digger was calm, collected, almost detached.

"Chevy is still there? Still in that small town?"

"I guess, unless Bass has moved her. In any event, I don't think she'll be there much longer."

Digger nodded thoughtfully and sipped his drink. "Cy had to take this chance," he said. "Sorry about Gage, but it really doesn't matter."

Ice let that sink in because he knew that was how it was with Cyrus. He'd learned years ago, after his first operation for Boss Cross, that everyone was expendable. And like Cross, the only person who truly mattered to Cyrus was Cyrus. That was why having enough money to disappear somewhere peaceful and quiet was so important to Ice. He was the only one he could count on to watch his own back.

"Any chance you were identified?"

"No, of course not, but things are hot right now."

"They won't be for long."

The statement took Ice aback. "Why?"

"Because things are happening quickly." He sipped his drink and held Ice's gaze. "We'll get Chevy and pay her back for her treachery, no matter what."

Ice started to speak but stopped himself. No one wanted revenge more than he did.

But it was too hot to go charging right back in to get her now. He could wait for the perfect time, not rush things, wait until everyone's guard was down, but he knew that Cyrus could not. Right now, Royal was tired, hungry, and aggravated. He'd keep his thoughts to himself for the time being.

Digger had turned the sound up on the TV.

"Grab something to eat," he said. "A very important story is breaking. Hurry, then come join me and watch."

Royal didn't need to be asked twice. He grabbed some bread and made himself a thick sandwich.

"Watch the television," Digger ordered as Royal took his first big bite.

Curious, Royal obeyed. Mouth full, Royal stopped mid-chew and stared at the set. The newscast was switching to a press conference. Royal recognized Agent Bass as he stepped up to a bank of microphones.

He started with a lot of legalese, something about a judge's determination about some evidence, so Royal continued eating. As Ice finished the first half of his sandwich, Digger shocked him still.

"The ankle monitoring has hereby been revoked. Cyrus Beck has twenty-four hours to turn himself in, or he will be remanded to custody."

Royal swallowed and turned to Digger, who grinned broadly. "That's a bad thing, isn't it?"

"It would be if Cyrus had hung around. The monitor is long gone; so is Cyrus. The Feds are behind us by twenty-four hours. We'll clean up this mess and join him."

"We?" Royal asked.

Digger stood and looked at Royal. "Yes. Cyrus gave me instructions for a big finale here. We will not fail, and that brat will not live to trouble Cyrus another day."

39

The shock didn't end when Tess stepped back out of the mobile home. Her phone rang, and she saw it was Agent Bass. What he had to tell her was beyond disturbing.

"Cyrus Beck is to be remanded to custody in the morning."

"That's good news, isn't it?"

"It should be. His lawyers were trying to get everything thrown out, but the judge ruled on the possible Miranda violation, granting us a good faith exclusion. Then we broke the encryption on every file on the tablet. I called for an emergency hearing. The money and resources Beck has overseas make him a flight risk."

"So why do you sound as if you lost? This is great news."

"We're on our way to Beck's now. There are indications that he disabled the ankle monitor. Chief, I believe he already fled the coop — maybe a couple of days ago. If he did, it's probably to a country with no extradition treaty."

She couldn't believe her tired ears. The body of Ken Blakely was a bad enough end to her day. This was like a bad horror movie where nothing would kill the ax murderer.

"What about Chevy?" Tess asked, conscious that Oliver was waiting to hear what was being said.

It took a few seconds for Bass to respond. "We're going to have to move her," he said. "I can't think that she's in any further danger because of this. But she has to be moved. I'm scrambling. Sergeant Logan called and filled me in on everything going on up there. I saw the fake ID. That was Charlie Gage who tried to take Chevy; he's well-known to us. And known to associate with Beck."

"Chevy also said that she recognized him as working for Beck. And the man we're looking for — she called him Ice, says he works for Cyrus. Do you know anything about him?"

"I'd sure like to talk to that Ice. I think he's the Piper I told you about. I'm sending an agent up there to help you with the search and to explain this turn of events to Chevy. Listen, I know you have your hands full . . ."

Tess got the drift. "I'll call Bronwyn, see if she'll hang on to Chevy at least until the second gunman is in custody."

"Or until my agent is up there. We may have a place to move her by then. Are you okay with that?"

"I'll have to be. When will your agent be here?"

"He's on his way. Name's Wally Ferguson. He's sharp."

They disconnected, and Tess told Oliver what he'd said.

Oliver brought a hand to his mouth in dismay. His breath appeared as puffs of vapor in the cold air. His concern was genuine — Tess knew him well enough to understand that. Pain rippled through her. In spite of the irritation and the bumps lately, she loved this guy, his heart, his commitment to people. Was there any hope for their relationship? Were they truly good for one another?

"At least they're going to find another place for her," Oliver said. "That's something anyway."

Tess nodded and swallowed her emotions about their relationship.

"I'll call Bronwyn for you if that's okay. You have a lot more pressing things to be concerned with."

"Thank you." Tess started to say something else — she so wanted to clear the air between them — but Bender asked for her on the radio.

"Curtis reviewed what he could of camera footage covering the parking lot and the entrance Janie always used. She never entered the store."

"Is her car in camera range?"

"Yeah, she parks and gets out of it as another truck pulls next to her. The other driver stays out of camera range, probably says something to her. She climbs into the other truck and they're gone out the north driveway."

The phone felt cold in her hand. "Blakely?"

"I'd say yes, but there's nothing clearly identifying him or the truck. It looks like his truck, but I don't have to tell you how popular that model is around here. The license plate is obscured. He knew how to avoid the camera."

Tess wanted to pound something. Janie leaving her children for another man — that made no sense to Tess. All her instincts screamed against it. But what would Blakely say to get Janie in the truck with him so easily? He could have threatened the kids.

"Find anything at the mobile?" Bender asked.

"Blakely, dead, execution-style."

"He bought it in there?"

"Yes, I believe he was killed here."

"Wow, you thinking he rescued our shooter and got a bullet for his trouble?"

"I am. But where does that leave Janie?" She looked back at the mobile. Exigent circumstances. "I've got to do a quick sweep of the mobile, see if Janie is inside." Part of her hoped she wasn't because if she were, she'd most likely be dead.

"Want me over there?"

"No, stay there. I'll stay connected."

Tess opened the mobile, stepped up and over Blakely. "Janie, Janie Cooper, are you here?"

As quick as she could, she walked through the place. "It's quiet as a tomb," she said to Bender. She saw a lot of stuff she'd want to go through later, but no Janie. She was on her way back out when a strap caught her eye. Holstering her gun, Tess stepped into the kitchen and knelt down. "There's a purse under the table."

"Janie's?"

Tess opened it up, pulled out a wallet, and saw Janie Cooper's smiling face on the ODL.

"Yep, it is." Dread enveloped her like a thick fog. She left the purse and made her way out of the mobile home.

"I'll need Jonkey here, early, to come stand by until the coroner arrives."

"10-4, I'll send her there."

"How is Garrett holding up?"

"I didn't tell him what I told you. His sister is here with him, and the friend who had the boys just came and picked up the little girl as well. What do you want me to tell him?"

"If Blakely had Janie, where would he take her?"

"I'll ask."

Tess considered her officer. He had to be as exhausted as she was. But she knew that like her, he'd probably want to see this through. Good cops were that way about their jobs, and Gabe was a good cop. Briefly she wondered if they'd need more help. She'd called in two officers, Del Jeffers and Sergeant Curtis Pounder, to help with the perimeter for the shooter at Faith's Place. Del she'd released earlier because it was his day off, but Curtis had stayed on because he had simply been called in early for his shift. Now he was handling calls for service. Since the sheriff's department was running point on the shooting at Faith's Place, she hadn't thought that she would need any other personnel. Ken Blakely's murder was related to the shooting at Faith's Place, she was sure, so they would step in. Calling in another officer would severely strain her staffing for the next week. No, she and Bender would have to see this through.

Like earlier, Tess thought, they needed to know where to search before they could mount an effective effort.

"No, I'll do it. Go get some coffee or some food or something. I'll make some notifications, tape off this trailer, and meet you back at the Coopers'."

"Fair enough. I'll see you there." He clicked off.

Tess turned to Oliver. His face was clouded with worry; she could see that in the dim glow of the mobile's outside lights.

"Blakely did take Janie?"

"Looks that way. From what I know of Blakely, he's just as likely to have killed her as not."

"Oh, Lord, for the sake of those children, I pray not."

Tess wanted to reach out, to touch him, hold him, maybe even pray with him, but all she said was "I agree with you there. What did Bronwyn say?"

"She's fine with Chevy staying as long as

she needs to stay. But . . ." He paused.

"What?"

"Harp is still there. She insists that Chevy come home with her."

"I don't have the strength to argue with her. Chevy is an adult. If she wants to go with Harp, I can't stop her. Harp's place is quite the fortress. I just want to be able to get to Chevy in a hurry if we need to. Agent Ferguson will need to see and talk to her in any event."

Oliver looked at Tess, an undefinable expression on his face. After a couple of seconds, he nodded. "I'll head over there then, after you take me back to the Coopers'. Harp seems okay with talking to me; so does Chevy. Maybe I can act as a go-between of some sort. I'll try to find out more about Harp."

Tess thought about that for a minute. She decided he was right. He had a rapport with both women. He'd be the perfect liaison.

"Okay, I just have a couple phone calls to make. Have a seat in the car."

By the time she was done with her notifications, it was dark and close to freezing. The clouds had cleared up, but that only allowed the temp to drop further.

Jonkey pulled up to wait for the coroner while Tess took Oliver back to the Coopers'.

"You know, Tess, this isn't your fault."

Tess sighed. She was so tired and wrung out, she couldn't stop herself. "Of course it is. I knew it was a bad idea to bring Chevy here, and I knew Ken Blakely was a bad actor. Not acting on what my instinct told me is why we're here. Two dead bodies and a missing woman." She slammed the steering wheel with a fist. "I have rules for a reason."

Oliver reached across the car and gripped her hand, forcing her to look him in the eye. "Tess, you were reasonably cautious. None of this could have been foreseen. You're tired. You need to go home and rest."

"I need to find a killer."

"You can't keep driving yourself to the end of your strength. Call the state police; they'll help."

"It's my job, Oliver, not the state police's. If you can't understand that I need to do my job . . ."

"Then what? I can't watch you kill yourself."

"I'm not asking you to." As soon as the words were out of her mouth, Tess regretted them. She saw hurt flash across Oliver's face and she felt her own pain deep in her heart.

"I'd better be getting to Faith's Place then."

He opened the door and climbed out. Tess

watched him walk to his car and get in. She wanted to call out, wanted to stop him and say that she didn't mean it, but she didn't. She simply watched him drive away.

40

Oliver drove away from the Coopers' mobile home feeling as if he'd left half of himself behind. Had he pushed Tess too far? She had to see how thin she was stretching herself, and he couldn't stop himself from pointing that out. He prayed as he drove. They had to find a happy medium. He realized that he loved Tess, but he couldn't dictate to her how to do her job. He needed to give this all over to the Lord and pray for direction. But he knew in his heart that he didn't want to lose her, to her job or because of her job.

He arrived at Faith's Place feeling tired and old and realizing that he should probably follow the same advice he'd given Tess. Taking a deep breath, he climbed out of his car and up the steps to the house. Inside, everyone was in the kitchen. He noticed that Chevy's small bag was next to her. So she was planning to go. He hoped that it was with Harp and not out on her own.

"Hi, all, what's up?"

Bronwyn looked worried, Nye noncommittal, and Chevy was chewing on a thumbnail. Livie Harp brought him a cup of coffee. The brew was welcome, and Oliver took a sip.

"Chevy is coming home with me," Harp said. "I know I can keep her safe."

Oliver waited a beat before responding, realizing that he considered that good news. "Bass is sending another agent. They're looking for a place to move Chevy. Why don't you wait until we hear what he has to say?"

"Why? That other gunman is still out there."

"Chief O'Rourke is doing —"

"I'm not blaming her; she is doing her best. And she's a good cop. But she'll play fair and I won't."

"What is that supposed to mean?"

"Just that I'm not constrained by a badge."

Oliver turned to Chevy. "You sure this is what you want?"

"I'm afraid of Ice. He's a scary guy when he's mad. Livie says she has a safe place for me." She shrugged, her eyes filled with tears. "I don't know where else to go."

In that second, looking at Chevy, Oliver

understood Tess's reckless, relentless drive. This young woman's entire life had been shattered by a cruel victimizer, and she'd just been let down by the justice system in a huge way. While his heart broke for the girl, anger ramped up at Beck and the shadowy fellow, Ice.

Catch them, Tess, he thought. *Catch them.*

Oliver's car was long gone before Tess climbed out of her car and up the steps to the Coopers' mobile home, the events of the day weighing her down — Chevy, Tami, Janie, Blakely, a madman called Ice. When it rained, it poured.

Gabe arrived with coffee and pizza. Tess went for the coffee first and drank half a cup before she looked at the pizza. When she did, she found her appetite had disappeared. As she continued to sip her coffee and watch Garrett pick at food, she observed that the young man was obviously distressed. His kids had been packed off with a family friend, and his older sister was with him, and Tess was glad for that.

She found guilt bubbling up again. If only she had paid attention to her instincts and not let Chevy be brought here. The regret was stifling, clouding her thinking. Oliver was right — she needed sleep, but she couldn't bring herself to leave for rest until she was certain she'd done everything possible to find Janie.

"What now, Chief?" Garrett asked.

Tess told him everything, partly because he deserved to know and partly because she hoped that it would shake some information out of him.

He crumpled, his head hitting the table, and said over and over, "No. No."

His sister came behind him and put her hand on his shoulders.

"Where would he take her?"

"I don't know. I don't know."

Tess leaned toward him. "Think. Something he said, something you saw."

He looked up at her, tears running down his face. "Oh, man, I wish I never had anything to do with Blakely. The money wasn't worth it."

There's plenty of regret to go around for everyone, Tess thought. Just then Jonkey called to let Tess know the coroner had arrived.

"As soon as the coroner gives me the okay, I'll tear that mobile home apart. But you have to help me, Garrett. Think, and think hard: where would Blakely hide Janie?"

He nodded weakly.

"Will you look after your brother, call me

if he remembers anything?" she asked the sister.

"I will."

"I'll call you as soon as we have anything. Gabe, you're with me." With that, she and Bender headed back to the Nelson place.

The coroner had just started photographing the scene. Tess told him she'd already done a quick walk-through.

"We're kind of in a hurry," she said. "There's a missing woman involved."

"I'll move as quickly as I can."

It was a little tight, what with the narrow hall and small doorway. After a couple of minutes, he put the camera down and donned a pair of gloves. It was during the inventorying of Blakely's property when things got interesting.

The first thing that came out of his pocket was a thick wad of hundred-dollar bills. The coroner counted out two thousand dollars.

"Where would he get that kind of cash?" Jonkey asked.

"The gunman who is outstanding, Ice, perhaps — he had a bunch of cash as well. My bet is, our suspect was aided by Blakely. How they met up, I don't know, but maybe he paid Blakely for his help, then killed him."

"And left the money?"

"He was running for his life."

"You think Blakely picked our shooter up and got him out of the forest?" Bender asked.

"Had to; it would explain a lot. And it proves that there's no honor among thieves. Blakely saved the guy's bacon and got shot for his trouble."

"Nice guy," Bender commented.

But the next item the coroner retrieved was the most disturbing. It was a handwritten note, addressed to Garrett Cooper.

I've got Janie. I want all the money you owe me or she dies.

The coroner looked up at her. "Is there going to be another body somewhere?"

"I hope not. But we need to tear this mobile apart."

He stood, scratching his nose with the back of a gloved hand. "Have at it. My crime scene is right here. It's obvious this is where he was killed. I've got lots of evidence bags you can use. It'll be a few minutes before I'm ready to move the body." He stepped aside.

Tess turned to Gabe. "You and I can take the back. Becky, you take the kitchen. Janie's purse is under the table."

They stepped over Blakely and went their respective directions. It wasn't long before they recovered a lot of evidence.

Gabe and Tess found wet, bloody clothing in the trash. Clothing that would fit a tall, lean man, similar to what Tess had pulled out of the knapsack. Becky recovered a Kevlar vest, pockmarked with buckshot, and a bloody, torn leather jacket.

"He's getting sloppy, leaving all this behind," Tess said. "We'll get some good DNA evidence off this stuff." She turned to Jonkey. "Look up vehicles registered to Blakely, put out a BOLO. Dollars to donuts, the killer took the truck."

"But where's Janie?"

Tess looked at Bender, heart heavy with the fear that Janie was now as dead as Blakely.

"Let's think: If Blakely was up on the farthest corner of the Scales property, close enough that he was able to help the shooter escape, why would he be there?"

Bender scratched his head. He looked as tired as Tess felt. Oliver had pointed out that she'd been going nonstop for far too long, and the same could be said of Bender. The hardworking guy had been at this just as long as she had. Oliver's solution was that Tess call in the state police for help.

But Tess resisted. This was her case. Maybe she was taking things too personal, but the shooter was hers and she was going to catch him, no matter what.

"There's nothing up there that I can think of. But Ken is a poacher. He's probably been all over after game. If he dumped Janie somewhere . . ." His voice trailed off.

"What?"

"There are some caves up there. I don't think he ever used them for poaching, too obvious. But if he were hiding something . . ."

Like a body, Tess thought but didn't say. Yet the information energized her.

"It's somewhere to start. We need to retrace his steps. Can we get to the back side of the Scales property from here? I know it's dark and it's cold, but I have to give Janie every chance. Blakely wanted money. I can only hope that he would have planned to keep Janie alive at least until Garrett got his note. He just never had a chance to deliver his note. But if she's somewhere exposed to the elements . . ." Now Tess let her thoughts trail off. They both knew that Janie could freeze to death if left in the forest overnight without any shelter.

Bender nodded. "I'll have to go get our

ATV, but I can follow the trail that Blakely came down to get here."

"Then go."

Tess turned to Jonkey. "Go ahead and go back into service. If we need you, I'll call you back."

Becky nodded.

The coroner loaded up his van with the body and the clothing evidence and was gone. Tess locked Nelson's mobile home up, then sealed it off with evidence tape, in case the sheriff wanted to send a crime scene technician in the morning to go over everything more carefully.

Filled with a lot of worry and not a little fear when she thought about Janie, she stepped back to her SUV and then remembered Yarrow's trail cams. Tess flushed hot with excitement. If she remembered right, at least one of the cams was up in this part of the forest, maybe not near Bronwyn and Nye's fence, but more west, in the direction Blakely and the shooter had fled.

She pulled out her phone and called Win Yarrow. It was after midnight, and she got his voice mail, so she explained the current situation, the search for Janie and the hope that the trail cams would be able to tell them something.

Then she drove back to the Cooper place.

She dreaded telling Garrett about the note, but she had to, and maybe, just maybe, Garrett would have a guess as to where Blakely might have taken Janie. He had, after all, been working with the guy.

Lights were still blazing inside the mobile, so she knew Garrett was still awake. She got out and knocked on the door.

"Did you find her?" Garrett opened the door, face full of hope.

Tess had to dash the hope. "No, I'm sorry; we didn't. But we know for certain now that Blakely was involved in her disappearance."

Tess stepped inside. Garrett's sister was curled up on the couch.

"How do you know?"

She told him about the note. Garrett paled and sat down hard in a kitchen chair.

"I think he was killed before he had a chance to give you the note, and I think that he's hidden Janie somewhere, up near the Scaleses' fence line. I have to ask again — do you have any idea where he'd take her?"

He looked at her with red-rimmed eyes, then ran a hand through his hair. "Ah, man, she could be anywhere. I . . . I, uh, never went with Ken when he poached. I'm no hunter, not even a hiker. I wouldn't know any landmarks."

Tess bit her tongue hoping that the caves

would be the place and that, by some miracle, Janie would be alive.

"He'd be gone for days, hiding in tents while he waited for bears. He used tents, bushes, caves, anything he could to hide from people too." He swallowed. "You think she's dead?"

Tess didn't answer right away. When Garrett said *caves,* she'd perked up.

"I'm not giving up on her. I don't want you to either. Gabe went to get our ATV. We'll head up the trail and look for her." Tess heard the whine of the ATV motor. "Try and get some rest, Garrett. I'll let you know the moment I have anything to tell you."

He nodded, and she stepped outside to where Gabe waited with the ATV. She saw that he'd also brought some powerful flashlights.

"I called Yarrow, left a message, asked him to check the forest cams he installed. Do you think we should give him another try?"

"He's a good guy to have along on a search in the forest."

Tess was still tapping her phone when a fish and game vehicle came tearing into the lot, jerked to a stop in front of them, and Win Yarrow jumped out.

"I got your message and came as soon as

I could."

"Well, your poacher is dead; coroner picked him up a little bit ago." Tess, feeling heavy with the full weight of fatigue and cold, told Yarrow about the events of the day.

"Talk about poetic justice. And you think Blakely kidnapped a woman?"

"Yeah, he had a ransom note in his pocket. He must have put Janie Cooper somewhere just before he ran into our shooter — or maybe after, I don't know — and he never got to deliver the note. Did you get a chance to review the forest cam tape?"

"Yes, I did. Caught an image of Blakely and another guy coming down the mountain earlier. I didn't see Janie Cooper, though." He held out his phone to Tess.

She studied the screenshot. Blakely was easily recognized. The other guy was vaguely familiar, but on the small screen, as good as the resolution was, she could not tell who the man was.

Yarrow rubbed his chin. "But you say he met up with your shooter at the corner of the Scales property?"

Tess nodded. "We're going to try and backtrack him now."

"I'll go with you. I know where Blakely crossed the cam. I've got a good idea where this woman could be if Blakely wanted to hide her up here."

Her phone rang, and she saw that it was Oliver calling. She considered letting it go to voice mail because of their last conversation but answered instead.

Stepping aside, keeping her voice neutral, she answered. "Yes?"

"I thought you'd like to know about Chevy."

She couldn't tell anything from his voice, but for a second she feared he'd tell her that Chevy wanted to leave, take off on her own. "Thanks. How is she?"

"She's shaken but okay. She's going to stay with Livie Harp."

Tess bit her bottom lip, not sure if this was good news or bad. She knew she had no power to force Chevy to do anything.

"You still there?"

"Yeah, I just don't know what to say. She'll be safe there. I just wish I knew more about Harp."

"I've got a contact number, but she doesn't want me to give it to anyone else, not Bronwyn and not you."

"Swell." Tess didn't have the energy to be angry.

"You sound dead on your feet."

He just couldn't resist, she thought. "I just

had some more coffee. I'll be fine."

"Any news on Janie?"

Briefly she told him what they'd found and their plan. There was silence and for a long moment she thought the call had dropped.

Then he said, "Tess, you can't keep going, running on coffee and adrenaline."

"I can't leave any stone unturned. If Janie is out there in this cold, I have to find her."

"Let Yarrow and Bender go. There's no need for you to go as well."

"Bender's been working all day like I have. No, I'm on this. It's my responsibility."

"You take too much on yourself."

"You can't tell me you wouldn't do the same if this were some church emergency."

"Maybe I would, but that is different. I don't carry a gun or worry that people will shoot me. I care about you, Tess. Your dedication is as attractive as it is terrifying."

"I have to go."

She disconnected. The cold hit hard, but for Tess the hit on her heart was the hardest. What chance did she and Oliver have if he didn't understand her responsibility to her job?

Tess had to take a minute while Bender and Yarrow discussed routes. She'd hit a wall thirty minutes ago, and if she didn't refocus, she'd be useless on this search. She asked herself a question: *What would my dad do?*

The answer came to her immediately: *He'd pray.*

Prayer had always been his default position, and tears threatened as Tess realized that was her weakness. Oliver's words about her taking too much on herself came blaring back to her. It wasn't a weakness to need help or backup.

Tess prayed, asking for strength, clarity, and most of all, for another miracle, for Janie's safety and a good end to this nightmare day.

41

Ice's eyes were heavy. He had a full stomach, he was warm and dry . . . it would be easy to drop off to sleep. But when his body shifted, pain stabbed him awake. His chest got more painful as the bruise settled in. It only served to make him angry and more committed to making the woman who'd shot him pay. Not to mention the fact that the cut across his cheek would ruin his looks forever.

"Women like scars. Don't worry about it," Digger had told him just before he left the plane, saying he had something to do for Cyrus. He and Cyrus had had quite the phone conversation. Digger hadn't said much, so it was obvious that Cyrus was giving the instructions and he had a lot to take care of in a short amount of time.

At this point Ice didn't care what women liked. He hated the angry red slash across the right side of his face.

He and Digger were still at the airport, in the plush private jet. This was a rental because Cyrus's personal jet had been impounded. Ice wondered if Cyrus had really left the country. He doubted it. Digger probably knew exactly where Cyrus was, but he wasn't saying. Royal hadn't spoken to Cyrus and hadn't asked to when Cyrus called. But he was reading between the lines and bet that Cyrus planned to go after Chevy himself. If he really had defeated the ankle monitor, he should get his butt out of the country. The last thing Ice wanted to see was Cyrus in Oregon with a string of marshals and FBI agents on his tail.

Besides, Ice had already been through amateur hour with Gage. If Cyrus did show up, Ice wanted to talk Cyrus out of what he was planning but figured he had at least a few hours before the man arrived. Till then, he needed to rest up, heal up, and plot his revenge against the crazy woman with the shotgun.

Tess felt a little heaviness lift after her prayer. Her dad and Oliver were what you could call prayer warriors, and she needed the strength they seemed to get from the practice. She even made a promise to try harder to go to prayer first, instead of after she felt all worn-out.

Once on the ATV, Tess saw there was a clear trail to follow behind the mobile home park, the remnants of an old logging road, and in spite of the dark, Bender chugged up the road without any problem. Tess sat next to him while Yarrow took a seat in the back cargo area. They traveled up into the forest for nearly an hour before Yarrow told Bender to slow.

"We need to go by foot from here. This is where I caught them on the cam. There's a big cave about a quarter mile in." The cave was directly on the route to the back of the Faith's Place property.

Yarrow had explained to them that he checked the caves regularly, thinking Blakely might use them. "I never caught him there or saw any evidence he'd been there. But one thing for sure: that guy always does the unexpected."

Stiff and cold, they climbed off the ATV and, with bright flashlights shining, followed Yarrow through the trees. Like Tami's rescue after an improbable trip down the river, Tess believed they would need just as big a miracle now where Janie was concerned. She felt a headache coming on at the thought of what Blakely might have done with Janie. What a stroke of bad luck that he crossed paths with a killer more cold-blooded than him before he could deliver his ransom note.

"Here!" Bender called out. Tess stopped, not certain what he was seeing. She followed his flashlight beam and still couldn't make it out. Blinking her tired eyes, she refocused and saw it — a dark opening in the hillside behind the trees.

A new fear gripped her. What would they find inside?

Both men stepped aside and let Tess take the lead.

She stepped between the trees. The stench knocked her back on her heels. It was reminiscent of the odor they'd detected at the cut fence. Tess prayed a dead body wasn't the source.

Tess, Bender, and Yarrow shone their lights into the black space. Off to one side something glinted — a sleeping bag, the lump making it obvious there was something inside.

Glancing to Yarrow, Tess said, "I've got this." Then she ducked down and stepped into the dark crevasse. She held her breath and knelt down to unzip the bag. She saw hair first and then the face, duct tape across the mouth.

Tess reached forward to check the neck for a pulse when Janie's eyes popped open, and Tess nearly fell back at the shock. The woman's eyes squinted at the light. First they filled with fear, and her body bucked; then she relaxed when Tess spoke.

"Janie, it's Chief O'Rourke. You're safe, you're safe." The woman's visible relief rippled through Tess like a wave. Finally some good news. *Thank you, God.*

With Bender's help, Tess freed Janie from the bag and duct tape that bound her. As she worked to get circulation back into her limbs, Janie began to cry.

"Oh, Chief, it was Ken Blakely; he stopped me when I got to work. He wants all of our money. He says that Garrett owes him —"

"It's okay. We know all about Blakely. He's not going to bother you ever again. Are you hurt in any way?"

"Just stiff. My throat is parched. Can I get some water?"

Yarrow handed her a bottle.

As she drank, Tess felt a lot of tension fade away. It looked like Blakely's attempt to conceal Janie actually kept her from freezing. While the woman hydrated and recovered from being bound and hidden for hours, Tess left the enclosure and radioed the news to Jonkey.

"We found her, she's okay, and we'll be heading back down in a few minutes."

When Jonkey responded with a 10-4, Tess took a deep breath. This was a second miracle.

But as they readied the ATV to accommodate Janie on the way back down to the mobile home park, Tess found her mind wandering to Oliver and the tension between them. The last phone call was crushing. Would it take a third miracle for their relationship to survive all this?

42

Following the emotional reunion between the Coopers, the paperwork, and tying up loose ends, Tess made it home as the sun was rising. Cold and tired to the bone, all she could manage was taking off her boots and jacket and falling into bed. But needed sleep was interrupted a few hours later when the phone rang. It was Steve Logan.

"Sorry to wake you."

Tess, stiff, bedraggled, and still exhausted, sat on the edge of the bed. "It's okay. What's up?"

"The gun you found in the knapsack. The guy didn't do a very good job destroying the serial number. We were able to figure it out and run the numbers. All kinds of bells and whistles went off. Gun was reported stolen years ago and used in three murders. It was actually a cop's duty weapon —"

Tess came wide-awake, her brain exploding with recognition. "It belonged to Isaac Pink."

"Well, uh, yeah, how did you know?"

Tess ran a hand through her hair, blinking away the last bit of sleep. "Because I know that case. Isaac Pink was a cop killed because he was sheltering a witness." She went on to explain to Steve the possible connection to Cyrus Beck.

"I'm not quite sure what to do with that. Do you think Cyrus Beck had something to do with Pink's death?"

"I wouldn't say it was impossible. And I'm sure Bass would be quick to make such a connection. Have you contacted LAPD?"

"I did. They're sending a team up here, just not sure when. With the gunman still outstanding, this situation is fluid."

"I'd like to talk to them."

"I'm sure they'd like to talk to you. One other thing: do you remember me asking Livie Harp to come to the station today to be fingerprinted? It's routine. She shot and killed a man; you know we need to identify her officially."

"Yeah, I remember that."

"She hasn't shown up."

Tess looked at the clock. It was close to 11 a.m. "What time was she supposed to be there?"

"Two hours ago."

"Do you think she doesn't want to be identified?"

"I don't know what to think."

Oliver hadn't been able to sleep. After tossing and turning, he finally gave in and got up. He opened the Bible but found that he couldn't concentrate. A check of the clock told him he could head for the hospital; by the time he got there, visiting hours would have begun and he could look in on Tami. All the way to Medford, Oliver replayed the events of the day before. As much as he did want to check on Tami, more than anything, he wanted to sit down with Tess and unravel all the problems they'd encountered. He refused to believe that their relationship was not fixable.

He stepped off the elevator and ran right into Alana. She must have been coming from Tami's room. She stood, hands on her hips, and gave him an earful about why she was unhappy with him.

"That woman is not the right woman for you."

"That woman? You mean Chief O'Rourke?"

She gave an exaggerated nod. "Pastor Mac, you need a woman dedicated to making you a good pastor. Chief O'Rourke needs to be a good police officer. The two don't mix. Anna was perfect for you; you need to leave it at that. If you don't, you'll suffer for it, and so will the congregation."

Oliver had no response for her.

Alana wagged her finger at him. "Mark my words — it will never work out with that woman." Then she walked away.

He watched her go before continuing into Tami's room. His attention was divided the entire time he was with Tami and her mother. This case had made him wonder if he and Tess could truly mesh. Alana echoed Don Cherry, and her words had stirred up a hornet's nest in his soul. Was she right?

There was no change in Tami, but the doctors had told Rosita that was a good thing. She was holding her own. If she wasn't getting any worse, there was a better chance that she'd recover.

Oliver was happy to hear that, but his thoughts were on Tess and the friction in their relationship. He admitted to himself that he was more concerned about how she jumped into things feetfirst than he'd let on. Running into the fire was bad enough, but then she put herself into the line of fire again searching for an armed and dangerous killer. He wondered at the irritation that had flared up inside. For a year he'd watched Tess work, seen her handle dangerous situations, and been completely amazed at her courage and dedication.

He stepped into a washroom on his way out of the hospital. He washed his hands and rinsed off his face. Drying off with a paper towel, Oliver studied himself in the mirror. "What is wrong with me?" he wondered out loud.

Her courage and dedication were a big part of what drew him to Tess. Why were they making him so angry now? Tess had not changed, yet Oliver found himself wondering if Alana was right. Yes, Anna had supported him completely and helped him to become the man and pastor he was today. But that was Anna — she loved being in the background, being his support.

Tess was not Anna — and Oliver didn't want her to be — but she was no less supportive.

Then it struck him hard, in the center of his chest, like a punch. He didn't love Tess because she was like Anna — because she wasn't — but he feared that just like Anna, she'd be taken from him violently.

"I can't go through that again. I can't." The realization shocked his whole system as if he'd just grabbed a live electrical wire and pulled it to his chest. Where was his trust in God?

It would be safe to break it off, not leave himself open to another loss like that again. But as he continued to study the man in the mirror, that idea was a nonstarter. God was trustworthy, gracious, and good.

And life was not about playing it safe.

After Tess finished talking to Steve, she knew she'd never get back to sleep, so she started a pot of coffee and took a shower.

As the warm water pounded away at tired muscles, Tess thought about the day before. It had been the strangest, busiest day ever in her law enforcement career. An attempted murder, then an attempted kidnapping and a self-defense shooting, followed by a murder and a kidnapping. With the exception of the self-defense shooting and Ken Blakely being dead, which solved the poaching and the kidnapping, nothing else was resolved and there was a cold-blooded killer loose in this valley.

What would today bring?

She finished her shower and dressed, trying not to think about Oliver. He'd been angry with her the last time they'd spoken on the phone, thought she was stretching herself too thin and needed to call the state police.

He couldn't understand her need to see everything she had started through to the end. And she'd come to see Oliver as someone who always understood her. Obviously she was wrong.

Was she wrong about their relationship as well? That thought brought a pinch of pain that made her take a breath.

After she finished half a cup of coffee, her thoughts cleared a bit. She realized Steve hadn't given her any updates on Tami's case or on the hunt for the killer. He would have if there were any news on either front, she knew. Maybe that meant she could deal with Livie Harp, find out why the woman didn't go in to be fingerprinted. She knew Oliver had a number for Harp, though the woman didn't want anyone else to have it. Tess could call him and ask him to call Harp, or she could just drive up there and hope Harp opened the gate.

Tess didn't really want to talk to Oliver at the moment. Her thoughts switched gears. She wondered about the agent Bass was sending. Was he here yet? If he'd shown up at the station, she would have been paged. She decided to call Bronwyn and ask if the agent had shown up at Faith's Place.

Bronwyn didn't give her a chance to ask a question right away. "What great news to hear about Janie Cooper," she said. "We really needed some good news after yesterday."

"Thanks, Bronwyn. We did need some good news." Tess paused, wondering how the Coopers were doing.

"Did I make a mistake letting Chevy go with Livie?" Bronwyn asked.

"She's an adult. You couldn't have forced her to stay with you. And I can't say that she's less safe with Harp. Has the FBI agent, Wally Ferguson, shown up yet?"

"No. The only federal agent here today was Mia Takano. She was released from the hospital, so she came, got her stuff, and left. She was called back to the office."

"Okay. Ferguson should check in with me first, but let me know if he does show up."

"I will."

Tess hung up, finished her cup of coffee, and poured another. There was so much on her plate this morning, she didn't know where to start.

She sat at the kitchen table and took out a piece of paper, numbering the issues in front of her. First, there was the situation with Chevy. What did the Feds want to do with her? That came first, rather than what

384

Livie Harp wanted. Tess needed to visit Harp and find out what was going on there.

Second, there was the issue of the handgun recovered, Isaac Pink's gun. That was huge. She bet the LAPD cold case guys would be all over that information. But did it mean that Pink's killer had been here in Rogue's Hollow, and was he the missing gunman?

Third, there was the gunman himself, presumably Ice. He'd obviously gotten away. Tess feared that he was miles away by now, and they had to figure out how to positively identify him. He had to be Blakely's killer. The only scenario that made sense was that Ken drove him off the mountain only to be killed for his kindness.

And last but not least, there was Tami Vasquez. What was her status? *And could she tell us anything at all about what happened to her?*

She perused the list, noting that she'd not gone in order of importance. The most important thing was finding the gunman. Finished, she stood and stretched. She hadn't yet eaten breakfast and already she had the whole day planned.

But niggling in the back of her mind was Oliver and the breach in their relationship. Could it be repaired? Did she want it to be?

"Do you really think you're any good for him?"

43

When Digger returned from his errand, he and Royal left the plane and checked into a hotel near the airport. Cyrus was all over the news. Bass discovered that the ankle monitor was disabled, that Cyrus pulled the wool over four agents tasked with watching him and he was long gone. Ice had to admire the move. He wouldn't have thought Cyrus capable of it. The Feds were scrambling and embarrassed.

Ice appreciated the time to soothe his wounds and rest up before the next phase of his mission. His shoulder was still sore, but the buckshot had really only grazed him. His ribs were another matter. The bruise had spread across his chest and hurt worse when he got up from bed, and he winced. He was getting too old for this. Ten years ago he'd already be healing. All the more reason to collect the rest of his money and disappear to some warm, sunny locale and relax.

And he *would* collect his money. Every time he looked in the mirror at the ugly, red-purple mark across his cheek, his anger rekindled. Thankfully, Digger had brought a bag of Ice's things; included inside was some makeup. He applied it liberally to his cheek until the mark disappeared. He'd make those women pay.

He heard a knock at the door of the suite and judged from the conversation that Digger had ordered breakfast. Ice threw on a robe and went out to see what was on the menu.

The coffee smelled great, and Royal saw an assortment of pastries. He also smelled bacon, saw pancakes and eggs. He was starved.

"Help yourself," Digger said when the bellman left. "We need to talk."

Royal filled a coffee cup and a plate, ignoring Digger's tone, but not liking it. There was a time when a side glance from Digger would have left Royal quaking in his boots. But that was a long time ago. They were both older, Digger at least thirty years older than Royal. And he looked every bit of his age. He didn't scare Royal at all anymore.

"What do you want to talk about?" Royal asked, his mouth full of bacon.

"This." He tossed a newspaper in front of Royal. The Medford *Mail Tribune.*

Royal swallowed his food with a swig of coffee. The headlines screamed at him.

Local Woman Survives Being Shot, Shoved over Midas Creek Falls.

There was a photo of the chatty cashier. He scanned the rest of the page, having to fight to keep his face blank when he saw a story about the shooting at Faith's Place, the women's shelter. There was a drawing of a man wanted for questioning, authorities said — code for "suspect" — and his nickname, "Ice."

Royal looked up to see Digger watching him. "What?"

"You screwed up all the way around, didn't you?"

Royal sat back in his chair and pushed away from the table. He swallowed again. "Gage screwed up. I'm a victim of his incompetence."

"This girl?" He pointed to the headline. "She's yours too, isn't she? You can't blame that on Gage."

"She doesn't know who I am. Even if she survives, she doesn't know anything. Cyrus —"

"I just spoke to Cyrus. He's not at all happy with you. Yeah, you're hot. You're kryptonite."

Ice sneered. "Me, kryptonite? From the guy who skipped bail? Cyrus is out of his mind."

Ice read the older man's body language and was ready to move a split second before the gun, suppressor attached, came out of Digger's robe pocket. Ice jerked to the right and the bullet missed, but the cup of hot coffee Ice tossed in Digger's face didn't.

Digger cried out in pain and stumbled back. Ice was up and on him, wrenching the gun easily from the older man's hand. Ice put his hand on Digger's chest and shoved with all his might, and the man went down onto the floor.

Ice stood over him. "Was that Cyrus's idea or yours?" he asked, pointing the gun at center mass.

"Does it matter?"

"Where is Cyrus?"

"You won't find out from me."

Royal could barely see straight, he was so angry, holding the gun on Digger, glaring at the man who taught him everything he knew. The pain that blossomed from the rapid movements he'd made caused his eyes to water.

Digger stared back. "Cyrus made you, and now you betray him."

"I can bury Cyrus. And I just might." He fired once into Digger.

After a minute, the pain in his body subsided, and Royal went back to his breakfast. He didn't think the pop from the suppressor would bring any unwanted attention. Digger liked small-caliber weapons. Now he contemplated this new development and wondered just what exactly his next move should be.

By the time he finished his breakfast, he had a plan. He showered, dressed, searched Digger's things, and took everything he thought he could use.

On his way out the door, he looked down on Digger. "You're right, old man. Cyrus made me."

He left the hotel room, remembering to put the Do Not Disturb sign on the door.

44

Tess had just ordered her late breakfast at the Hollow Grind when her phone rang. It was the deputy working Shady Cove. He'd found Ken Blakely's pickup truck. But where he found it gave Tess pause. It was at the Maple Leaf Hotel.

She took her breakfast to go and headed down to the parking lot of the Maple Leaf. She remembered that was where she was when she got the call about the shooting at Faith's Place. She'd planned to check on Jim Smith, a member of the work crew. He'd listed his residence as room 10.

What a coincidence that the stolen truck belonging to murdered Ken Blakely would be found at the same hotel where a potential suspect in Tami's shooting had been staying.

"I haven't gone through the truck yet," the deputy told her when she arrived.

"Thought you might want to take a look first."

"Thanks."

The hotel manager was also in the parking lot. "This truck was never registered here," he said. "All my guests register their vehicles."

"Did you see who parked it here?"

He shook his head.

"What about the occupant of room 10? Has he checked out yet?"

"No, but he paid through the month, in cash. He doesn't have a car; he has a motorcycle." He handed Tess a registration card with all the information Smith had given him.

Tess noted that there was no motorcycle in the lot. She called the work crew supervisor and asked about Jim Smith.

"He wasn't home when we came by to pick him up this morning. I put him down as a no-show. Today was the last day anyway." He gave Tess the phone number he had for Smith. Tess remembered the burner phone in the knapsack; it was unlikely that the number would get her much.

Though Tess doubted she'd find any evidence, she went to her computer and applied for a warrant to search room 10. Once she was able to access the room, she found the place as clean as if housekeeping had recently been there. Frustrated, but glad that she had a name to go with her suspect, Tess had the truck impounded and room 10 sealed in order for a crime scene team to process the room more completely than she could.

The elation she felt at recognizing that Jim Smith was her man was tempered by the knowledge that she'd been one step behind him for far too long. Was Jim Smith the gunman in both Tami's shooting *and* the incident at Faith's Place?

Her phone rang, and she saw it was Steve.

"Good news," he said when she answered. "Tami came around. She was able to give the deputy on her room a statement. The guy you're looking for is part of the temporary work crew. His name is Jim Smith."

"That is not a surprise." She told him where she was and what she had found so far.

"What?"

"Yeah. Did Tami say anything else?"

"Only that when she went out with Smith, he was very interested in the woman who made a scene at the market. That was Chevy, correct?"

"Yep." Tess felt the click of things sliding into place. Poor Tami. She was in the wrong place at the wrong time. Smith pumped her for information about Chevy and then tried to kill her.

"It all fits, Steve. Now we just have to find Jim Smith."

"Working on that. You sent me the information from the work crew. His driver's license picture is there. I'll get a press release out right away."

"Thank you, Steve. I appreciate that."

"No problem. We'll catch this guy. If anyone deserves to be caught, he does. According to Tami, he shot her cold, never said a word, never showed any emotion. His nickname is fitting."

Tess ended the call and got back in her SUV. Her thoughts drifted to Oliver. She hadn't spoken to him that morning, which was unusual. Emotions conflicted, she didn't want to argue, she didn't want friction; she simply wanted to share her thoughts and plans with someone who would understand.

45

Ice left the hotel room cautiously, hoping to avoid contact with anyone. Makeup covered the mark on his cheek, he was clean-shaven, and he'd buzzed his hair very short. He needed to be a ghost now.

He relaxed a bit when he stepped into an empty hallway. Taking as deep a breath as possible while still avoiding pain, he strode toward the elevators. As he got closer to the elevator bay, he could hear a male voice talking. Slowing, Ice paused before stepping from the hallway into the vestibule that held the elevators. Last night, he remembered that there was some problem with them; maybe this was a technician.

Then he heard something that hit him like a brick and made him stand stock-still, straining to catch every bit of what the man was saying.

"Agent Bass gave me instructions to convince the girl that we can protect her better at a different locale."

Then quiet; the man was listening. Ice held his breath and leaned forward slowly to peer into the vestibule. The man's back was to him, phone to his ear.

"Hmm." He nodded.

It was a Fed — the suit, the haircut, the shoes all gave him away — and Royal fought the urge to turn and flee down the stairs.

"Right, I spoke to the sheriff before you called. He says the girl is staying with some prepper. . . . Uh, what? . . . Yeah, apparently the woman lives on some sort of self-contained compound."

He jammed the elevator button impatiently two or three times. "Well, I have to get out there before I can give you a full report on the situation, don't I?"

Ice tried to figure out how this could work to his advantage. He could follow the Fed right to Chevy before eliminating him. Ice didn't mind ridding the world of another Fed.

"There's a liaison, a local pastor who can take me to the girl. Look, there's a problem with the elevator here. I'm taking the stairs. I'll call you back after I make contact with her."

He shoved the phone into his pocket, and Royal turned, reaching the door to the stairwell first. He pulled the door open for the Fed.

Affecting a British accent, Ice said, "Shoddy elevators, yeah?"

The agent brushed past him, clearly in a hurry. "You said it."

Ice stepped into the stairwell after him, and before the door closed behind him, he leaped forward and shoved, hitting the agent in the back as hard as he could.

The agent's startled cry was drowned out by the sound of him and his briefcase falling down the metal and concrete stairs.

Ice waited for the echo to die out and then walked down after the agent while reaffixing the suppressor to Digger's gun. But when he reached the spot where the agent had landed, he could see the gun was not necessary. The unnatural angle of the man's neck told him that the fall had done Ice's work for him.

Heart beating rapidly, Ice put the gun away and looked up the stairwell and then down. No one else was in sight. He'd already noticed yesterday that there were no cameras anywhere. He knelt down beside the dead agent, went through his pockets, removed his ID, his phone, his wallet, car keys. The man was about Ice's height and weight. Ice studied the ID photo and believed he could sell it — he could be Agent Ferguson.

This was a stroke of luck.

The briefcase had fallen a few more stairs below. Ice took out his own ID and put it in the agent's pocket. Then he continued down and collected the briefcase. He opened it and put the agent's things inside, then snapped it shut. Straightening his jacket and running a hand over his short hair, Ice picked up the case and started down the rest of the stairs. He didn't hurry, but he walked with a purpose, working hard to not draw attention to himself as he exited the hotel and entered the parking lot.

He found the agent's car not far from Digger's Cadillac Escalade. As much as he preferred the luxury car to the nondescript sedan belonging to the agent, he knew that taking the agent's car was the wiser choice. He'd do what he needed to do and ditch the car anyway.

46

On his way back to Rogue's Hollow from the hospital, Oliver got a call from Bronwyn.

"Just wanted to let you know, I talked to Agent Bass, and now, as far as all law enforcement is concerned, you are the official liaison between Chevy and Livie and everyone else. You are the only one she trusts with her contact information."

Not sure what to make of that, Oliver thought for a moment. "Has the FBI agent arrived in town yet?"

"No," Bronwyn said. "The chief asked about that as well."

"I assume he'll want to go check on Harp and Chevy."

"Most likely. Chief O'Rourke will call you when he gets here."

"You're right. I'll wait for her call."

He rang off and headed to the home of Janie and Garrett Cooper, to see how they were doing after the trauma of the night before. Garrett was quiet, subdued, and Oliver knew from Tess that there was a very good chance he'd be charged with a crime for what he did for Ken Blakely. Janie, considering what she'd just been through, was doing well, seemed calm sitting in the living room, holding her little girl and watching the two older boys play.

Oliver took Garret aside to the kitchen. They sat together at the small table.

"I'm sorry, Pastor Mac."

"Sorry for what, Garrett?"

"Everything. The situation with Blakely, helping him poach, lying — everything."

"I think you should be telling Janie that."

"It's hard to say that kind of stuff to her. I feel weak."

"It's not weak to admit the truth to the one you love. And she needs to hear that from you. You want this marriage to work, don't you?"

Garrett faced Oliver, expression earnest. "More than anything, Pastor Mac. I didn't realize how much I loved Janie until I thought of life without her." He sniffled and ran a hand across his nose. "She's a great mom. She's my other half." He held Oliver's gaze as his eyes filled with tears. "Does it make me weak to admit that?"

"No, not at all. It makes you human." He put a hand on Garrett's arm. "Do me a favor, Garrett. After you put the kids to bed tonight, tell Janie what you told me. The two of you need to talk honestly and for a long time. It's not just about you; there are also three little lives who depend on an honest conversation. Will you do that?"

A tear fell, and Garrett quickly wiped it away. "I will, Pastor Mac. I promise I will. I never want to lose her."

Before he said good-bye, Oliver prayed with the couple, for healing, for the family, and for the bad memories of the last few days to be erased.

He left the mobile with a much lighter heart than he'd woken up with. He believed there was hope for Janie and Garrett. It was too bad that it took the kidnapping of Janie to make Garrett wake up.

He couldn't help but think about Tess. Oliver thought about how irritated and angry he'd been with her the day before. But she could be so stubborn when she wanted to be.

Oliver smiled. He loved that about her — her dedication, her heart, and her commitment to her profession. Why had he gotten so angry? He was frightened. He could admit that now. It was pure fear. He'd lost

Anna, and now just as he was beginning to realize how much he loved Tess, the fear of losing her hit hard.

His own advice echoed in his mind: *"It's not weak to admit the truth to the one you love."*

I'll call her, he thought. *As soon as I get home, I'll call her.*

But his day was interrupted when he reached the church grounds. Tami had regained consciousness, and local news crews had descended on the town, asking not only about Tami, but about the shooting at Faith's Place. And Oliver saw the press release. They had a name and a picture of the missing gunman. That made him relax. In today's digital media, that picture would be everywhere, and the man would be caught soon, he was sure of it.

Tess, Oliver learned, was in Shady Cove, where they'd found Blakely's truck. It was late in the afternoon before Oliver actually entered his home. He hadn't heard from Tess, and that bothered him. He picked up the phone to call her and then set it down. Better to do this in person. Oliver decided to drive to her house. Once there, he planned to pour his heart out and, hopefully with Tess, figure out their relationship once and for all.

Oliver showered and changed his clothes. When he checked his phone before leaving the house, he saw there was a message from Tess and his heart sang.

"Oh, Lord," he breathed, "help us to make this right."

He was just about to listen to the message Tess left when a knock at the door distracted him. Maybe it was her. He pulled the door open, smile dying when he saw a tall man wearing a dark suit standing on his porch.

"Pastor Macpherson?"

"Yes."

The man held up an ID card. Oliver saw FBI before the man quickly put the ID back in his pocket. "I'm Special Agent Ferguson. Agent Bass sent me to investigate the shooting yesterday. I was told that you helped find a safe place for Roberta."

Tess arrived back home at dinnertime, still tired from the day before. She planned on making a bite to eat and filing her reports at home. It was frustrating that they now knew who their suspect was, but they couldn't find him. But his picture was everywhere. Steve had sent out an urgent BOLO, highlighting the fact that this guy was armed and dangerous, so it would just be a matter of time.

Her phone rang as she climbed out of the SUV.

"Steve, tell me you caught him."

"Well . . ."

Tess stopped at her front door. "You found him?"

"I was called out to assist Medford PD at the airport Marriott. Guy fell down the stairs, looks like he broke his neck. They found an ID in his pocket, California DL, issued to Jim Smith."

Tess stood stock-still at her front door. "Our gunman died falling down the stairs?"

"Well, there is no way this guy is Jim Smith. Coroner turned him over, straightened him out. Height and weight are close, but that's it."

Tess frowned. "So what do you have?"

"This guy checked into the hotel as Walter Ferguson."

Tess felt her heart drop, her mouth go dry. "Oh no. That's the agent Bass sent. What you're telling me —"

"Chevy said that Ice liked to think of himself as a chameleon. Jim Smith killed Ferguson and sure as shooting, he's going to try to pass as Agent Ferguson."

Tess froze as that sank in. Smith was after Chevy, and the only way Tess could get word to Chevy and Livie was through Oliver. Tess quickly said good-bye and called Oliver as she hurried back to her car, praying she'd get to him before the fake Agent Ferguson did.

47

Oliver brought a hand to his chin, scratching his beard, hoping this request from Agent Ferguson wouldn't take long. He heard his phone but wanted to finish with the agent first. He'd check messages in a minute.

"Yeah, she's with Livie Harp. Harp's home is very secure; no one is going to get to her there."

"Can you take me to this Livie Harp?"

"Now? Can't it wait a bit?"

"No, it can't. And I was told that you were the only person to speak to. I certainly don't want to arrive there out of the blue and frighten the girl. After all, she has been through a lot."

"Yes, she has." Oliver knew he was the only one who had Harp's phone number. Realizing that he'd have to wait to see Tess, Oliver swallowed his disappointment. He didn't want Chevy frightened either.

"I can call them —"

"I'd rather go in person. A phone call is too cold, impersonal." The agent smiled.

Resigned, Oliver said, "Okay, sure, I can take you there. Let me grab my coat."

When he returned to the porch, Agent Ferguson was on the bottom step.

"My car is in your church lot." Ferguson gestured toward the lot, indicating Oliver could walk in front of him. Oliver lived on the church grounds, and the parking area was a short walk along a stone path. He started up the path, Agent Ferguson on his heels.

As they approached the lot, Oliver saw a gray sedan. The only out-of-place vehicle there, it must be the agent's. He was headed toward it when a Rogue's Hollow PD SUV pulled into the lot and parked next to it.

Tess. Oliver's heart skipped a beat.

"Ah, the chief is here," he said to Ferguson without taking his eyes off Tess.

She stepped out of the car and started toward them. Something was wrong — Oliver could see that right away. There was something in her body language that made Oliver tense up. He felt the agent at his shoulder.

Tess's eyes never left the agent, even though Oliver was trying to catch her gaze.

She said, "Hello, Oliver, going some-where?"

"This is Agent Ferguson. Agent Bass sent him to check on Chevy. We're on our way there now."

Tess nodded. But Oliver saw her hand unsnap her duty weapon just as Agent Ferguson wrapped an arm around his neck and pulled him close. In shock, Oliver felt the arm tighten against his neck and the cold steel of a gun barrel as it pressed into his temple.

Tess tried to hide her terror when she saw Oliver with Jim Smith. They were way too close together. She knew that there would be no negotiation with this man; he was a no-hesitation killer. Her gaze went straight to the blue eyes of the tall man, and she saw the murderous calculation there. Her only hope was to get some distance between him and Oliver and hopefully take him down.

But it all went wrong. As she approached — at a loss for how to get the message to Oliver that he was in danger, there was a killer at his back — she saw Smith move even closer to Oliver, and she had no choice but to draw her weapon. She cleared leather the same time Smith wrapped his arm around Oliver's neck and pulled him close, gun to Oliver's head.

"Drop it, Smith. This is the end of the line. You have nowhere else to go." Tess took a shooter's stance. She knew backup was en route. Surely Smith had to see there was no endgame here.

Then again, he was a cold-blooded killer.

"No, no, Chief. You drop your weapon, or this town will be minus a clergyman."

Tess couldn't look at Oliver; she kept her eyes fixed on Smith.

"Not going to happen. The sheriff's department, state police, and officers from my department are going to converge on this spot in seconds. There is no way out for you."

As if to punctuate her point, sirens became audible in the distance, growing closer.

He fidgeted, and Tess saw indecision cross his face, but it was quickly replaced by a hardness, a resolve. He wasn't going to give up easily. She tried another tack.

"Look, we know Cyrus Beck sent you. He's the one we want. Let go of Pastor Macpherson, give up, cooperate, and things could go easier for you."

He chuckled mirthlessly. "Snitch? Not likely."

A patrol vehicle screamed into the lot. Tess

didn't turn but knew it was most likely Del Jeffers.

The siren died, and Tess tightened her grip, sharpened her aim. She was confident in her shooting ability, but Smith wasn't giving her a very big target.

As if reading her thoughts, Smith stiffened his hold on Oliver.

"I want out, simple as that. I —"

It was Oliver who acted. Tess jumped, nearly fired as Oliver brought his elbow hard into Smith's ribs, causing the man to cry out in pain. Everything happened at once — Oliver lurched to the left. As Smith crumpled in the opposite direction, he fired the gun toward Oliver. Tess saw Smith try to swing his gun around toward her, and she fired four times, not stopping until the man was down and not moving.

But then, the same could be said for Oliver. He was down and not moving.

48

Tess rushed to Smith's downed figure, wanting to be certain he was no longer a threat. He wasn't. She picked up his gun, holstered her weapon, and leaped to where Oliver lay. Del was already kneeling next to the prone form.

"Oliver!" Sliding to her knees, she felt fear fill her, nearly split her apart when she saw blood. Fireworks exploded in her head. But Oliver moved. And groaned.

Tess saw that the blood was coming from his face, a slice of red from where the beard on his chin had been creased by a bullet.

"I think he's okay," Del said. "It's a nick, that's all. Like he got socked in the jaw."

Tess didn't take her eyes off Oliver.

"I better manage the crowd," Del said.

"What? Sure, yeah." Tess didn't even look up.

Oliver groaned again, and she focused on him.

"Are you okay?"

He looked dazed, but his eyes cleared rapidly. He brought a hand to his chin and Tess helped him sit up.

"I'm fine. Feels as if I got coldcocked." He looked at the blood on his hand. "Did he shoot me?"

Tess sat back on her heels, relieved beyond belief and a little irritated that Oliver had taken such a risk.

"Looks like the bullet grazed you. You might need a couple of stitches." She pulled a handkerchief from her pocket. "Here, apply pressure."

He did as she directed.

"Oliver, what were you thinking hitting him like that? The bullet could have just as easily gone into your head."

Two fingers pressing the cloth into his chin, Oliver gave her a lopsided grin. "I remembered hearing you and Sergeant Logan talk about him being hurt, that his ribs probably didn't feel so good. I took a chance that I could distract him. It worked."

Tess stared into his stormy green-gray eyes, emotions swirling. She grabbed his face in both hands. "Oliver Macpherson, I love you."

She pulled his face close and kissed his

413

lips, not caring about the blood or who was watching.

Steve arrived on scene a short while later. The state police were handling the shooting investigation, and Tess was fine with that. There were plenty of witnesses to the shooting. Alana was one of the first to run up to Tess and Oliver.

"I can't believe that just happened! I mean, you saved his life!"

The newspeople had been there for the purpose of interviewing Rosita Vasquez about Tami and her ordeal. They were putting stuff away, getting ready to leave when the shooting started. Needless to say, after the shooting, their cameras were up and rolling.

Tess had been so focused on Oliver that she'd not even noticed the crowd until after everything was code 4. As for the shooting of Smith, Tess herself felt confident that she'd had no choice, considering what she knew about the man. Briefly, she wished that she'd had a chance to interview him, but it was doubtful he would have talked. He killed people too easily; there was no room for half measures.

"Medford PD found another body in the hotel," Steve told her.

Tess was sitting in one of the chairs on Oliver's porch. The weather was balmy, in transition, the cold front having moved on, a warmer one moving in, so it was pleasant to be outside, and she didn't want to be closed in. Jethro had taken Oliver to the hospital to get his chin stitched.

Steve sat in the other chair.

Tess turned to him. "Smith killed someone else?"

"We think so, yes. Dead guy is Doug Dugan. According to Agent Bass, who will be here shortly by the way, Dugan was Cyrus Beck's girl Friday."

Tess smiled. "That's a funny way to put it."

"I know. I thought we needed some levity. The guy was actually a decorated Vietnam vet, had worked for Beck for years."

"Smith bit the hand that fed him."

"Apparently."

"There's something else. What's the matter?"

He gave a tilt of his head. "You always could read me. I've got some good news and some bad news."

"I'm too tired to pick what I want to hear first. Just give it all to me."

"Okay, first the good news. LAPD is sending up a couple of cold case detectives right

415

away to collect the gun we recovered. They've had a couple of dinosaurs working the case for years and they've uncovered some fresh clues and leads. They weren't surprised about who had the gun."

"Really? They knew about Smith?"

"Jim Smith is not his real name."

"No surprise there," Tess said. "Who was he?"

"Real name, Royal Redd. There were prints on the .357 we recovered. And since they had Redd's prints on file, it was easy to make the comparison. He had minor arrests back when he was eighteen, but no police contact since then."

Tess arched her eyebrows. "Seriously? That dirtbag hasn't been in trouble with the law since he was eighteen?"

"He seems to have been good at staying off the radar. As far as Isaac Pink's case goes, after speaking with the LA cold case guys, they've come a long way in twenty-five years."

"New evidence?"

"Yeah, and help from new forensic tests. How much do you know about the Pink investigation?"

"The basics. I never read the whole thing in detail."

"Well, one thing they recovered was some

blood found at the back door of the kitchen. It didn't belong to any of the Pinks, but the blood was preserved and eventually matched to a dead body that was pulled out of the LA River. Denton Young. Moniker of Devo. He was from Long Beach, a drug addict and burglar, found in the trunk of a stolen car that surfaced in the LA flood control channel as water from winter rains subsided. And there was a slug recovered from his body, .357. It matched Pink's gun."

Tess stopped the gentle rocking she'd been doing. "Pink killed him?"

"The evidence points that way. Young bled in Pink's house, so he was shot there. And breaking into houses with security systems was his MO. Had an extensive record in Long Beach. He was detained once in Pink's San Pedro neighborhood about two weeks before the Pink killing. Field interview cards recorded that he and Royal Redd were thought to have been casing cars. But cops found no evidence of any crime, so after they were questioned, they were released."

"Whoa." Tess leaned forward as the picture crystallized in her mind. "Those two dirtbags killed Isaac and his family."

"That's where the cold case guys are going. They've wanted to find Redd for a long time."

"Any connection to Beck or Cross?"

"Cross, yes. The guys found travel records showing that Redd left the country with Cross some twenty-five years ago, but it's not known when he returned."

"He must have returned and assumed the Smith identity," Tess said. "Or maybe he got the ID somewhere out of the country."

"He got it somewhere. Redd had a passport; none has been found for Smith. And Redd is known to be an associate of Cyrus Beck. The cold case guys really wanted to go the distance with Redd in the box."

Tess leaned back. She understood that. The LAPD detectives probably had a whole script for the interview if they'd ever gotten Redd into an interview room. Almost made her sorry she'd had to shoot him. Almost.

"Needless to say, the investigators are anxious to get up here and do more digging, hopefully close the case as solved. It's actually amazing that this guy, at his age, has been able to avoid even a traffic ticket for all these years." He fidgeted, and Tess finally picked up that something was wrong. She realized she'd been distracted by fatigue and thoughts of Oliver.

"Why are you telling me this, Steve?

What's the bad news?"

"Ah, this is where it gets dicey." He stood, wiping his palms on his thighs. "You know Livie Harp never came in to be printed. And with everything that's been happening, I haven't had a chance to find out why. So I pulled some prints off the guns we recovered from her." He swallowed.

Tess froze. "What is it?"

He shook his head. "She's not Livie Harp; she's Heather Harrison. LAPD will be all over her if they find out."

Tess stood and faced him. "You didn't tell them? Or Bass?" A knee-jerk reaction in her wanted to rush out and arrest Heather Harrison; for years she'd believed the woman was a vicious murderer.

But now, after all she'd learned, was Livie Harp really a cop killer?

"No. I found out after I talked to LA, and Bass is more interested in Redd and the bodies at the Marriott. And . . . well, Tess, I can't believe she's a murderer. She saved everyone in Faith's Place from a couple of cold-blooded killers."

Tess did a circle on the porch, one hand on her hip, one on her forehead. She remembered the day before, thinking at the time, when Steve was interacting with Livie, that something had sparked. Was that interest on his part? Was it clouding his judgment?

Maybe it's clouding mine as well, she thought, *because I'm kinda glad he didn't tell the LAPD detectives.*

"We have to confront her — you know that. It's not up to us to decide whether she's guilty or not. Is there still a warrant in the system?"

"Yes, there is."

"I knew she was hiding from something," Tess said, "but I have to admit, I don't see her as a killer. Yeah, she shot someone, but it was clearly self-defense. She did it to protect everyone at Faith's Place. To me, there's a difference."

"We have to go talk to her. We can't keep this quiet," Steve said. "Can you call her?"

"I don't have her number. Oliver does."

"I'd really like to talk with her before I say anything to the cold case guys. I know it's not procedure. If you want to step away, I won't blame you."

"I'm as curious as you are." Tess smiled. "Besides, you covered me over the whole Faith's Place fiasco. We can drive up there now or —"

She was interrupted by the arrival of Agent Bass.

"Chief, glad to see that you made it out

okay after tangling with Smith. I just left one young agent who wasn't so lucky." He nodded toward Steve and then faced Tess, his features grim, and Tess imagined that she knew how he felt. She prayed she'd never have to oversee the line-of-duty death of one of her officers.

"Sorry about Ferguson."

"Yeah, looks like he never had a chance. And I'm afraid I have more bad news. We found the forger, the man who made Gage's fake creds. He gave up Beck; we know Beck paid him for the paperwork."

"How is that bad news?"

"It's just another charge. But without Beck in custody it's empty. The man has disappeared. As I said before, it's obvious now he fled the country, and bringing him in will be no easy feat, especially if we have to deal with extradition issues."

Tess closed her eyes and sighed. "Is he still a threat to Chevy?"

"I won't say no until he is in custody. And I'm not giving up looking for him. This guy needs to go down."

Tess considered this news, not sure what to feel. Relief? Anger? So much death and destruction attributed to the man over the last few days . . . She felt numb and prayed that Beck would face justice soon.

The shooting investigation chewed up the rest of the day. Tess and Steve decided they'd confront Livie Harp in the morning. It was cutting it close, with the cold case guys on their way, but everyone needed to take a breath after the incident with "Jim Smith."

49

Four stitches were required to close the crease in Oliver's chin. They didn't hurt as much as having to shave his entire beard off to avoid looking silly with simply a shaved patch where the stitches were. He'd had the beard since his twenties and felt decidedly naked without it. But the pain of shaving the beard had been tempered by two things. First, Oliver had been able to call Livie and Chevy and tell them that Jim Smith was dead and no longer a threat. And second, finally, he had Tess alone and could pour out his heart.

"Wow, what a look," Tess said, eyes dancing with mischief. They were in her office. So much had happened since the shooting, they hadn't had a minute to themselves until now.

Tess put a hand on his freshly shaved cheek. "It makes you look so young. Now I feel like a cradle robber."

He pulled her close. "As soon as the stitches are out, the beard comes back." Oliver hugged her tight and she hugged back. He loved having her close. Now was the time to have the talk that Jim Smith had so rudely interrupted.

It had been only a day since Jim Smith had held a gun to his head. Oliver knew there was still a lot of dust that needed to settle, but he couldn't let what he needed to say go unsaid any longer.

He released Tess and held her at arm's length, loving the light there in her vivid green eyes. "We need to talk. I wanted to find you yesterday, was on my way to your house when that man came to my door. I still can't believe I was so gullible."

"Don't be too hard on yourself. That was what he did, conned people. What did you want to talk about?"

"I wanted to apologize. I've been so irritable with you lately, questioning your judgment, giving you a bad time about how you do your job. I realize now, more than ever, how hard that job is. But I confess I was operating a little out of fear."

"Fear? You?"

To Oliver, Tess seemed truly perplexed by his confession. "Yeah, me, afraid. I lost sight of the big picture and I stopped trusting

God." He gripped both of her hands in his. "Yesterday you told me that you loved me. Well, I realized a long time ago that I love you too, Tess. No, let me finish." He held his hand up when she started to interrupt.

"You're such a hard charger, jumping feet-first into everything. That's a very appealing quality. But because of everything that happened here the last few days — and before, with the fire — I let fear creep in that I could lose you like I lost Anna." He pulled her close, noting the mist in her eyes. "But I have to practice what I preach. You're in God's hands, and I can't interfere in the way you do your job. I have to trust, not fear."

She freed one hand from his grasp and wiped her eyes before holding on again. "Well, since we're confessing, I have one of my own to make."

"Really?"

"I had — have, because it's still lurking — this fear that I can't truly be good for you because of my career. I can't be totally devoted to supporting you —"

He put a finger over her mouth. "Tess, if you think that's what I want out of a relationship, you're wrong. I love you because you're you, and I wouldn't change a thing." He pulled her close again, and his heart fluttered when she whispered in his ear.

"Ditto."

And then the inevitable happened: they were interrupted by a knock at the door.

Tess grinned. "Duty calls."

"As usual." He let her go and she stepped to the front of her desk.

"Come in."

When the knock on the door came, Tess was expecting Steve Logan. She hadn't had a chance to tell Oliver about Livie Harp. But it was sure to be big news, and with the cold case crew already in Medford, reviewing evidence there, she knew that she and Steve didn't have much time to talk to Livie before LAPD arrived in Rogue's Hollow and put two and two together. Tess didn't see Livie refusing her and Steve access, but she'd planned to ask Oliver to call and announce that they were coming. Both Tess and Steve wanted Harp/Harrison's explanation before they turned over what they knew to the LAPD.

But it wasn't Steve at the door; it was Sheila.

"Sorry to interrupt, Chief, but there's another FBI agent here to see you."

Tess frowned. "Not Agent Bass?"

"No, but he's from the same office; it's an

Agent Archer."

"Okay, send him in." Tess turned to Oliver. "This can't take very long. Stick around? I have something I need to tell you."

"Sure." He nodded and took a seat.

Tess moved back behind her desk as Sheila showed the agent into the office.

For a minute, Tess was taken aback. This guy was older; he couldn't have been a regular agent. As she looked closer, there was something familiar about him. And as he smiled and closed the door behind him, horror dawned.

This was no FBI agent. This was Cyrus Beck.

50

"I suggest we all stay calm, Chief." Beck held up what looked like a garage door remote in his hand. He was a tall man, taller in person than he ever appeared on TV, and he looked well built in the expensive suit he wore. His head was shaved smooth — that was different . . . and probably why it took Tess so long to recognize him. But the face, that sardonically cold expression, was what couldn't be changed and what gave him away.

Tess stared at him as Oliver got up and moved quickly behind the desk with her.

Hand on the butt of her gun, Tess asked, "Why should I stay calm and not arrest you right now?"

"Keep your hand away from your weapon. Because in my hand I hold a detonator."

Tess forced her hand to drop. "Detonator?"

"Yes. When he arrived here in your neck

of the woods, my friend Digger did a favor for me. He packed a rental car with explosives. It's parked right outside, on your main street, in front of a very busy coffee shop. I press this button and half of your little hamlet goes up in smoke."

Tess started to speak, then stopped. Rule #1 — LTS — applied here in spades. She doubted Beck had such a sophisticated knowledge of explosives, but then she remembered Steve saying that the man called Digger had been a decorated Vietnam vet. Anything was possible there.

"Why should I believe you?" she asked.

"Because I have nothing to lose. You've ruined me. My best people are dead. If I blow up your town, you shoot me." He shrugged. "I win because I stay out of prison."

"How can you say that you win by causing the deaths of innocent people?" Oliver asked, clearly disgusted.

"Because I don't care about them. At all. You can save those innocent lives, Chief. You and you alone have that power."

"How can I do that?"

"Take me to Roberta. You do, and I'll give you the detonator. Lives saved, everyone happy."

"What about Roberta?"

"I have a score to settle. Your choice is one death or many."

"You can't expect me to make that choice."

He arched an eyebrow. "I expect you to do just that. I'll count to ten. Either you take me to Roberta, or I kill everyone within a one-block radius of my vehicle. Some damage may even occur here. Digger always was one for overkill." He held the remote up again. "One, two, three . . ."

Tess listened to him count, a mix of negative emotions choking her, knowing he might well be lying, but realizing that she just couldn't take that chance. He got as high as eight.

"Wait." She put her hand up. "What do you think happens after you settle your score with Roberta? Do you think that you'll just walk away?"

"Tess, you can't." Oliver gripped her arm.

"Oh yes, she can," Beck said. "She's pragmatic; she can't have the deaths of thirty or forty people on her head when one will suffice. I expect you'll try to arrest me. Good luck with that."

"You're crazy, Beck." Tess's heart was pounding in her ears, and her thoughts scrambled for a way out of this situation. She could shoot Beck dead right now, but suppose he pushed the button as he fell? Or pushed it in the time it took to unholster her weapon?

"Maybe I am. Call the woman who has Roberta. Tell her we're coming; tell her an agent will be with you."

He must have seen the shock on Tess's face because he laughed. "Yes, I know very well you've hidden her with some insane prepper. Digger did a lot of what he was good at — he dug up information for me before his unfortunate demise. Just call the woman and don't do anything to alert her or —" he snapped his fingers — "boom."

Tess turned to Oliver. "Call Livie."

"Tess . . ."

"Trust me, Oliver, call her. Tell her we're coming up to visit and talk to Roberta." Tess needed time to figure out how to disarm Beck, look for an opening, and only by making him think he had the upper hand could she do that.

Oliver took a deep breath. "If you're sure . . ." He pulled out his phone and called Livie Harp.

51

"You can leave your gun belt on," Beck said with a smirk just before they left Tess's office. "But turn your radio off, no accidental notifications. I want this jaunt to look perfectly normal and natural. I can press this button faster than I can blink."

As she switched her radio off, Tess realized there was no way she could draw her weapon before Beck pushed the button. Part of her wanted to call his bluff, but she could never live with herself if a bomb did, in fact, explode on River Drive. So she walked out of the station with Beck and Oliver, planning, hoping, and praying for an opening.

Livie was expecting them. Tess had the duration of the drive, maybe fifteen minutes, to figure out a way to get the remote from Beck. He'd already dashed her hope that Livie's home would be out of range for the remote, telling her that his technology was as advanced as anything used by the US military. Tess knew he could be lying, but she didn't want to risk innocent lives on it. No, she had to get the remote away from him, eliminate the threat.

Tess's phone buzzed as she, Oliver, and Beck left the station. She looked at the caller ID. It was Steve.

Beck gripped her arm. "I suggest you answer it, on speakerphone."

"I think I should just let it go to voice mail, safer that way." She held his gaze. He relented.

"For the sake of your town, I hope you're right."

The buzzing stopped; then the phone chimed with a voice mail. Tess put it in her pocket.

They reached her SUV. Beck climbed in back. "Better to watch the both of you," he said.

Oliver took the front passenger seat.

Tess drove out of the lot, mind whirring. Beck hadn't disarmed her; she supposed he figured the threat of the remote would keep her from shooting him. He was right on that count. And other than the remote, she couldn't see that Beck had any weapons on him.

She drove slowly, stalling. Hoping Steve

would be perplexed by her not answering. They were supposed to be contacting Harp together today. What would he do if he thought Tess had stood him up? She prayed that he'd think something was wrong and do something to throw Beck off-balance. She glanced at Oliver on her right. She knew he was praying as well, and that gave her hope and, surprisingly, peace.

Who said a cop and pastor wouldn't make a good team?

They reached the gate. Tess pressed the intercom and announced their arrival. The gate swung open. As Tess drove through, she remembered the cameras; they were everywhere. Was Harp watching? She knew who Cyrus Beck was. Would she recognize him and be ready?

I have to grab that remote.

"When we get there, you and the pastor walk in front of me. I won't hesitate to push this button if either of you do anything I don't like."

Tess said nothing, just nodded. They reached the front of the house and she parked. Oliver climbed out first. Tess followed and walked around to the passenger side. She caught his glance for a brief second, and in that look, she knew he would follow her lead. Whatever she decided to do, he'd be with her.

Beck climbed out. He pointed at her with the remote. "Now, hand me your weapon, very carefully, Chief."

"What?"

"Tsk, tsk, you didn't think I would leave you armed?" He held his free hand out. "Carefully now."

Tess stared at him for a moment. Finally she unsnapped the holster and drew her weapon. She placed it in his hand.

"There, wasn't that easy?" He sneered. "I've covered all bases. Now —" he gestured with the remote — "let's get going. You first."

Tess and Oliver walked up the stairs to the front door. The door was partway open. Tess grabbed the knob, pushed the door fully open.

"Livie? It's Chief O'Rourke." She stepped over the threshold. All three of them entered the house. The room was empty.

"You warned them!" Beck shoved between Oliver and Tess, furious. "You warned them! How did you do that?"

"You heard Oliver when he called. He told them nothing but what you wanted said." Tess's eyes were on the remote. Dare she call his bluff?

He waved the gun around, and with the

remote in one hand and the gun in the other, he stepped to the middle of the empty room.

"Roberta! Come out from wherever you're hiding. It's time to pay for what you did. I swear you'll never get away from me!"

When there was no response, he turned back to Tess, fury in his eyes. "You just killed half your town!" He squeezed the button on the remote with a flourish.

For Tess, time stopped. She felt as if her head would explode in horror. There was no way to know right at that moment what had happened in downtown Rogue's Hollow, but she knew she had to stop Beck cold now. He was mad with rage, and she was unarmed, so she went with the unexpected.

Tess jerked her baton from the ring. Beck raised her gun to fire. She stepped to the side and brought the baton down hard on Beck's wrist. He howled even as he squeezed the trigger. The gun fired into the floor and then flew from Beck's hand, clattering down on the floor with the remote. He bent down, cradling his injured wrist.

"You broke it." He looked up, fury in his eyes. "You'll pay — I swear you will pay."

It took all of Tess's restraint not to smack him again. She quickly replaced the baton in its ring and stepped forward. Grabbing hold of his uninjured forearm, she jerked it toward her, causing a howl; then she bent the wrist and twisted it back in a textbook wrist lock, spinning him forcefully face-first into the wall so she could apply the handcuffs, even as he hollered.

"I will not stay behind bars, I promise you."

Tess applied the cuffs quickly and roughly, mind overcome with dread about what had happened in downtown Rogue's Hollow.

"It's over, Beck, and you are the one who will pay for what you just did. You are under arrest."

He cursed. "If it's the last thing I do, ahh . . ."

Tess ignored him and locked the cuffs in place, her focus now shifting to her radio so she could find out what had happened in the Hollow.

"Darn right, it's over."

Tess, grip tight on Beck's upper arm, stepped back and turned. Livie Harp stood there, shotgun up and ready.

"Move out of the way, Chief. It's time to end this for good. And you, Pastor Mac, stay back."

Reflex made Tess step in front of Beck. "Livie, no, don't. There's no reason to do this. He's a threat no longer."

"As long as he's breathing, he's a threat." Harp tried to move around, get a clear shot at Beck.

Tess moved with her, blocking the shot, a fleeting thought crossing her mind: *My dad died protecting an innocent woman. Do I want to die protecting evil?*

52

Harp had fury in her eyes and a death grip on her shotgun. Tess scrambled, knowing that she had to derail the anger, defuse the moment.

"I can't let you kill him. He deserves to be in a cage." She put a hand up. "Surely you can see that will be worse than a quick death, Heather."

Harp's glare flipped from Beck to Tess. "What did you call me?"

"Heather. That's your name, isn't it? Heather Harrison."

Tess saw surprise flicker across the woman's face and her resolve waver. In her periphery, she also saw shock hit Oliver.

"I haven't been her for a long time. She was stolen from me — by him, by Porter Cross. You could say that they killed her. Cross met his end, but he —" she jammed the gun toward Beck — "he deserves to die for that and for so many other crimes."

Tess held her hands up, making certain that she blocked the shot. Oliver had picked up the remote and her gun. Tess shot him a glance, hoping he understood that she wanted him to stay back, not to try anything.

Her concentration returned to Harp. "No, he deserves to rot in prison. Killing him now, like this, will put you in prison. *That* would be wrong."

"If you know my name, then you know I've been blamed for something a man like him did. So either way, I'm going to jail. Might as well make the trip worth it."

"No, Livie."

Harp's attention shifted. Steve Logan stood in the doorway. Behind him, two unfamiliar, older men.

"We know you had nothing to do with Isaac Pink's death. We can clear your name, but not if you shoot Beck like this, in cold blood."

Tess watched the indecision seep in as Harp turned back her way. The shotgun lowered slightly. Steve stepped into the house; the two men stayed in the doorway.

"These are LAPD detectives. They have evidence. They know you didn't kill Isaac Pink. Come on — the other day you were the hero. Don't throw that away for the likes of Cyrus Beck." He kept coming slowly and

440

put a hand on the shotgun. "Let it go, Livie."

The two stared at one another for a long moment, until finally Livie released the gun. She turned away, tears streaming down her face.

Tess jerked Beck toward the door with one hand and turned on her radio with the other.

"Did you just come through town?" she asked Steve, turning up her radio, listening for emergency traffic.

"Yeah, I did. Sheila told us you were out here. What's going on?"

Oliver stepped forward. "There was no explosion?"

"No, not that I heard." Steve frowned. "Why?"

Tess felt her gut unclench. It had been a bluff. She told Steve about Beck's threat.

"If there are explosives in a rental car, they didn't detonate."

"Thank God," Tess said. "Can you secure him in my car while I contact Gabe?"

Steve nodded. "We'll need to get the bomb squad out just in case." He took Beck by the arm and jerked him to the front door.

As he passed the LAPD officers, he said, "These are Investigators Flores and Black. They've been waiting a long time to talk to

Livie — er, Heather."

The two men nodded toward Tess and then walked to where Livie was being comforted by Oliver.

Tess hadn't seen her come in, but there by the door stood Chevy. The teen looked Beck up and down.

"You'll never get away from me," Beck sneered.

"I think I already have," Chevy said, flipping her hair and continuing toward Livie, Oliver, Flores, and Black.

Steve tossed Tess a grin and continued out the door.

Tess radioed Gabe, the officer on duty, to check and see if there was a rental car in front of the coffee shop. There was one, a large black Cadillac Escalade. Tess asked him to clear the area while Logan called the bomb squad to check out the vehicle.

"Thank you for taking him away," Chevy said.

Tess nodded, still on edge and knowing that she would be until she found out the truth about the explosives.

"Where were you two hiding?"

"Livie has a panic room. There are monitors in there for all the cameras. We were watching when you came up the drive." She sniffled. "On the monitor, I saw it was Cyrus in the car and we thought you'd betrayed us at first."

"No, he just threatened me with a bomb."

"Livie was going to ambush him, but I didn't really want to see him, until . . . Well, when he was in handcuffs, he looked so much smaller than I remember. I opened the gate for Deputy Logan."

"He never was what you thought he was. There was nothing good in Cyrus Beck."

Chevy looked at her, seemingly unsure, the hard adult gaze Tess had seen at the shelter gone. She looked smaller and younger somehow. Tess hoped the girl would recover from this chapter of her life with minimal ill effects.

Tess turned to regard Harp, who was sitting on the couch. Oliver had gotten her some water. The LAPD guys wanted to ask her questions, but she looked at Tess.

"You know what happened, what that man did. He and his buddy Porter Cross killed Isaac Pink and his whole family." Livie's voice broke. "They were good people. He's a monster."

"Yes, I know. But you couldn't bring the Pinks back by killing Beck. This way, we are denying him freedom like he denied Chevy and who knows how many other women.

Talk to these men; tell them the truth."

Livie nodded and gave the two investigators her full attention.

By the time Flores and Black had finished with Harp, Steve let Tess know that the bomb squad was en route.

He left to meet them in town, taking the cold case guys with him.

"We'll get the warrant quashed," Investigator Black told Tess as he was on his way out. "I never thought she had anything to do with that killing; now I know for sure. Thanks for your help on this, O'Rourke."

"I'm just glad you can close the books on this case. My dad would be happy to see it resolved."

"Your dad? You mean Daniel O'Rourke?"

"Yeah."

"Nice to see that the apple didn't fall far from the tree. Good work, Chief."

With them gone, Tess was in a hurry to get Beck booked and to see to the conclusion of the bomb threat. But Harp had a question and Tess realized that so did she.

"What's going to happen to me now?"

"You heard Black. They know you're not a killer." Tess sat on the coffee table across from Harp. "How on earth did you get to this place in life? How did you survive?"

Harp was composed now, back to her

confident self. "It wasn't easy. I made it to Vegas on what I took from the Pinks. Got a job, went to school at night, and learned about computers. I worked my way up at a big casino as their tech person. I thought I'd pulled it off. But one day I was on the strip, and I saw someone I thought I recognized, someone who worked for Cross. He didn't see me, but I was spooked. I quit my job and fled to Atlantic City. There, I met a man who was a lot older than me and I married him. For the first time I felt reasonably safe from Cross."

"I searched your background. I never found that you were married."

"Because his name wasn't Harp. I was so freaked that for a while I was even agoraphobic. After he died, he left me a boatload of money. I used it to buy a new identity. And by hacking, I removed as much of my past from the public record as possible. I discovered that I had a talent for hacking. It was more out of a need for self-preservation because it was how I kept tabs on Cross."

"Wait." Tess stopped her, something Bass told her about catching Cross clicking. They'd been tipped off to all the porn on his computer by an unnamed source. "Were you by chance the anonymous tip that tripped Cross up?"

A faint smile showed. "Well, he was a sloppy man. It was only after he died that I truly felt alive. But in keeping up with what Cross was doing, I also found out what Beck was doing. He wasn't nearly as sloppy as Cross. And he had Ice working for him. He really scared me. That was why I came here, to live off the grid. I was afraid because I knew Beck was worse than Cross."

She leaned back against the couch, closed her eyes, and stretched, raising her arms in the air. "Oh, wow, is it really over now?"

Tess stood. "It's over. He can't worm his way out of this one."

Oliver stepped close. Tess could see that his brow was furrowed with worry.

"Do you think he was telling the truth about the bomb?"

Hands on her hips, Tess shook her head. "I don't know. All we can do is wait and see."

Oliver brought a hand to his face as if he were going to scratch his stitches and then changed his mind.

"What is it?" Tess asked.

"I just remembered our conversation, a while ago. We spoke of Beck and evil and God's forgiveness. I have a confession to make."

"Oh?"

"Beck, so nakedly evil. Casually talking about taking innocent lives." He held Tess's gaze, pain in his eyes. "I saw no shadow of hope, and it breaks my heart. But I will pray for him. Because even though I can't see it, I still believe God is able to break through to him."

Tess stepped forward and put her arms around Oliver's waist, pulling him close. "That's one of the things I love about you, always trying to find the good in people."

She felt his lips on her forehead and he whispered, "And one of the things I love about you is that you never give up fighting for justice."

53

Cyrus Beck began his jail career at the Jackson County Jail, and according to Gabe Bender, who transported him for Tess, he complained and screamed for his lawyer all the way into Medford.

"He says he'll beat this case like he's beaten all of the others," Gabe told Tess when he called her from the jail. "What about Harp?"

"Cold case guys cleared her."

"Wow. Wonder if she's still going to be a recluse?"

Tess considered the question after she ended the call. Her last glimpse of Harp was of a woman who looked as if the monkey was finally off her back. Her phone rang again — Steve this time. He'd returned the cold case guys to their hotel.

"What do you think? Livie is totally in the clear. Good news, huh?"

"Yeah, it is. And she's got a new project.

She's going to help Chevy catch up on her education. It seems like Livie is inching her way back into society."

"That's good to hear."

"You like her?"

"I do. I know there's an age difference, but she is very intriguing."

Tess smiled, thinking that they would be good for each other. "Thanks, Steve, for all your help."

"No problem."

She and Oliver were at the perimeter of the bomb-safe area, just outside Wild Automotive.

The sheriff's bomb disposal team had evacuated the town center. It turned out Beck wasn't lying about the explosives in his rental car. It was indeed wired and packed with enough explosives to take out half of downtown Rogue's Hollow. The bomb squad commander told Tess the reason it didn't go off was that, for all his bluster, Beck's device had a range limit after all.

"The amount of explosives in that car would have leveled half your town," he said.

"What now?" Oliver asked.

"I guess we wait."

A good hour passed before the squad defused the bomb and called all clear.

Just before they climbed out of the car, Oliver asked, "Did you ever think that maybe Beck was bluffing and you should call him on it?"

Tess rolled her eyes. "Maybe for a second, but there were too many lives to roll the dice. Besides, I had a secret weapon."

"What's that?"

"My favorite pastor was with me, and I know he was praying."

He put his hand on hers and smiled. Tess loved his smile . . . his green-gray eyes . . . everything, really.

"I got more than I bargained or prayed for. Livie — or should I call her Heather? — is now free, just like Chevy."

"Yep, she is."

"What a big secret she's kept all these years."

"True, but she proved something that I think I may add to my rules list."

"Oh yeah, what's that?"

"Big secrets never stay buried."

EPILOGUE

It took time for things in town to settle down again, but the people of Rogue's Hollow got a good start when Tami was released from the hospital. Shot twice, but somehow neither bullet hit anything vital. She had a lot of scrapes, scratches, and bruises from her trip downriver, but everything would heal.

Oliver threw a coming-home party for her at the church. She thanked Tess for ending the life of Jim Smith.

"He gave me no choice, Tami. But do me a couple of favors?"

"Sure, what?"

"First, don't let Smith occupy your thoughts or life for another second. I think Oliver would agree with me. You need to let go of any anger or hurt; it will only affect you and your life, not Smith's."

Tami's eyes misted, but she held Tess's gaze. Finally she said, "Okay, Chief, I promise I'll try. Maybe Pastor Mac can help."

"I'm sure he would."

"What's the other favor?"

"Promise me that you'll never go down the Rogue River again without a raft."

Tami burst out laughing and gave Tess a hug. "You have my word."

A month later, Tess could say that things in town were back to normal. Cyrus Beck had been remanded to federal custody, where he was going to be kept despite his plea to be released back to an ankle monitor. The judge was having none of it. At the bail hearing, bail was denied. It would still be a long time before the trial, but everyone in Rogue's Hollow was happy to hear that Beck was behind bars and he'd stay there.

One night while watching an old movie, Tess pressed Pause and turned to Oliver. "Would you work with Cyrus Beck like you worked with Don Cherry?"

"That's a little random, isn't it?"

"Not to me. I'm still struggling with redemption. You told me to keep asking questions."

He shifted on the sofa to face her. "If he asked me, yes, I would."

"Still think he's redeemable?"

"Not on his own, no. But with God, all things are possible, and everyone is redeemable. Does that bother you?"

"On one hand, yes, it does. But on the other hand, I think if he did repent and change, like Cherry did, he could apologize to all the people he's hurt, maybe heal some wounds, in a small way do some good. But he can never bring back the people whose deaths he caused. I guess I don't want him escaping punishment."

"I understand, but even if he truly did ask the Lord for forgiveness and change, it would not negate the consequences of his misspent life. He is looking at a long prison term, maybe a death sentence. There's no such thing as a get-out-of-jail-free card."

Tess grasped Oliver's hand, realizing that as much as she struggled with men as evil as Beck being redeemable, it touched her deeply that Oliver believed it was possible.

"I love that about you, you know that?"

He smiled, brought her hand to his lips and kissed it. "What's that?"

"That you can look at what looks completely hopeless and see hope."

"I can do that because I serve a big God, and with him there is always hope."

"Yeah, Tami, Chevy, and Livie would testify to that. So I guess the police chief can come around in agreement."

"Amen to that," Oliver said and then leaned forward, this time pressing the kiss to her lips.

Winter was coming, and the temperature reflected that fact. Normally, Tess didn't mind the cold, but on this particular Sunday she was going to be baptized, so she whined a little about the cold.

"Ah, my tough friend," Oliver teased, "the baptismal is heated. You won't feel the cold."

"I'll hold you to that," Tess said.

She'd been baptized years ago, in her teens, before her father's murder, but since Tess knew that she was rededicating her life, she wanted to be baptized again, and she loved the fact that Oliver would do the dunking.

He or one of the other pastors did baptisms every fourth Sunday, so Tess wouldn't be the only person, but when she saw the list, she was pleasantly surprised.

"No kidding — Livie Harp and Chevy are also going to be baptized?"

"Yeah, and one other late arrival. Garrett Cooper added himself to the list this morning."

"Oh, speaking of him, I talked to Win Yarrow about Garrett today."

"Good news, I hope."

"Yeah, fish and game isn't going to charge him with any crime."

"That's nice of them."

"Not really. There just isn't any evidence. Blakely is dead; everything Garrett hid for him burned up." She hiked a shoulder. "No evidence, no case. But I'll tell you what is nice."

"What?"

"Yarrow really surprised me. I always thought he was a jerk. But he did the nicest thing. He put Janie Cooper's name in for the poacher reward money."

"You're kidding!" Oliver's eyes sparkled. Tess knew that he'd been worried about the Coopers' finances. Twenty-five thousand dollars would go a long way to help.

"Yeah, he wrote up a memo that just about made Janie sound like Superwoman, helping end a prolific poaching career. They should get the check soon."

"That will truly be a blessing to that family."

"You know, I would have said they didn't have a chance."

"I know."

"And . . . I've kinda thought that about us from time to time. My friend Jeannie doesn't think we're a good match."

"Yeah? Well, according to Don Cherry, we're oil and water."

"Really? Both sides of the spectrum count us out?"

Oliver nodded, then pulled Tess close. "You know what that means, don't you?"

"No, what?"

"We're just going to have to prove them wrong."

She stood on her tiptoes, and he bent over and pressed his lips to hers.

When the kiss ended and he released Tess just a bit, she smiled, holding his warm, stormy-gray eyes, and said, "Piece of cake."

DISCUSSION QUESTIONS

1. As *Cold Aim* begins, Chief Tess O'Rourke is bucking the advice of fire officials to make sure the residents of Rogue's Hollow have evacuated the danger zone. Oliver Macpherson tells her not to take such risks. Are Tess's actions reckless or part and parcel of her job? Why do some people (both in this story and in real life) opt to remain in their homes despite official advice? Do Tess's thoughts about the inherent danger in her profession change her actions at all throughout this story?

2. Neither Tess nor Oliver knows what to make of Livie Harp, the mysterious recluse living under tight security. What did you think of Harp? Is Tess right to wonder if the woman is hiding something or is even guilty of some crime, or do her years of police work make her overly suspicious of people? How much does a first impres-

sion color your opinion of a person?

3. Like other seekers, Harp has questions about the Christian faith, and she specifically asks Oliver to show her proof of God in a broken and sometimes ugly world. What does Oliver tell her? How would you prove God's existence?

4. During one of his jailhouse visits, Oliver considers the difference between justice and mercy. In what ways are these two traits "opposite ends of the spectrum"? Do you agree with Oliver's conclusion: "All fair justice is dispensed with some mercy"? Name other qualities that might aid in mercifully dispensing fair justice.

5. The FBI asks Tess to shelter a key witness before an important hearing. Why is Tess reluctant to say yes? What convinces her to agree to the request? As events unfold, what makes her wish she had followed rule #4: "Always trust your gut"?

6. Though Tess believes in the justice system, she recognizes that there are weaknesses to it, that sometimes people are able to "buy justice." How does this play out in *Cold Aim*? In the real world? Is it

possible to protect the justice system, to make it impervious to outside influences?

7. San Diego, California, was one of the first jurisdictions to adopt a "no drop" policy that allows the state to prosecute even when the victim is unwilling to testify against the perpetrator. Is this an example of government overreach or a helpful tool to protect us from ourselves? Is there an aspect of your life where you know that what you're doing or thinking is unhelpful or even harmful? What steps could you take to change your behavior or thought patterns? How would you hold yourself accountable?

8. Both Tess and Oliver worry about the Coopers' marriage. Oliver turns first to God, believing that "prayer is the first best answer for everything," but Tess feels it might not be enough in this case. Where do you tend to turn first when facing a crisis? Are there times to act, as well as times to sit back and allow your prayers to work? How do you decide which course to take?

9. Throughout the story, Tess wrestles with the evil she encounters in her job, espe-

cially in victimizers like Cyrus Beck. What does Oliver tell her when she asks whether there's anything redeemable in Beck? What did you think of his response? Do either Tess or Oliver change their opinions of Beck?

10. Several people cast doubts on Tess and Oliver's relationship, leaving both to question if their differences are too great to overcome. Are their fears valid? Should occupations that seem to clash with each other — like a pastor and a police officer — play any role in the success or downfall of a relationship? In what areas is it most important to be on the same page? Where do you see Tess and Oliver's relationship going?

11. After a shooting incident at Faith's Place, Tess suppresses the urge to rush out after the suspect and waits until she has backup with her. Does she make the right decision? Are you more likely to run headlong into a situation or to sit back and observe things before making a move? What are the pros and cons of each?

12. Tess contemplates adding a new rule to her list: "Big secrets never stay buried."

What secrets are revealed in *Cold Aim*?
Can you think of an example from your
own life when a secret was revealed? What
resulted from keeping the secret and then
its discovery? Read Mark 4:21-25. What
do you think Jesus meant when he said,
"Every secret will be brought to light"
(NLT)?

ABOUT THE AUTHOR

A former Long Beach, California, police officer of twenty-two years, **Janice Cantore** worked a variety of assignments, including patrol, administration, juvenile investigations, and training. She's always enjoyed writing and published two short articles on faith at work for *Cop and Christ* and *Today's Christian Woman* before tackling novels. She now lives in a small town in southern Oregon, where she enjoys exploring the forests, rivers, and lakes with her Labrador retrievers, Abbie and Tilly.

Janice writes suspense novels designed to keep readers engrossed and leave them inspired. *Cold Aim* follows *Crisis Shot* and *Lethal Target* in her latest series. Janice also authored the Cold Case Justice series — *Drawing Fire, Burning Proof,* and *Catching Heat* — the Pacific Coast Justice series — *Accused, Abducted,* and *Avenged* — and the Brinna Caruso novels, *Critical Pursuit* and

Visible Threat.

Visit Janice's website at www.janicecantore.com and connect with her on Facebook at www.facebook.com/JaniceCantore.